THIS COUNTRY I CALL MY OWN

This Country I Call My Own

Julian Roup

Copyright © 2023 Julian Roup

Paperback ISBN: 978-1-915490-17-9

This edition published in 2023 by BLKDOG Publishing.

This is a work of fiction. Names, characters, businesses, places, events, locales, and incidents are either the products of the author's imagination or used in a fictitious manner. Any resemblance to actual persons, living or dead, or actual events is purely coincidental.

A catalogue record for this book is available from the British Library.

No part of this publication may be reproduced, stored in a retrieval system, or transmitted in any form or by any means, electronic, mechanical, photocopying, recording, or otherwise, without written permission of the publisher.

All rights reserved including the right of reproduction in whole or in part in any form. The moral right of the author has been asserted.

www.blkdogpublishing.com

To my brother Herman Roup, who opened the door to Idaho and the USA for us in 1992; and to my brother-in-law Guy Louw, who keeps the home fires burning in South Africa.

And for my wife Janice Warman, who left behind her beloved journalism career in London to give me the space to follow my dream in Idaho.

Other titles by Julian Roup for your consideration:

Life in a Time of Plague:
A Coronavirus Lockdown Diary

Into the Secret Heart of Ashdown Forest:
A Horseman's Country Diary

A Fisherman in the Saddle

First Catch Your Calamari: Travels with an Appetite

ACKNOWLEDGEMENTS

I wish to thank my first readers, Herman Roup and Guy Louw, for their input and encouragement. Thanks to my wife Jan for endless advice, encouragement and superb editing. And thanks to our son Dominic for his wonderful work on the cover.

Thanks as ever to Nicky and Carol at BLKDOG, my publisher, for their support.

CHAPTER 1

Commander Ross McCallister, former SEAL and later a member of Task Force 20 (Special Ops), now retired, was, at 42, not as young and fit as he once was, able to leap onto a horse from the ground. His lithe 6ft 2in frame, muscled from years in the saddle, was now hurting in parts and his days of vaulting onto a horse were past him. But women still stared, or rather gave that glancing appraisal they do, that returned covertly two and even three times to see if he'd noticed. He was used to it and took no great pleasure in it.

Ross had been proud to make it as a Navy SEAL, a military unit established by President John F. Kennedy in 1962 as a nimble, elite maritime military force suited for all aspects of unconventional warfare. In this role they offered immediate military relief in crises around the world. But for Ross those days were long gone.

What he wanted now, what he lusted after, longed for, was the silence of deep wild country where nature ruled, brutally but impartially, and where only the wise survived. He had spent too many of his best years putting his life on the line for his country in the Middle East or dealing with the security issues at the end of wars, lucrative work he took on, buying into the financial scramble for security. What he wanted now was to immerse himself in the wild, to find a nature cure for his ills, in the ancient tradition of traumatised men.

He was still connected to a few political players, but he placed little value on these contacts. His own experience of the world had taught him the bitter truth about connections, permanence and security. His military years had drummed it in deeply. War, global financial disasters and epidemics had given added depth to his understanding that we all live on the edge of a precipice. To believe anything else was delusional.

On his 40th birthday two years previously he had bought a small 500-acre ranch in the far north of Idaho's Panhandle, close to the Canadian border, heavily wooded in pine, deeply ravined and rocky in places, cut by two streams that held trout and bordered by some acres of meadowland. His neighbours were few and, like him, shared a desire for privacy; they were not the visiting kind. A nod in the coffee shop he frequented in Sandpoint was about as far as it went for socialising when he went in for groceries. He also bought shells for his rifle, a McMillan Tac-50 used by the US SEALs, accurate up to 3,000 metres with a sound suppressor, and cartridges for his Holland & Holland 'Royal', an heirloom shotgun inherited from his grandfather, probably the most valuable thing he owned. His town visits also provided fuel for his old Jeep and a couple of jerry cans for the generator, though now he was converting to solar to help him stay completely off grid. He picked up sacks of oats for his two geldings, Rincon, a chestnut quarter horse, rock solid on the trail, and Buddy, an old flea-bitten grey cow pony that served as his pack horse. Both went unshod with no ill effect.

He had spent his first year on the property under canvas in the summer and autumn. For winter, he had towed in a beaten-up Airstream caravan he'd painted green to blend into the landscape. He installed a wood-burning stove with a metal chimney which rather spoiled the lines of the caravan but kept him warm and which he justified as function over form.

He spent weeks building a wood pile as tall as the caravan, which he covered with lengths of corrugated iron and then a tarp to hold it braced against the weather. It would be his life support when the snow threatened to engulf the van. It had seen him through the tough winter just past, during which he spent much time shovelling snow from around the caravan and snow-ploughing a path the mile back to the metalled road into town which lay 20 miles distant.

The horses managed with a field shelter he'd constructed from fallen seasoned pine. A second shelter held enough hay to see them through the hard months. Now that spring had arrived, he was felling timber for a robust single story log cabin that would see him out, he reckoned. He sited it in the lee of a tall hill where shy wild bighorn sheep liked to graze the ledges and bed down in the deep brush crevices.

He had felled and debarked enough pine trunks to get started and was using the tried and tested method of fitting each log snugly into the one beneath it with a saddle notch, using a triangle hoist he'd constructed to lift them into place. To limit any movement in the structure he was using steel spikes, nailing each log to the one beneath it at the corners. His aim was to have a bedroom, living room, kitchen and bathroom, with an attic for storage and an earth cellar for keeping food chilled. And he planned a tunnel that would exit the cabin higher up the hill in thick brush. Old habits died hard with him.

As he worked, he noted the bird life around him, a constant coming and going that added life and vitality to his solitary days. There were robins, one of whom became a companion as he cut logs, totally unafraid, and on parade, present and correct, when Ross arrived, chainsaw or axe in hand. Other regulars included black-billed magpies, woodpeckers, northern flickers, European starlings, and sparks of colour provided by red-winged blackbirds and gold finches. He loved the bird songs, whose music formed part of his soundscape. To encourage them to stay close to the cabin, he put out water and birdseed.

This morning he was heading into town for more steel pins and a cooked breakfast at the Hoot Owl Café, described boldly as quite possibly the best breakfast in the Panhandle. The place provided no-frills, good old-fashioned food in a charming rustic atmosphere. The country fried steak breakfast was something he craved once in a while. And, despite his introverted nature, he enjoyed being in a crowded roomful of people, part of the buzz but not part of any conversation. He was slightly thrown by his waitress.

'Hi, I'm Sandy, what can I get you?' she said, touching her name badge on her chest. She was not one of the regular motherly waitresses, but evidently a new arrival. She had a collar-length bob of shiny mahogany brown hair and an athlete's trim body; she could be anything from 25 to 35, he judged, with some Native American Indian blood or Italian possibly. Briskly she wrote down his order and as she walked off, he noticed one of the other servers winking at her.

As he waited for his meal, he scanned the café, an old life-saving habit he had never lost, much like the old sniper's trick of holding his breath and slowing his blood pressure, something that alarmed some medics looking at his readings. The odd night sweat and flashbacks also came with the territory, but, on the whole, he was in reasonably good shape physically, if one discounted the knee and shoulder twinges that also told him of incoming weather.

The food as ever was homely, filling and delicious, and he had to stop himself wolfing it down. His own cooking was adequate, but he missed some of the many great meals and cuisines his travels had provided.

He ate, but all the time kept up his scanning and he noted that Sandy's other tables were all grouped near the windows. She had been sent to him by one of the other servers to see his reaction. It explained Sandy's slight terseness when taking his order. He grinned inwardly. The motherly crew who manned this place never lost an opportunity to quiz him about whether he'd found an Idaho girl to keep him company out in the wilds. The rarity of his visits and his air of mystery kept tongues wagging.

But now his life was different; his buzz came from silence, in the space and light of the high country. To achieve this, he had invested his earnings wisely and this helped, but he had to supplement it with some summer hunting and guiding on forestry commission and public land. He specialised in offering horse packing trips with clients bringing their own horses if they wished. But more usually he hired horses for the summer, as needed, from a farm nearby. He provided mountain camp accommodation using large wall or bell tents. Most of his guests simply wanted to enjoy early morning or evening wildlife rides, heading out on scenic trails or hiking where elk, deer, antelope and an occasional mountain goat or sheep could be viewed and photographed. Riding at an elevation of 6,000 feet past beautiful, secluded mountain lakes loaded with native trout offered some pleasant fishing too for those who wished to try.

His biggest problem was the guests, who, despite being on holiday, brought their problems to the wilderness. There had been marital and teenage tantrums and the occasional wife who made it plain she would prefer his bed to her husband's. His favourite guests were the young couples in love with each other and nature who made guiding a pleasure. He managed it all with the quiet self-assurance he carried with him, plus some humour and self-deprecation. After two summers in the area, he was getting repeat business, which pleased him.

As he paid his bill, some slight deviltry made him say to Sandy, 'If ever you fancy a horse to ride, let me know and I will take you up to the prettiest lake you've ever seen.' She looked slightly startled but smiled and thanked him. He gave her one of his cards which said Ross McCallister – Idaho Horse Safaris. That would get them talking, he had no doubt. If she mentioned the invitation.

He got into his beaten-up old Jeep Cherokee and drove to collect more steel spikes from the hardware store and then meandered slowly out of town, full of breakfast, his eyes passing over the rustic saloon just before the edge of town. He thought back to his damn fool younger self, who'd been beaten up in many such places and done some beating up himself. 'Damn fool!' he muttered. The big Cadillac V8 engine he'd fitted to the Jeep made a sound that was pleasing to his ear with its promise of surprising grunt and lightning speed when needed.

The battered Jeep said much about him. His father had lived in Dallas, Texas and bought one of the first two-door Cherokees to come off the production line in 1974. Ross and his father spent many happy times driving into the woods in the Jeep to go camping, hunting, and fishing – every dent and scratch held memories for him. When his father died, he could not bear to part with it, so he placed it in storage on jacks. When he bought his land in Idaho, he retrieved the Jeep and found that the narrow street tyres and worn-out engine would not cut it in the wilderness. So he took the Jeep to the Gas Monkey Garage in Dallas and told them not to touch the bodywork, but to flare the wheel arches to accommodate wider off-road tyres and to fit a reconditioned V8 engine. It pleased his ancestral Scottish frugality to save something good and to improve it to suit his needs.

The rhythm of his days on the ranch were slow but purposeful. There was time aplenty now with the lighter days. He kept all his machinery from chain saws to guns perfectly serviced and in meticulous condition. The Airstream was given a spring clean and his generator topped up. He worked some hours each day with the horses, bringing them back to a semblance of fitness after their winter lay-off. Both had wintered well, even Buddy, who was now 14, and the much younger Rincon. Both were full of themselves and tore around the paddock. He looked over each horse with the care and deliberation of someone who saw them as friends who would stand between him and disaster if necessary, bringing him home if injured.

Work on the house went apace and his fitness grew with the exercise of wrangling logs. Within a month he had the walls up and was working on the roof gable ends. Life was good. On finally leaving the armed services, Ross had been lucky to find himself in the hands of a horse-riding psychiatrist who not surprisingly, assessed him as suffering from PTSD (post-traumatic stress disorder).

An ex-military man himself, the man had said to him, 'When life bites you in the butt, a horse will help you at least as much as the Samaritans. Our equine friends make for good therapy. Hell at work, a failing marriage, bereavement, not enough money for the mortgage or the children's school fees, coming back as you have from war, all these things that life sends when it bares its teeth, are helped by horses. How, I cannot fully explain, it's just so.' Ross agreed wholeheartedly.

The therapist mentioned the writer John Irving. 'He gave sage advice about surviving this world in his book *Hotel New Hampshire*. He wrote, "Just keep passing the open windows". Those windows are always there, Ross, they beckon and promise release, and sometimes it takes more courage to walk past them and live, than to dive out through them and die. Horses help you move past them more quickly – they have longer strides.' Grinning, he added, 'A wise Englishman – there are a few – once said that the best thing for the inside of a man was the outside of a horse.' Ross was in complete agreement. In his experience, their beauty and their presence brought healing, and the landscapes they took you to only added to the cure.

'We poison ourselves with information and stimulation, like too many uppers. They leave us buzzing and nauseous, twanging like a tuning fork. Horses earth you once more. They will make you stop and stare, take in the view, dream a little, and then magic happens, peace leaks quietly in. They make you whole.'

Ross was surprised to hear this coming from a psychiatrist, but his words touched something in him that had experience of just this phenomenon. His words proved a turning point for Ross, who began to improve as the mission to find land and horses took an ever-greater hold on him. Horses had always been his medicine. Back in his youth in Texas, a half-hour with his horse at night, standing by its shoulder, watching over the stable door as the northern constellations wheeled across a winter sky, or at the moon scudding between clouds, or just the wind, coming from across the world, brought quiet, and peace and joy. Now and then his horse would rest its head on his shoulder, snuffle into his neck, and Ross would feel touched by blessings.

And now he was in search of an Eden, an Arcadia, a

place of deep untouched nature, after the horrors of war and, encouraged by the therapist, he instinctively sensed from experience that it would be a journey made better with horses. Perhaps that was why great kings and warriors lay buried with their horses, not only as a sign of status, but as a means of transport to another world, to Heaven. After all, when the final window beckons, wouldn't it be good to take that final leap with a horse beneath you?

Chapter 2

Ross was the first to admit he had been lucky and that this quality had stood him in good stead during his years of soldiering. He was also deliberate and patient. He knew that these two qualities had come to him as the result of living on the edge – that however careful, smart or lucky you were, if you played that game of cards, sooner or later you would come up a loser. It was just a matter of numbers and probability.

Now when asked what he did, he told people that he'd knocked around a bit after his army service, which had been uneventful. He said he'd done some offshore oil drilling, worked for a while as a car salesman and motor racer, even had a season of rodeo riding, none of it entirely untrue, but all the other stuff, he figured, was his business and his business only.

He spent two winters setting up a sophisticated security system on the place. Nothing and nobody moved on those 500 acres without him being aware of it. He also used a drone to let hunters and anyone else know there were eyes in the sky, and he was watching. This did not help the hunting and they knew it, so they veered off immediately, mostly. Once or twice, a hunter had fired at his drone and he had scared them off with a couple of shots from the Tac-50, so close that they realised he could well have killed them had he so wished. News spread and he was seldom bothered. Thanks to the technology, he got to know the ways of the animals, the elk, the bear, the deer, the odd cougar and the mountain goats and sheep. The biggest threat to his drone were the eagles who would stoop on it and then slide past.

He was disciplined about staying offline, generally keeping away from social media. It was just too easy now to be in someone's crosshairs and not even be aware of it. When he was forced to, he used some electronic coding and interfering kit that his ex-Mossad friend Mordechai 'Motke' used in his sensitive business dealings. They trusted each other, having had each other's backs on more than a few occasions. Each had reason to be grateful to the other.

All of this stuff was driven by a mindset that was shaped by his past twenty years. He had first-hand knowledge of just how real realpolitik was and how big the political threats were. He feared the ever-widening gap between rich and poor and just how easy it was to rile people up who felt they had been given the bum's rush by government and big business.

He wanted out of it all. And he wanted to be able to live as independently as possible and to defend himself if the need arose. He was not unusual in this; many people shared his feelings and this created an environment that largely respected privacy and was deeply suspicious of strangers. His neighbours were a mix of miners and loggers, some old-fashioned hippies, and a sprinkling of back-to-nature types wanting to live off-grid as much as possible, like him. There were writers and artists too and one or two trappers who scraped a living.

It was mountain country and Schweitzer, the local ski resort, pulled in tourists throughout the winter ski season. Lake Pend Oreille was big enough for good sailing and in summer there was a lot of water sports activity. For a slightly rough-around-the-edges town there was enough sophistication and visitors in Sandpoint to keep the local economy ticking over.

He had thought seriously about getting a dog, a Weimaraner like those he had grown up with, but for now he felt it would limit his freedom to come and go. The horses were another tie, but they helped him earn a living and provided all the company he needed. Once the cabin was complete, he might think about a dog again.

His plans for the homestead included a vegetable garden and a polytunnel to extend the growing season. He had already laid a pipe from the stream that ran down the hill and filled a couple of 500-gallon tanks. He aimed to back this up with rainwater off the roof when it was up. He had no problem feeding himself with grouse and deer and fish, much of it smoked to make it last longer. Bottled, canned and dried foods completed his provisioning and the berries in spring and summer were plentiful.

Ross was just back from a few days in the high country with the horses, checking the trails for tree falls and landslides. At the ranch he found all pretty much as he had left it. His discreet 'tell-tales' were all still in place and the cameras showed nothing untoward. His clothes carried the scent of woodsmoke and trees, lodgepole pine, Engelmann spruce, white bark pine and subalpine firs. He'd found the country in good heart. He was just finishing his breakfast dishes when his phone rang. It was Sandy from the Hoot Owl Café. He was surprised; he had not thought he would hear from her.

'Hi Ross, it's Sandy from the Hoot Owl Café. I'm calling to ask if your invitation to go riding still stands?' She sounded a little unsure of herself and a bit shy, uncertain what kind of reception she would get.

He was reassuring. 'Hi Sandy, yes, of course, you would be most welcome. Good to hear from you. I'm just back from a few days on the trails, stretching the horses' legs after the winter. When would you like to come up?'

They arranged for her to come out on Sunday, her day off, and he gave her directions.

'Is there anything I can bring you?' she asked.

He said, 'Just as long as you let me pay you, I'd like some pastries and some biscuits from the bakery in town. 'And one last thing,' he added. 'Sorry to ask, but how well do you ride? I'd like to match you with something that suits.'

She laughed and said, 'That's a fair question. I've been around horses most of my life. I grew up just outside Quebec where I learned to ride, and then again on a ranch near Bozeman where I studied.'

As he cleaned the horses' bridles and saddles, he found himself wondering about Sunday. She would have no trouble with Buddy if she rode as someone who had grown up with horses.

Rested by his days away from building he got stuck in once more and by the end of the week he had the cabin's two gable ends linked with the ridge pole and eight roof beams. The place was beginning to take shape.

Spring had come with a rush, and he had to take a day off to get some of the plants he'd been nurturing into the ground. He had created a number of boxed raised beds that received sun throughout the day, and he looked forward to eating his own home-grown salads and vegetable crops. He had potatoes in as well as beet, carrots, spinach, cabbage, squash and beans. As a newcomer to farming, he was reading everything he could find on how to be self-sustaining and his veg boxes showed he was learning fast.

As he worked on the cabin and his gardening or with the horses, he was always aware of the many ghosts who walked with him, friends who had not made it back from various theatres of war, or those who had, but could not adjust and who took their own lives. And then, more dimly in the day but much more demanding at night, the faces of those he had hunted and who had hunted him. Now and then he found himself simply looking into the distance, a thousand-yard stare once more.

He had willingly accepted the psychological support he'd been given on his return, and it had helped him enough that he was able to get back to active duty but in a different capacity, working undercover for some years. But a growing exhaustion with a double life and an ever-greater conviction that this was not the life he wanted had brought him to this big sky country. He was grateful that he had made the transition. And the friendly ghosts were good company of a kind.

When Sandy arrived, she disarmed him with a gift of a chocolate cake that she had made herself. 'Probably not as good as the stuff from the bakery, but I felt it was the least I could do.' He was touched.

'Well that's three things I know about you now. You can ride, cook and you are not scared of a challenge.'

'What do you mean?' she asked.

'Well, when the ladies at the café suggested you come serve me instead of your usual tables, you did not say no.' She blushed and they both laughed.

They were lucky with the weather and were on the trail shortly after she arrived. She had asked to use the toilet and did not seem fazed by the outhouse. After greeting Buddy, she swung up into the saddle with practiced ease and rode with the relaxed seat of an old hand and Buddy looked happy and calm with her. As ever, once in the saddle, conversation was easy and the silences comfortable. He discovered that she was a teacher, a history major from Montana State University in Bozeman, and was teaching school in Sandpoint. She had been waiting tables at the Hoot Owl Café to earn some money during the vacation after a holiday on Captiva Island off Florida's Gulf Coast. She smiled when he asked if she had developed a stoop looking for sand dollars on the beaches. They spoke about her teaching, and it was evident that she had a vocation; it was more than just a job.

She rode ahead at his urging. His horse Rincon danced a little, used to being boss horse on the trail, but soon enough settled down. Ross noted her old but well cared for cowboy boots and the way she held her reins, barely touching Buddy's mouth. Her back was straight and elegant. And he liked the swing of her shiny hair. She was slim and athletic, her fine boned face showing empathy and intelligence.

He teased her, 'If you teach like you ride, your pupils are very lucky to have you.'

She laughed and said some of them thought she was a holy terror. 'My homework assignments have to be in on time!' He felt the strength of her personality, warm and gentle though she was.

After some hours, they swung for home and loped the horses along the valley bottoms and water meadows. The girl could ride.

Back at the half-built cabin he gave her a tour and she complimented him on managing the work on his own. He realised that she had not asked him a single question about himself, happy with what he was prepared to mention. He appreciated her tact.

He made her a cheese omelette served with hot rolls, a salad, and a glass of white wine for lunch. They ate with appetite, the food on their laps, sitting in the camp chairs outside the Airstream. And she praised his cooking.

'That omelette would have my mother's approval. It was delicious.' And that led them to discussing a mutual love of France. As it happened, her parents were French Quebecois who had come south for work before heading home to retire.

He told her of his time in Paris and on the Brittany coast. She smiled and said, 'But that's amazing! My people came from Brittany, they were Bretons before they were French!' She explained, 'The Bretons are a frugal French farming and fishing stock as you will know. They made a living off the land and the sea for centuries in the old country. They are my history.' She said that as a result of a few years of bad harvests, sea storm disasters and the loss of men during war, her family had come to the New World around 1880 seeking land and a new start.

'It was the very lack of information about my family history beyond these bare facts that made the study of history such a compelling subject for me. It was so personal at first and then once I had some of the answers I searched for, it became a fascination with the broader discipline of history itself.' She had inherited all the canniness of her French peasant ancestry and the bravery of her fishing folk who worked small boats far out to sea. But it was her very name that held the biggest clue, Sandrine Deschamps – Sandrine of the fields – that gave an insight into what her people held most dear. Land.

'But in Canada, instead of land we found education and that changed things for us. My grandfather became a horse dealer and then expanded to sell agricultural products as well and my father is an accountant, now retired. They both married women of Breton stock who could live off the smoke of a cooking stove and also hold down jobs as seamstresses and in my mother's case, bookkeeping. So land remained a dream.'

Before they knew it, they had finished the bottle of wine. He offered to open another, but she said she would not trust her driving. So, instead, he made some strong coffee to go with the cake she had made, and they sat quietly enjoying the dessert and basking in the spring warmth, both aware that something good had begun.

Around 6 o'clock she said she felt confident now to drive back and he walked her to her car, a small white Toyota. He opened the door for her and thanked her again for the cake.

'It was such a lovely day,' she said, looking at him directly. And she added, 'You must be aware that you are seen as a man of mystery in town. But the ladies I serve with at the Hoot Owl Café have a thing for you, so I thought I would risk taking you up on your offer to ride.'

'And what will you tell them about this visit?' he could not help asking.

She grinned impishly and said, 'I will tell them that you remain a mystery… but one that is most partial to my chocolate cake!' They laughed.

He took her hand, touching her for the first time, and said, 'Come again. I could do with this kind of break more often.' He released her hand slowly and waved her off as she drove out of his yard.

The next time Ross saw Sandy, it was in Sandpoint, and she

looked much more like Sandrine Deschamps, a French woman raised in Canada, but with no hint of the wilderness about her. She wore a simple stone-coloured dress, but it was cashmere, he noted, and beneath it a cream silk shirt, whose collar and cuffs peeked out from the three-quarter sleeves. With this ensemble she wore elegant grey suede pumps with silver buckles. A simple turquoise necklace, one of the December birthstones, with a central oval of red coral, set it all off to perfection.

She would not have been out of place in an art gallery in New York or having tea at the Savoy in London. Her look stopped him dead in his tracks. She looked… he searched for the word… aristocratic. He had not noticed or thought that before when she arrived at the ranch in jeans and cowboy boots. But this quality carried on beneath her clothes too, in her body's elegance, the clean line of her jaw and the high-bridged nose. She took his breath away.

Sandy said she had been at a teacher-parent meeting at the school, and he wondered how she was perceived by her students and their mothers and fathers. The word that came to him along with the French accent was 'formidable'. It was something he noted too and filed away for the future. She was a woman who expected respect and got it in spades. He greeted her warmly.

'You look ravishing.' She smiled, content with his reaction, but she had an appointment and had to run.

'I'm so sorry. I hope to see you soon.' And she was gone, Ross gazed after her as she walked to her car. He admitted it to himself, he was surprised, but pleasantly so.

As someone who had spent years in the Middle East, he was finely attuned to the cues that dress provided. Although garbed in virtually all-enveloping and disguising clothes, the women of the region still managed to project touches of individuality that flashed from beneath their strict dress code, the quality of material, the way a scarf was worn, discreet jewellery, kohl to highlight the eyes. Dress was a much more subtle language there, but no less intriguing.

Ross was no stranger to shopping for women, most of

whom were very happy with his choices. It was a skill honed in New York, London and Paris as well as the Middle and Far East. He had 'an eye' as they said in the art world, an ability to appreciate beauty, line, elegance, understatement and that something else, a quality of uniqueness that arrested your attention. But there was something innate too in him, an ability to perceive beauty, however unusual in a woman, a landscape, a painting, or indeed in a horse. It was something that spoke to his emotions. As a result, he enjoyed clothing women, almost as much as its opposite.

He could not help but wonder in which outfit Sandy was her truest self – the black and white waitress uniform, the cashmere dress or the jeans and blue shirt she wore for riding. He hoped it was the latter.

CHAPTER 3

Relatively remote though his place was, there were times when Ross felt hemmed in. But he had known and expected this so had bought land wisely, land that gave him close access to millions of acres of untouched national forest land in the 2.2-million-acre Kootenai National Forest located in the extreme Northwest corner of Montana and Northeast Idaho and the 1.5-million-acre Colville National Forest in Northeast Washington, east of the Cascade Mountains. In either one of these forests, one could simply disappear off human radar if you so wished, or get dangerously lost.

The spectacular landscape of the Kootenai National Forest was shaped by continental and alpine glaciers leaving lakes and valleys behind, a mountainous retreat and home to the early American Indians who lived by hunting and gathering. Traces of their life here over the past 8,000 years were discreetly evident if you knew where to look, the remains of fish weirs in the rivers and some rotted log shoots for funnelling big game to killing points. They had lived lightly on the land. The European history of the Forest began with the arrival of the early explorers and fur traders then railroad construction, mining and logging activities flourished in this vast land rich in resources. The same was true of the Colville National Forest. These cool northern forests were seemingly untouched bear country and the grizzly still ruled here.

But now and again civilisation called, and Ross took off on a book-buying spree to Spokane in Washington, where he would spend the best part of a day browsing the bookshelves of Auntie's Bookstore on Main Avenue or, by way of a change, he'd do a book dash to The Well-Read Moose in Coeur d'Alene. Driving home, his passenger seat loaded with his finds, their weight forced him to click in the passenger seatbelt to stop the car beeping. These days he read mostly non-fiction, travel writing and books to educate himself about his new home, its history and inhabitants, both human and animal. House building, farming and food gardening books, cooking, fishing and hunting. After two years in the area, he could have held down a job as a geography lecturer at Gonzaga University in Spokane or Montana State University in Bozeman.

He read for days at a time, letting his house building schedule slide. And then he drank himself into near oblivion. It was something that happened from time to time, his way of coping with the remnants of his PTSD.

He had become almost inured to the flashbacks, reliving the traumatic events, the intense feeling it was happening again, with a racing heart and sweating. At night he wrestled with repeating memories or nightmares linked to those almost buried events. Distressing and intrusive thoughts and images came with sweating, trembling, pain or feeling sick. He felt that he was torn in two, needing to keep busy all the time, and at the same time using alcohol and drugs to avoid the memories. He felt numb and detached from his body but was sufficiently in control to recognise what was going on, and watched himself as though from a distance, able to some extent to observe the trauma with one part of his mind. It was as if he was two separate beings. He did not eat properly. He disconnected the landline and switched off his mobile.

So it came as a surprise to hear a gentle tapping on the door one day. When he opened it, gun in hand, he found Sandy on his doorstep. She summed up the situation immediately, having expected some trauma had befallen him when she could not reach him on the phone. She took him by his hand and ran a bath for him and helped him undress. He went in like a child and when he had lain some time in the warm water, she washed him like a child. She watched his eyes focus on her as he returned to himself from somewhere unknowable. She towelled him dry and put him to bed in clean pyjamas and held him while he slept. When he woke, she made coffee and fed him breakfast. In all this time, they barely spoke. After they had washed up the dishes, he started to tell her why he was as she found him. She put a finger to his lips and then kissed him.

'You don't have to explain. I know this thing. My brother had something similar after a summer of fire-jumping in California. He saw a lot of dead folks.' Then she made love to him slowly, gently, lovingly.

Within a day he felt quite himself again and started once more with his much-delayed building work on the cabin. Sandy stayed two more magical days and then took off. The intensity of the experience was such that there was no need for talk of commitment or meeting up. They felt a joint future opening up before them. What would be would be.

In one of Sandy's weekly calls to her parents, offering her news and checking in on them, she admitted that she had met someone she liked. She described Ross as a former soldier and now a rancher in the dude ranch business. She said he'd grown up in Texas and was very tall.

'*C'est un grand homme maman, de plus de six pieds et un bon cavalier. Et il a sa propre terre, cinq cents belles acres!* He is a big man, Mom, over six foot and a good horseman. And he has his own land, five hundred beautiful acres!'

In reply there was a typically sharp inquiry from her mother, asking how old he was. When Sandy explained the twelve-year age difference, she heard her mother make that 'Pffft' sound the French make to accompany the gesture of throwing their hands in the air.

'*Tu l'aime?* Do you love him?' her mother asked.

Sandy replied, 'It is too soon to say, but I think this is a man I could love. You are right of course about the age difference, but he is emotionally intelligent, he is sensitive, kind, generous, wise in many ways and brave. He has a distinguished war record. And he is funny, he makes me laugh!'

'Ah oui, that is nice, but will he be able to support you or will you be working to your dying day?' she asked with all the pragmatism of her French farming past.

'*Mamere*, he has a good pension from the army and he is ambitious to grow the ranch business. And he can cook!'

'But *cherie*, does he love you?'

'I think so, a little. Time will tell.'

And that ended that conversation. She thought it best not to mention the PTSD issues he faced.

Chapter 4

Like all of us, Ross was the product of his genes and his environment. His Scottish and Viking forbears had ended their fight by settling amicably in his DNA which, however peaceful that may sound, carried its own consequences. His childhood in Texas had been a seminal influence, bullied in a number of schools till a growth spurt at 13 and a love of wrestling and boxing put him beyond the reach of his tormentors.

His biggest challenge during his active service army years was learning to control the blood madness that descended on him in a fight, be it in a barroom when a friend was picked on, or in the field in a fire fight. His every instinct – one his blood ancestors would have understood and respected – was to welcome the onset of the berserk and run directly at the enemy wielding a battle axe, or in his case, a high-powered rifle. He was lucky to survive those early years, but in the end he learned to harness his fury and fight clever, a boxer who had tired of the canvas.

A day came when he was in charge of a four-man team tasked with taking out a group of Mujahideen holed up in a remote house in the mountains of Afghanistan. In the past he might have worked the group into close quarters under cover of darkness and simply stormed the building, but he'd learned the hard way and responsibility for the lives of his companions had taught him a wary, canny caution. They waited till first light when men started coming out to relieve themselves and with silenced weapons lowered the odds considerably. With the rest of the group in the house now aware that they were under attack, he moved the offense up a notch with a volley of mortars followed by stun grenades and as the survivors exited the remains of the house, they were clinically picked off. All that remained was for a search of the property for the one or two survivors who would inevitably be sheltering in a cellar or under the collapsed roof beams. A toxic smoke bomb took care of them and as they ran coughing and vomiting out of the remains of the house they too were eliminated. After an hour, as the smoke cleared, he went in with one man to find, as expected, that the only remnants of the group were those killed in the mortar fire. It was a cold and controlled business, much like a rat shoot in a farm barn.

His days of running amok were over and men followed him with total commitment. He became a master at tactical withdrawals and false feints, boxing clever. And it served him well. In pub fights too, he now walked away and if followed outside, would end it quickly with a range of close quarter combat skills which included a vicious chop to the carotid artery in the neck that would drop a man quicker than a punch. An effective self-defence technique, which was useful in close range situations. When executed correctly, the so-called *carotid strike* caused the assailant a sudden loss of oxygen to the brain, followed by fainting and collapse. When they come to some minutes later, they were usually unaware of what had occurred.

Being able to maim or kill with his bare hands made Ross ever more cautious, but there was now something in his eyes and posture that sent a danger signal to would-be attackers, who mostly left off immediately. None of this gave him any satisfaction but simply added to his wish to be gone forever from those theatres of war or espionage where such behaviour was common currency.

Nor did he miss his leadership role. Writing to the parents or wives of dead men put an end to that pleasure. It had been a fierce joy to lead squads of SEALs, the best of the best, but even with such mutual support and the respect he saw in their eyes, there was only so much killing a man could stand before he became an animal or a monster.

Ross completed tours of active service in the Iraq War and terms in Afghanistan and then transferred to the US mainland, where he ran a training camp. He found life at the Navy Recruit Training Center, the Navy boot camp, where SEAL candidates start their training with the 10-week Navy boot camp in Great Lakes, Illinois, pleasant enough, if boring, and after a year he exited life with the SEALs for a very different kind of brief, serving with Special Ops in a number of capacities that required initiative, tact, diplomacy and the ability to turn on a dime and kill if the need arose. He seldom had to take a life again and that suited him fine. His tasks were security oriented, guarding facilities or dignitaries, but every now and then an off-radar project would come his way in which he would find himself rubbing shoulders with CIA, Mossad or MI6 operatives. He learned a great deal and a number of new languages and life was stimulating, with plenty of R&R in exotic places in Asia.

By the time he quit, he could as easily host a diplomatic dinner at an embassy as he could run a team of agents to extract someone from behind the lines. There was seldom a dull moment, but he drank too much and slept badly and as his 40th birthday loomed, he knew it was time to seek pastures new. An altogether quieter life beckoned. And it was then that the words of his friend Stiegs came to mind. 'Land is true wealth, Ross.'

CHAPTER 5

He now turned his energies to finishing the cabin between horse packing client trips. The weather held good and he made steady progress. His carpentry, plumbing, electrical and structural skills might not have been that of an expert but were sufficient to his needs. And his highly developed appreciation of line and architectural aesthetics took care of the rest.

By the fall, he had a low-slung ranch house, rather more than merely a cabin, and he was pleased with the look of the place, part Montana log cabin, part shuttered French farmhouse. It was both sturdy and elegant in its simplicity. He spent some time scouring farm sales, antique shops, junk shops and small local auctions to furnish the house in an eclectic style, part Western, part Mexican with earth-fired tiled floors covered in kilims and oriental rugs.

Sandy approved and when she could, joined in the search for soft furnishings that added a sense of comfort. A massive chimney breast of smooth river stones dominated the living-dining room. It was functional too, retaining and releasing heat for hours after the fire had died. They found soft caramel-coloured leather couches and men's club easy chairs and one or two early Swedish wood, metal and leather recliners. His pride and joy on the walls were a series of Western cowboy landscapes, some naïf work by local artists of the mountain terrain in the vicinity and a few river trout-fishing scenes. Ross was more than happy with the effect. Sandy added some Mexican serapes as wall hangings, and in one corner of the living room they stacked four century-old western saddles. The place had atmosphere.

One hot afternoon he found her just out of the shower stretched full length on her stomach on one of the leather couches and her beauty struck him an almost physical blow. She looked up and smiled, knowing full well the effect her nakedness had on him. 'You look like cream spread on caramel,' he said, and the old caramel leather couch took some hits.

Ross brought in triple-glazed weather windows that guaranteed to keep the place cosy in winter while opening up the views. They also had the ability to take a bullet, the middle pane being bullet-proof.

His last client trail ride of the season was a three-day affair with a young couple in their thirties. It was patently the idea of the wife, Claire, a former event and distance rider introducing Ben, her new husband, to the joy of riding and deep country. On the phone she said he had been riding now for six months and had made good progress. Ross hesitated to confirm and she sent him a flurry of emails assuring him that Ben, a former football and ice hockey player, was fit and able and very much up for the challenge. Something made him delay confirming, but he was busy and as it was the last trip of the season, he finally said yes.

When Claire and Ben arrived he saw that they were indeed young and athletic and Ben seemed as enthusiastic as his wife. But after a few hours on the trail he noticed that Ben was looking uncomfortable. Ross ordered a halt for an early afternoon rest and they all had a brief doze in deep grass under some shade trees. When they moved off for the last two hours all seemed well again and they found a good place to camp by a stream. It was a place he'd used a few times. Ben helped him erect the tents and set up camp and soon they sat by a fire grilling steaks and sipping red wine. The conversation flowed and by 10pm they all turned in.

Ross was awoken by the sound of raised voices around

This Country I Call My Own

2am and he slipped out of his tent to check the horse lines and to listen more closely to the argument. This was not the first time he had experienced marital discord on a trail ride. People brought their problems with them. It was one of the challenges you faced in this business, and he was normally good at diffusing such discord. He approached his client's tent cautiously and was close enough to see Ben storming out. He waited in the darkness and saw Claire emerge from the tent and reach out to Ben who struck her a blow that sent her sprawling backwards. It was all Ross needed to see. He strode to Claire and asked her if she was OK.

'Keep out of this cowboy!' Ben said in a voice thick with fury. He lunged for Ross who sidestepped and put his man down with an almost unseen strike. He checked Ben's breathing and went to help Claire up.

'Is he alright?' she asked. He assured her that Ben would sleep for a while, and wake up probably remembering little of what had occurred. Claire said, 'I think we'd better go back in the morning. This trip was not a good idea. I'm sorry to have inflicted our problems on you.' He reassured her that he had seen much worse and asked if Ben was often violent towards her. Her tears answered his question.

The ride back the next day was tense, but Ben seemed subdued and avoided eye contact. When they reached the homestead that afternoon, Claire and Ben took their leave in a reasonably civil way and he thought no more of it. She had said he was to keep the payment for the full three days, for which he was grateful.

That night, after he had let the horses out to pasture and made supper, he sat outside looking at the stars wondering if he should call a halt to this way of living and simply become a hermit full time, just living off his pension and some investments he had. But he brushed such thoughts aside, recalling the many successful trips he'd made with clients, some of whom kept in touch, planning repeat visits. He wondered what compromise Claire had made in her marriage and how long it would last. He knew of old that making deals with the Devil was not a winning hand; cashing in your chips and getting out of the game was the smart call. Far in the mountains, a coyote howled at the rising moon.

Chapter 6

And then, as though summoned by his thoughts, the devil himself arrived at the ranch unannounced, as grim-faced as ever, and bearing a gift that could well be a poisoned chalice. It was his former boss, head of the Agency that orchestrated some of the bloodier threads of the war tapestry in the Middle East that the US Government did not wish to leave its own fingerprints on. He'd earned his nickname, the Devil, for his constant interference with plans that had been agreed and signed off. He rode two horses, one political and one military, hence the constant shifting of priorities that so frustrated his team at times.

Ross smiled grimly, recalling his thoughts about making a deal with the devil that had come to him following the debacle with his clients, Ben and Claire, as he watched the dust trail of his former boss's car dissipate in the still afternoon air. He had come to offer Ross a deal that would clear his debts, his mortgage and put some decent money into his savings account and his investments, but the price was high for this promised last job for the old firm.

He was under no illusion as to the rights and wrongs of the thing he'd been asked to take on. His old outfit had been tasked with finding a way for federal officials to walk away from their obligation to properly clean up a massive quantity of radioactive nuclear waste in Idaho and Washington states, left over from nuclear weapon production dating to the

Second World War and the Cold War.

The process of avoiding the clean-up – which would save the Government billions – had been quietly underway for some time, but now a lobby group of antis had sprung up led by Jack Freemantle, an articulate, Harvard-educated, media-savvy lawyer and author of *Our Nuked Country*. The book had won plaudits and awards and its writer was building a growing following, rallying people and support to the anti-nuclear environmental cause. Some political pundits were saying that Freemantle was ambitious and had his eye on a Senate seat and then possibly even the Presidency itself, but his short-term goal was the Governorship of Idaho and the nuclear waste clean-up fight was a handy means of generating media interest and building a constituency of support across the Democrat-Republican divide. Nobody wanted children who glowed green and had two heads. But that political ambition was a pipe dream. Idaho had voted Republican for six decades.

And now the Agency wanted him to run a blocking tackle on Freemantle and the clean-up lobby. As Ross sat in the deepening night, watching the stars, his mind as ever walked him back to his childhood. He had read enough literature on the subject to know that our childhood is ever with us, in its experiences and the deep subliminal subconscious messages it has taught us. If the brain was a blackboard, then the writings on it of the early years were not so much chalked on it as gouged deep into its surface, the rest merely a light scribble by comparison.

Ross spent some time figuring the angles and trying to work out how he would buy off his conscience if he accepted the Agency deal. As ever, the image of his father sat at the gate of his soul, his conscience and his spirit.

When Ross was five, his six-month old brother Angus died, and it was recorded as a cot-death. His grief-stricken mother, Sarah, never got over the loss and blamed herself. One day she walked off into the desert, took a handful of sleeping tablets and died of dehydration on a rocky outcrop. Her desiccated remains, much mauled by predators, were found by hikers three weeks later. Ross's father never remarried, the double tragedy killed something in him and now he simply lived for his remaining son. It was just the two of them against the world, and a deep and unbreakable bond developed between them. Jeb McCallister was a righteous man of no religion but with a cast iron belief in right and wrong and with an independent streak inscribed on his bones. Not surprisingly, worshipping his father as he did, Ross learned to fend for himself at a young age and think for himself, taking his lead from his father. And though he no longer felt so sure of being on the right side of history in his two bloody decades at war and then working for the Agency, he had always believed that he could look his father squarely in the eyes.

But now his peace of mind, fragile as it was, faced a threat embedded in the offer from his old handlers. And he knew it was not really an offer, it was a demand. Their hold on him had not entirely ended the day he left their employ. His great abiding wish to be gone from his past was now under threat. The US government's plans to reclassify some of the nation's most dangerous radioactive waste to lower its threat level was outraging critics, who said the move would make it cheaper and easier to walk away from cleaning up nuclear weapon production sites in Washington state and Idaho. Some three million gallons of waste were due to be moved to New Mexico.

The Department of Energy said that labelling some high-level waste as low level would save $40 billion in clean-up costs across the nation's entire nuclear weapons complex. The material that had languished for decades in the two states would be taken to low-level disposal facilities in Utah or Texas, or New Mexico, the Department said. This would maintain standards set by the independent Nuclear Regulatory Commission, with the goal of getting the lower-level waste from the production and storage of nuclear weapons out of these states without sacrificing public safety.

Critics of this scheme, like Freemantle and his cohorts, were saying it was a way for federal officials to walk away from their obligation to properly clean up a massive quantity of radioactive waste left from the production and storage of nuclear weapons.

The calm, rational, persuasive voice of his former boss, the man he had been led by for years repeated, 'Ross, we want Freemantle discredited, stopped. The guy is bringing huge pressure to bear on health officials in both states. He is fundraising for a legal fight to halt the light clean-up. If he succeeds, it's going to cost the administration billions, money they are reluctant to spend on this issue when experts are telling them it's not necessary. We simply need to move three million gallons of toxic waste to Texas or New Mexico, bury it and be done.'

Ross asked, 'Discredited or dead?

'Discredited, not dead, Ross. You have a week to say if you are in or out.'

Ross was not a scientist, but his gut instinct told him the job brief was clearly something that a court of law would find troubling. The McCallister mind and ethics shied away from it like a very skittish horse. He decided to head into the mountains on his own to think it through.

CHAPTER 7

The following day's weather promised rain, but Ross felt the call of the mountains and was not going to be put off by the chance of a shower. Whenever the weather offered challenges, his mind took him back to his basic training. His old drill sergeant was fond of the expression 'Pussy weather', explaining that rain kept the pussies indoors.

This male locker-room talk set his teeth on edge, but it was just another part of basic training. He found that when he got into fieldcraft, his handler was of the same opinion. 'Wet is good. It washes your tracks away and the wildlife like to lie up out of the weather. If you know their secret shelter spots, you know where to get a meal.'

Animals, Ross discovered, were as habituated to their own range as much as any person living a suburban life. They kept largely to their own patch, to their own runs, their own paths, their own places of rest, their own watering places. It was up to him to read the land and see its messages, its words, its animal and botanical life, to make something of it to put in his fire or his pot. It was an open book, all there before you if you had the eyes to see it, and the knowledge. His training was his Rosetta Stone, the key to unlocking landscape, so that what looked like indecipherable runes turned out to be as clear as a song.

He had worked hard at survival training, learning just

how many calories it took to keep going in all weathers, learning to trap, fish and snare. He learned to move like a ghost through a landscape, leaving virtually no trace of himself behind, cooking if he had to in sheltered places where his fire could not be seen and carrying the cooked food with him to be consumed cold in the following days. It became an instinct as much as moving unseen through a city was second nature to him, always backtracking and checking for tails, marking and noting security cameras, finding those places where crowds provided cover to disappear. Sometimes he felt that living with his senses on red alert all the time had turned him into a wild animal himself.

The horses were not happy as the weather broke but they put their heads down and trudged on somewhat grumpily. They were definitely not best pleased to be so wet, but they worked with a will, trusting Ross to bring them to a good place up ahead, as he always did. Once clear of his own land, he felt them become more alert as they entered country they knew less well, or not at all. He was headed for the high country, on trails he was sure would keep him clear of walkers and riders from one or more of the other riding outfits, dude ranches with up to 100 horses and horse packers with almost as many. This region was prime country for city folks seeking a 'wilderness experience' and they were well catered for by ranches that in some cases had been five generations in the same family. There were some very good folks out here, he knew. The Ruby Ridge shootout between the US Marshals and a group of survivalists which had left dead on both sides, had done the area no favours but it was an exception, though there were still pockets of survivalists, people deeply suspicious and hostile to government, and those with radical and sometimes racist doctrines. The Sons of Aryan were headquartered in the area, although how many adherents they had these days was anyone's guess. The Twin Towers attack in New York a few years back had been a great recruiting sergeant for them, so he figured numbers could well be up.

These thoughts drifted through his mind as he picked

out the best way to work the trail he had chosen. The horses were sure-footed but he kept a watchful eye as they emerged from the bottom land, largely meadow with stands of trees, climbing into hill country that had much heavier tree cover. Now and then, out of pure habit, he stopped, dismounted, and put his binoculars on his back trail. He was looking for people but now he was in the realm of moose, elk, wolves, bald eagles, deer, wild mountain lions, a landscape of mountains and meadows, secret canyons, streams, waterfalls and rock pools and he scanned the land with meticulous care.

There was nobody on his trail. This high mountain land was at the emptiest it had been for centuries, its natural human inhabitants wiped out by the army, by settlers, by sickness and disease brought by the newcomers, and by their impact on the resident animal population. It was a story as old as man. One human group wiping out another. Science was now indicating that this was how the Neanderthals had died out, in the same way as a handful of Spanish Conquistadores had taken over much of South America aided by horses, bullets and germs. The land was largely free of humans. Ross looked up and the lines from Psalm 121 came to him as they had so often before when he was troubled and had taken himself off into deep country:

> *I will lift up mine eyes unto the hills, from whence cometh my help.*
>
> *My help cometh from the LORD, which made heaven and earth.*
>
> *He will not suffer thy foot to be moved: he that keepeth thee will not slumber.*
>
> *Behold, he that keepeth Israel shall neither slumber nor sleep.*
>
> *The LORD is thy keeper: the LORD is thy shade upon thy right hand.*
>
> *The sun shall not smite thee by day, nor the moon by night.*
>
> *The LORD shall preserve thee from all evil: he shall preserve thy soul.*
>
> *The LORD shall preserve thy going out and thy coming in from this time forth, and even for evermore.*

The weather matched his mental state – much disturbed – as he debated with himself. But repeating these lines brought him a certain peace, as it always did. It was a psalm his father had taught him. He, like his father, was not a churchgoer and did not think of himself as particularly religious, but in the mountains something of their grandeur lifted his spirits to a place where something in nature and the beauty of creation made him connect with his deepest self, and a sense that he could not name but which brought comfort. The sense of some intangible presence, some 'Other' that he felt here was almost tangible.

Looking at the magnificence around him, he spoke aloud to his horse. 'This is all I want, Rincon. This is all I want. Now and for as long as I breathe. And I mean to have it and to keep it!'

An image of the lawyer, Freemantle, came to him. It seemed clear that the guy was riding the nuclear clear-up issue as a vehicle he hoped would carry him all the way up the political escalator, not really giving a care either way for the subject itself. The nuclear waste issue was a new departure for the man; he'd had no previous involvement with this before. It was just politics, and though Ross was sympathetic to the cause of keeping any wild environment clean, he was far from sure that Freemantle was a committed long-term environmentalist.

Everyone he knew who'd made money or had gained power of any kind had compromised somewhere along the way. There were no clean hands anywhere, whether it was offshore tax havens, child labour in the Third World, dodgy advertising claims, or financial chicanery. Success in the world's terms came at a price. He was in no position to be picky. His own hands were dirty enough. He was not sitting on some high horse or hill of moral principle.

And yet? Back and forth he argued the issue as he moved between meadow and timber, lowland and mountain, looking out for rockfalls and windfalls and dangers of all kinds, predators and weather. He worked across two maps, the Idaho wilderness and the moral wilderness in his head. But he could not see the chasm that awaited him.

Then he disappeared into the timber like an injured wolf seeking refuge, and was gone from view.

CHAPTER 8

It was high summer in the high country and there was a great stillness over the ridges and valleys. Ross estimated his length of vision at around 30 miles that morning, and no sign of smoke.

Rincon and Buddy were bushed after their long climb to the mountain meadows and after checking them for cuts and bruises or any rubbing from the tack, he hobbled them and let them roll and graze. All was well with them; after rolling they did their usual buddy bumping with ears back, but soon settled down grazing, heads close together. He was pleased that neither showed any sign of alertness or wariness. They were his best early warning system with senses of sight, smell and hearing far superior to his own. Watching them, he was alerted to danger far sooner than his own senses set alarm bells ringing.

Quickly and efficiently, he set up camp at the foot of some tall pines that offered shade and pinecones to use as kindling. He gathered a few rocks for a fire pit and then set up his tent alongside a nylon rope line between two huge pines to hitch the horses to during the night, that would allow them to graze a little but keep them close to camp.

Once he had washed, he removed his boots so that his feet could have the pleasure of grass underfoot. Then he reached for his binoculars and quartered the country carefully. It was not really necessary, but it was an old habit that brought him calm. He thought of scrambling down to a nearby stream to cast for trout, but decided to heat some tinned beef stew he carried to add to potatoes and onions. After eating, he lay on his back watching a pair of eagles criss-crossing their territory. Other than the thin piping of birds settling in for the night and the dim sounds of the stream, all was quiet. Up here the most likely interruptions would come from wolves or bears, predators, rather than the deer and elk that would give the camp a wide berth.

As he lay back in his sleeping bag looking out at the stars, his thoughts returned to the offer hanging over him. His mind roved forward for the next twenty years, the endless horse packing trips it would need to service his mortgage and the issues of dealing with clients, most of the time pleasurable but occasionally upsetting enough to make you wish you were not tied into this way of earning a living. The huge chunk of money he had been offered would finally mean true freedom and with it the time to ride, work with horses and his land and to feel himself as removed from the world as he chose to be.

He still had moments when he was overcome by amazement that he was alive. He had lived a charmed life, making it to 42 with only minor physical wounds and scars, although mentally he was far from whole. When these thoughts came to him, the face of his old buddy, Charles 'Stiegs' Stiegler III, rose crystal clear and his words played back on the memory loop that never went away. 'A small ranch, Ross, not huge, but land to call your own. That is true wealth. That is what I dream of.' This dream was one both men shared and was the subject of many a long discussion, building ranch houses in the air, stringing fences, backing horses.

Stiegs was old Boston money, trying to prove himself to himself and to his family too, instead of taking the old family hustle, straight out of college making Old Money folk richer and keeping them that way. Stiegs of the impeccable manners was something of an aberration to find in Afghanistan and for Ross he was like fresh cold water in the desert. Someone who truly had his back and also the best Cuban cigars, none other than Cohiba Behike, a cigar that every cigar aficionado craved, considered by many the perfect cigar, the holy grail of cigars. One would end up killing Stiegs when he lit up one night after an early evening strike on a hamlet close to the Afghanistan border with Pakistan, the bullet entering an eye and exiting the back of his head. And the cries of jubilation 'Allah u Akbar' echoing from the hills as the American mortars opened up.

Sitting on a camp chair high in his Idaho heaven, sipping Jack Daniels, Ross could hear Stiegs cussing as if he was sitting right by him.

'Ross, for heaven's sake, show some respect man! What you have in your mouth now is something majestic. This stuff is made with a portion of *medio-tempo*, as they call it, a type of tobacco that grows on top of the plant where it catches the sun. Note the creamy flavours and the earthy notes.'

Ross would growl, 'I will cream your flavour and put your nose in the earth. Leave me be, let me enjoy this fat brown cigarette my own way.'

What he would have given to have Stiegs along on this trip! How they would have savoured the big country, the sense of freedom, of release from danger, the joy of simply being alive. Both of them had made their peace with death. You could not live that life without going mad if you had not made that accommodation with the Grim Reaper. It went with the territory. Doing what they did and hoping and praying to live was not conducive to remaining sane. So they thought of themselves as already lost and with that some strange peace was gifted to them.

In the days that followed, Ross took his horses deeper into the vast spaces of this border land with Canada than he had ever been before. One morning shortly after leaving camp they had a close shave with a grizzly bear and her cubs. He had walked the horses carefully across a stream feeling the bottom with his own feet and then led Rincon and Buddy into heavy brush on the other side. Just as they emerged into an open glade the bears appeared, headed for the same stream he and the horses had just crossed. They were rooting around for grubs and berries with the wind blowing from them to Ross and they were totally taken by surprise when they saw Ross and the horses. The big female rose up to her full commanding height, just long enough for Ross to unsheathe his rifle from its leather scabbard on Rinc's side, before both horses pulled hard away from him. He managed to hold on and to get a shot off into the air at the same time. With the rifle crack echoing in the mountains, the grizzly dropped down and shepherded her cubs to safety. The incident had shaken them all up and it took a while for Ross to persuade the horses to follow him once more.

That night they camped by a long, narrow-waisted lake and Ross brought in three fat rainbow trout that he smoked over the fire. As he ate, he thought of Sandy. The money from this job would also free her from teaching if she so wished and they might build a life together. He smiled, acknowledging the fact that he missed her. She had brought a certain calmness and sanity to his days and nights and he found that he slept better than he had for years when she was with him. Her unquestioning presence beside him when he woke shaking from a nightmare helped him settle back into sleep much faster than had he been on his own. There was too her strength of character and integrity that spoke to his heart. She was, he sensed, someone on whom he could depend in a fight. His years of surviving wars had honed that instinct to an edge that could be relied on. She was without doubt the right stuff.

The return journey from the high country was uneventful. They went slowly, taking their time, enjoying the good weather and the plentiful grass and forage. The horses knew they were headed home and were in good spirits. Ross too felt buoyed up by this time alone with his horse companions. He struck camp early each day and by mid-afternoon called a halt, making it much less of a gruelling trip than on their way in, when he had pushed the horses to make the maximum distance. Now he felt easy with a sense of accomplishment and proud of the horses who knew the drill and made life easy for him.

His time alone in the wilderness always had an effect on him he found hard to describe, he felt lighter, cleaner, clearer, more at peace with himself. The quality of the place was half of it, but it was also fed by the feelings of what it was not – it was not the busy souks of the Middle East, the streets of New York, the teeming presence of other men in the army camps he had spent time in, the prisons he had worked in getting information from his country's enemies, the strangling claustrophobia of relationships gone wrong. The woods in the high country were all of that for him too, a place of escape he never wished to leave.

He always said to those who asked, 'Why Idaho?' that the place had chosen him rather than the other way round. During time off from the army, he had been brought to the Panhandle by Stiegs and they had skied the mountains in winter and hunted in the fall. Slowly, over the years, the place took a hold on his heart in a way that Texas never had. There came a point in which its beauty was not the only emotional impact it made on him, there was also an ache when he was away from it, come fresh to it after being away and when leaving it once more. It was an ache he learned to call love. The place had beguiled him. He felt at home here, he felt himself here, he simply felt more here. And he could read its moods, its colours, its tastes, its land, its skies, its mornings and its midnights. Wakened suddenly in Idaho, he not only knew where he was but how the land was. Its being, its soul, had become one with his.

Stiegs would tease him for the small snuff box of Idaho earth he carried round his neck alongside his dog-tags, his 'sacred relic' his friend called it, and he was not far wrong in that description. It was how Ross thought of the place, his sacred place.

By the time Ross reached the ranch, his mind was made up. He would accept the job his former boss had offered him and spend the rest of his life a free man among his beloved mountains on his own land. Then truly he would feel that he was gone from all that he had lived through before.

CHAPTER 9

As he rode into the property it was dusk and he saw lights on at the cabin. Sandy was as good as her word, she was here. She stood framed in the open front door waving to him, the light behind her illuminating her slim frame. He set the horses free in the paddock after rubbing them down and giving them a feed. They looked tired but well and his heart lifted, thinking of how they had handled the miles and the heights. 'Good horses,' he murmured, 'good horses.'

He washed his hands and face and neck at the water trough and walked up to the open front door. Wonderful cooking smells greeted him before he went in. Sandy came to him, a wooden spoon in her hand.

'Hello, Texas' she said, teasing him once more about his origins. She was in cut-off jeans and a short tank top that ended just below her breasts, revealing her tanned stomach. 'I have made my grand-mère's coq au vin. You hungry?'

He hugged her and took deep breaths of her glorious smell. 'Just let me have a shower and I will come eat,' he said, but she held onto him.

'Don't shower just yet. Let that old coq stew a few minutes more,' she said grinning. He scooped her up in his arms and carried her into the bedroom.

'Supper was as delicious as the entrée,' he told her,

smiling, later. 'How delicious?' she asked. 'And which poulet did you prefer?' That was all it took and they were on the couch this time. The dishes stood in the sink till morning. As they lay in bed drinking coffee watching the sun rise over the trees, she asked him, 'Ross, what is it about the Panhandle that you love so much? Besides me of course?'

He kissed her, once more taking pleasure in her morning scent. He was silent for a minute, thinking how best to answer her question. 'It's so many things, large and small, that just add up for me,' he replied. 'I suppose it's the smell of the place, the mix of pines, grasses and lake water and something more subtle that blows in from the mountains. Sometimes it is very simple things, like the grass seed fields on the way across the prairie on the way to Spokane. And the smoke when they burn the fields. The smell of freshly milled lumber. The look of the wooden log cabins and the wood cladding of the houses in the trees.' He paused, sipping his hot coffee.

Sandy urged him to continue. It was not often that he would speak like this.

'It's also the people. Neighbours give you space, they keep apart but when help is needed, they are there for you. And it's not just the Mormon community that does that, it's everyone. And the crazy stuff. I've never before seen such displays of Christmas lights that blow out the transformers. The groups of people picking blueberries with bells on the milk jugs to let the bears know where they are. And the last of the old-timers, the few left-over trappers. The bow men. The black powder rifle men. It's different up here, almost as if the past, the settler past is hanging on, still making space for loners, the land-hungry and the slightly odd. I also like the different people who come in from other states with their own expertise, writers, artists, the IT crowd. There is a creative hub here that is unexpected and that adds to the mining and lumber culture. I even like the tourists, well, some of them anyway. It gives me pleasure seeing them get blown away by this place.'

She watched him closely. He had never said this much

before and she knew she was seeing into his soul.

'It's the taste of the clean, clean water. Sometimes I think it's better than anything else I've ever drunk. I love watching the deer coming down to drink in winter and having to break the ice with their hooves. The sound of the ice expanding up onto the banks of the lakes and the withdrawing again in spring. And when I first got here, I was amazed by the little seaplanes flying down from Alaska, landing on the lakes to winter in milder conditions. I used to watch them for hours. Once I met a guy who took me up for a spin and looking down, I could not believe how beautiful it was, the lakes, the rivers, the pine hills, the prairies. It just crept up on me and before I knew it, I couldn't do without it. Bit like you really.' And he hugged her.

He saw that there were tears in her eyes. She took his face in her hands and looked deeply into his eyes. 'I love you, Ross. I love you. And I also love this place for all those reasons and more.'

He kissed her gently and asked her a question that had been worrying him. 'Sandy, I love you too. You are so much more than I deserve. But there is something that I must ask you.'

She looked at him quizzically. 'What is it?'

'How do you feel about hooking up with an old man, a rather wrecked old man? I'm twelve years older than you.'

She paused a moment and then replied, 'Can I quote my mother? "You are an ample sufficiency"! Your age is just not an issue.'

The horses had to wait a while longer for breakfast that morning.

After a day or two of catching up on ranch chores, Ross made the call that he had been delaying to his former boss. He finally reached him and said he would take on the job.

He asked him what he would need, and Ross asked for a payment of expenses up front. There would be some travelling needed, people to see, places to go. The payment

should be sent to his offshore account in the Bahamas.
'Good! Consider it done. And, Ross, don't do anything wild. Discretion please.'

Ross threw himself into briefing himself on the nuclear waste issue and discovered that a nuclear site known as Hanford was established by the Manhattan Project during the Second World War to make plutonium, a key ingredient in the atomic bomb dropped on Nagasaki, Japan. The site lay 200 miles south-east of Seattle and contained about 60 per cent of the nation's most dangerous radioactive waste, stored in 177 ageing underground tanks, some of which had leaked.

It was time to get a handle on Jack Freemantle. One aspect of the man's political campaign – his book on the threat of nuclear waste – gave Ross slight pause. It was not the action of someone who came into an issue lightly, intending to use it as a political springboard. A book was just too much damn hard work, even if using a ghost writer. It was something he would look into.

CHAPTER 10

Two things delayed him from taking a more active pursuit of the Freemantle job, one of them planned and one unplanned and unexpected.

A few days after getting back from the mountains he was working on the Jeep, draining the sump and replacing the old oil with clean. It was 6pm and he was not expecting anyone. The sound of a racing vehicle made him look up and he saw a pick-up truck barrelling down his drive, trailing a cloud of dust. His first thought was that it was a UPS delivery, but he dismissed this immediately as the fishtailing pick-up was being driven too aggressively for any normal delivery driver. More likely a neighbour in trouble with stock seeking help, he thought. But he held back in the shelter of the workshop garage, waiting to see who the visitors were. The truck pulled up in a sliding stop and two lanky men sprang out, baseball bats in hand. These were not friendlies. Ross picked up a tyre iron which had a sharp edge to its flattened end and he stepped out to meet the men. They were nonplussed seeing him come to them and hesitated just long enough for him to ask what they wanted. As he spoke, the beer fumes reached him, and he relaxed a notch.

The skinnier one of the two, he noted, had a very pronounced Adam's apple and a broken nose; his sidekick was heavier, over six foot, and looked like a football player slightly gone to seed.

This Country I Call My Own

The big guy shouted, 'What the fuck do you think you are doing with Sandy, you old prick? We are gonna teach you a lesson you ain't gonna forget!' And with that he ran bull-like at Ross, who side-stepped the charge and as his assailant passed, struck his head hard with the tyre iron. The man fell like an ox.

Now the lighter man was on him, heaving the baseball bat at his head. This time the tyre iron connected with the Adam's apple and the man fell to the ground gasping for breath. He had never been much of a threat, the 'suckerfish' to his pal, whom he tagged along with, like one of those weird fish which travelled with sharks, feeding from what they ate. It was a phenomenon as old as time and its two-to-one dynamics had been part of Ross's hand-to-hand combat training. The whole thing was over in seconds.

He dragged the big guy into the back of their pick-up, and then his friend. He tied their hands with plastic baling cord, threw a lasso rope into the back and took off for the most wooded part of the ranch. The cab stank of fast-food containers and empty beer cans. He drove the truck right up against a tree and in minutes had both men well roped to neighbouring trees. By now the suckerfish could speak, but all that came out of his mouth was cursing. The big guy was conscious but woozy and made a low moaning noise.

Ross took a good look at his assailants so that he would remember them well. He took out his phone and photographed both of them and then reached for his hunting knife on his belt. Both men, seeing the knife, thrashed as best they could as he methodically cut their clothes off. Both were now sufficiently aware of what was happening to object violently, but they were not going anywhere soon. Once they were butt naked, he photographed them again. Then he checked their wallets for ID. He did not recognise the names, which he memorised.

He grabbed the suckerfish's pecker and made as if to geld him. The man made a high-pitched scream. He was still screaming, trying to look down at his 'wound' when Ross took hold of the big guy's dick. He let him feel the cold steel of the knife on his testicles and as expected the man began to beg for mercy. Holding the knife hard against him, Ross said, 'Listen up! If I ever see you two anywhere near here again, you will be gelded good.'

He showed them the phone. 'I will be sending the pictures of you two having your Brokeback Mountain picnic to the *Spokesman Review* if I ever hear a single word from you. Enjoy your night in the woods. You'd better hope a bear doesn't find you.'

He left the pick-up and walked back to the cabin listening to the shouts and screams of the two men. He called the sheriff in Sandpoint and explained what had gone down, providing both men's names and the truck's licence plate. He explained exactly where they were tied up and asked the sheriff to leave them there for a few hours.

'You bet, Commander. I know those two very well. Let them stew awhile.' He asked if Ross wished to press charges. Ross declined and bid the sheriff a good evening. There was silence from the wood.

He then called Sandy to explain what had happened and to warn her to be careful. He reassured her that he was fine and that everything was under control. When he mentioned the names of his assailants, she said the men worked in the garage where she had her car serviced. She promised that she would change garages.

At midnight, he heard a car approaching and saw the flashing of its blue light. The men would be spending the rest of the night in jail, no doubt.

The next morning, Ross loaded the Jeep with some essential supplies he had long been meaning to take to the mountains. Now and then he took sportsmen to the high country when asked to arrange an elk hunting trip. On occasion, they had ventured above the 8,000-foot altitude and one or two of his clients had experienced mountain sickness. In such instances, he always brought them down to lower levels and gave them a day to recover. But he wanted to cache a few oxygen bottles as well as some emergency rations, just in case the need arose.

Getting enough food and oxygen were the two single biggest issues facing sportsmen who had hunting fever on them. This led them to push themselves too hard, too fast, too high, leading to the loss of appetite that accelerated their physical decline. He had made it his business to know the highest major summits of Idaho. There were ten peaks exceeding 11,000 feet and thirty-four peaks exceeding 9,000 feet, enough height to make the fittest hunter dizzy.

His own military experience had taught him the hard way how he could prevent altitude sickness naturally, but it was a task at times to convince his clients. He would urge them to move higher over a period of two to three days to acclimatise, to eat regularly, carbs in particular. A tough one was to avoid alcohol, to always drink water, to take it as easy as possible and to drop down at night to altitudes below 8,000 feet to sleep.

He carried acetazolamide, altitude sickness tablets, ibuprofen and paracetamol for headaches, and promethazine for nausea. And the failsafe standby was to take oxygen to make up for the lack of it, hence the oxygen cannisters he was trucking in and carrying to the heights where he would stash them securely at sites he marked on his GPS.

High altitude cerebral oedema (HACE) could be a killer; he had buddies who had come close. The problem was caused by a swelling of the brain as a result of a lack of oxygen. Its symptoms were headache, weakness, feeling or being sick, loss of coordination, feeling confused and finally hallucinations – seeing and hearing things that were simply not there. A hunter with HACE would often not realise they were ill, insisting that they were OK and wanted to be left alone. Left alone and not treated, the condition was fatal in a few hours.

And then there was the challenge of food. Ross was all too aware of the physical stress travel in high country placed on human physiology. Height brought with it mountain or altitude sickness from the elevations involved; the body does not get sufficient oxygen above heights of 8,000 feet. And with the illness comes a lack of appetite which leads to a daily calorie deficit of between 1,200 and 1,800 calories if not immediately addressed. Seasoned hunters and mountaineers know this well and take measures to ward off the ill effects of high-country travel which can impair moods, create headaches and ultimately affect good decision making.

Ross was an old salt in this respect and made frequent stops to eat, whatever his appetite was. He used food that he enjoyed at home as the basis for his rations, with the result that he operated at optimum efficiency mentally and physically above the 8,000 feet line and kept a careful watch on his performance and those travelling with him. He knew he was a glorified nursemaid at times, having to reason with unruly children.

Leaving the Jeep, he spent two days caching the oxygen bottles and the extra emergency ration packs under huge rocks that were easy to recognise, sprinkling used motor oil and pepper spray on the earth to warn off bears that scented food. He knew none of this might be needed, but it gave him peace of mind that he had safety nets built in and that in an emergency he would have the satisfaction of having options. One day they might save his life or the life of one of his clients.

CHAPTER 11

Ross wrote to Jack Freemantle at his Seattle office address, a fancy-sounding building downtown. He kept it brief, stating his interest in the lawyer's position on the nuclear waste clean-up issue, explaining that he was based near Sandpoint in the Idaho Panhandle, running an ecologically sensitive business – a horse packing, hunting and fishing operation – and would welcome an opportunity to discuss the issues.

He was surprised to receive a reply in days. Freemantle said he would be speaking at a public meeting at the Coeur D'Alene Resort about the subject in a fortnight's time and that Ross would be welcome to attend and to seek him out afterwards for further discussion if he so wished. The letter was courteous and to the point; there was no politicking involved. Despite himself, Ross was impressed, though he thought the resort was a strange place to speak about environmental issues, being an 18-storey eyesore in a pristine environment.

He had finally come clean to Sandy about the offer his former employers had made to him and at first she sounded very dubious.

'Seriously Ross? This goes against everything you say that you want! Peace and quiet and distance from your past.'

But once he explained that the Agency believed Freemantle was just riding the issue to raise his political profile, she started to come round and listened carefully to what he outlined.

'They want me to check him out for anything compromising, to see if he really is so squeaky clean.' He told her that his coming to Idaho was driven by a wish to escape his previous life and all the morally questionable and stress inducing work it entailed, but that the money involved would make them independent for life. Sandy heard the 'us' pronoun and looked at him.

Ross noted the look and addressed the unasked question. 'There has been a question I wanted to ask you for some weeks now, and it is this – will you marry me? I know I am not to everyone's taste, and you know just what damaged goods you'd be getting, but, Sandy, I have loved you almost from the day you served me that coffee in Sandpoint and it has just grown and grown.'

'Damn! Ross McCallister, that is the most romantic proposal I've ever heard, and I've had a few!' She made to speak further, but he stopped her gently.

'Let me finish my piece. The reason I haven't spoken before is that this issue has been bugging me so much. It's the reason I took off for the mountains. By the time I got back, I had decided to accept the job. I didn't want to ask if you'd marry me without your knowing what I've decided to embark on. I would understand if you said no to me because of it. If that is how you feel I will walk away from this job in a heartbeat. But the money would free both of us to do what we wish with the rest of our lives. If you want to continue teaching, as you get such a kick out of it, then fine, but it will become an option for you, not something you have to do to earn a living. And for me, it would mean less client work or no client work if I so chose. I would truly be free and be gone from the world in a way I could only dream about before.'

Sandy reached her arms around him and said, 'Yes, yes and yes! I love you, you know that, and I will follow you wherever you wish to go, through hell if needs be.'

They stood for a long time simply holding each other and both felt an enormous burden lifting from them and a growing sense of excitement.

The lunchtime meeting in Coeur D'Alene Resort was something of a revelation. Freemantle had done his homework and had all the facts at his fingertips. Some of the worst ground and water pollution in the country due to silver mining and air pollution due to wildfires, the result of climate change, nuclear dumps poisoning the aquifers, and the thorny issue of the navy submarine testing presence in Lake Pend Oreille. The Panhandle might look pristine but there were a lot of nasties in the landscape, he said.

Freemantle cut a short, slight, boyish figure; not what Ross had been expecting. He spoke quietly and calmly, painting a picture of dire environmental impacts as a result of mining, logging, tourism and military and naval experimentation over decades. He quoted from a raft of distinguished research papers published by the country's leading academics and scientists. He described his boyhood in Sandpoint, his love for Idaho, his belief that a Democrat in the Governor's mansion would bring good things.

'We've not had a Democrat running Idaho since 1964 and I know we have a mountain to climb. But I am ready, willing and able to climb that mountain.' And then he made his pitch. Jack Freemantle spoke quietly but passionately, with an underlying fury. 'Not many new arrivals in the Panhandle have any idea of the history of this place, other than the sketchiest information. Like all of us, they fall in love with the wilderness, the mountains, rivers and lakes, the affordable housing, the cute towns. We keep getting nominated for the best place to visit, the most liveable area etc, etc. But few understand the environmental bomb that went off here thanks to the logging and silver mining industries in the past, the presence of nuclear dumps, and now the new interest in mining for cobalt to make electric car batteries. Sure, there have been attempts to mitigate the lead, arsenic, cadmium and zinc poisoning of the soil and water, but the human cost has been devastating. People carry a load of metals in their system and the fish have malformed skulls in some areas.'

Ross saw and felt that, like him, the audience was

hanging on every word. The subject was close to their hearts. Freemantle was a compelling speaker, telling a story that many were dimly aware of, but few understood the full ramifications of what had occurred across the region.

'Do you realise that until recently there were 500 mine shafts and trenches on US Forest Service land in the Panhandle, and to date, they've closed 242 of them. God knows how many people have died falling down those shafts when out hiking or hunting. Many of the miners and mining companies that followed left behind shafts and tunnels that still dot North Idaho. Even in operating mines, shafts pose particular dangers. In his 2003 book, *From Hell to Heaven*, the late Gene Hyde, who spent his career as a mining geologist, documented the deaths of 204 miners killed by falling down mine shafts between 1890 and 1998 in the Coeur d'Alene Mining District alone. Idaho's Silver Valley, the Coeur d'Alene mining district in the South Fork of the Coeur d'Alene River, has had one of the world's largest concentrations of silver metal. Since 1884, the district has produced over 1.18 billion ounces of silver, along with major amounts of lead, zinc, copper, and antimony. In total, more than $2.89 billion worth of metal has been produced from veins in the district.'

As Freemantle spoke, the hotel waiters started discreetly laying out coffee and refreshments and there was the odd chink of china. Ross could only wonder at the strangeness of life. A man was outlining the poisoning of a land and its people, and yet despite the gravity of the occasion, coffee would shortly be served.

'Gold was discovered on the South Fork of the Coeur d'Alene River in 1878. The gold rush lasted only a few years. In 1884 the first major lead-zinc-silver discovery was staked, and all of the major mines were found within a year. Of ninety mines historically in the district, only two were still operating in 2007 (the Lucky Friday and the Galena), and another (the famous Sunshine mine) was being targeted for reopening. The Coeur d'Alene district contains the largest underground mine in the United States, the Bunker Hill

Mine, with over 150 miles of workings, the deepest mine, the Star-Morning, which is over 7,900 feet deep and the richest silver mine, the Sunshine, which has produced over 367 million ounces of silver.

'And as a direct result of this mining and the chemicals used to extract the metal, children in Kellogg, for example, average 50 micrograms of lead per decilitre of blood. Medical experts consider five micrograms high enough to warrant concern, and children with levels above 45 micrograms are advised to undergo chelation therapy, which involves administering compounds like dimercaptosuccinic acid, either orally or intravenously, to remove heavy metals from the bloodstream.

'Lead is a neurotoxin linked to schizophrenia, poor academic performance, low cognitive ability and attention deficit hyperactivity disorder, ADHD. Once the metal gets into the blood, it concentrates in the brain, kidneys, liver and bones; in pregnant women, lead can cross into the placenta, poisoning their unborn babies.'

There was utter silence in the room as the audience hung on his every word.

'For decades, Silver Valley's mines were extremely profitable. Then the price of silver sank, and by 1982 they all closed, leaving thousands jobless. Millions of tons of sediment polluted with lead, arsenic, cadmium and zinc remain in the Coeur d'Alene River, groundwater, lakes, floodplains and hillsides. In 1983, the U.S. Environmental Protection Agency designated a 21-square-mile area of Silver Valley the Bunker Hill Mining and Metallurgical Complex Site. Locals call it "the Box". In 2002, the EPA expanded the site to encompass the entire 1,500-square-mile Coeur D'Alene Basin, recognizing it as among the largest, most polluted places in the nation. But over a decade later, Lake Coeur D'Alene is still filled with lead, wildlife goes to the basin to die, and locals suffer a litany of mental and physical disabilities that make it difficult to get through each day.

'And of course, we have a whole new generation of horrors awaiting us as they start to mine the rich deposits of minerals for electric car batteries. Idaho's Cobalt Belt is a 34-mile-long stretch below the Salmon River Mountains that is considered "globally significant" by mining companies. A new mine will open soon and we are talking billions of dollars in value. And we are in bed with the Chinese, who will actually produce the batteries. There are global forces at work here that are after cobalt, lithium, nickel, copper, and rare earth elements used in so-called clean energy applications. These horrors are starting all over again and we are up against some of the most powerful and ruthless interests on the planet. These interests don't want us interfering with their plans, they want us gone.'

As Ross listened, he could not help but wonder who he thought he had been working for. Who was really funding the Agency? Were some of these shadowy mining interests behind his 'last job'?

Freemantle continued, 'If you are content with the status quo and happy for the powers that be to keep raping and despoiling your home, then leave now, I have nothing to offer you.'

Nobody walked out.

'Thank you for coming today. As no one has left, I can only assume that you are as concerned as I am about what our representatives have allowed to happen, waved through unopposed very often. The prize offered to us always being jobs, jobs, jobs and the economic improvement of the state. If you are as concerned as I am, then please support me. I am asking for your vote to get elected as your new Governor so that I can start changing things in Idaho.'

There was polite applause. One man called out: 'But what are you offering us?'

Freemantle held up a hand and continued, 'How did they sell this abomination to our grandparents, our parents and us? The answer is jobs. The promise of jobs in the only industries available at the time, mining and logging. And our people raised families on the delivery of those jobs, and they also died young as a result and it damaged many of our children too. I understand that it is easy to stand here and criticise, but the question is, what will I replace it with? My offer is also jobs, many more jobs than these wrecking and wrecked industries now offer, industries that devastated our land and our health. I have many people from the new environmentally friendly industries who say they will gladly move their businesses to Idaho if we subsidise the move. The IT industry, the creative industries, they all love the location and the opportunities they see here to expand. These are industries that will not poison our land or make you ill or damage our children. It can be done and I promise you I will make it happen if you help me.'

For the first time, there was a counterpoint to the sound of Freemantle's voice as the audience picked up on this offer. People were commenting on this promise.

'This is not going to be easy. We have some serious big money opponents. My family and I have already received some not very pleasant threats to cease and desist, to walk away. But I can see that I am not alone in my concern and that encourages me to make this run for Governor. Together, I believe we can change things for the better, so that one day our children and grandchildren will live in a better, cleaner, happier place than we have inherited.'

Now the applause crashed out loud and long. This was no John F. Kennedy but he looked, sounded and felt like the real deal, Ross had to admit. The guy really did sound sincere, did seem to care deeply and he really sounded as if he had a plan. And he had balls, coming here to say these things.

He and Sandy joined the small group of well-wishers around Freemantle after the venue had emptied and as the crowd thinned, Ross introduced himself and Sandy. Freemantle's handshake was firm and he said he had wondered if they would make it. 'You guys run a horse packing/hunting operation up near Sandpoint, I recall.' He introduced his wife Michelle, a botanist, who was equally warm and friendly.

Once again, Ross was impressed. The guy had remembered his letter expressing interest. They spoke briefly and to his surprise Ross heard himself invite Freemantle to visit if he would enjoy a day in the saddle. He thanked him and said he would really enjoy that and would call to set a date that worked for both of them.

Later, over a coffee with Sandy at the Sandtrap Café in Hayden Lake, Ross asked what she had made of it.

'Well, I must admit I rather liked them both. This is not going to be as easy as we thought. But he is a politician already. Very smooth, very aware, very switched on and actually very likeable. If he'd asked me out on a date before he met his wife, I would have said yes!'

'But he is such a short-ass!' Ross grinned and laughed at himself. 'Listen to me. And we had our asses kicked by the Viet Cong. But seriously?'

Sandy poked him in the chest, 'Not everyone has to be a side of beef to attract a woman, Texas! He has a quiet confidence that is very attractive and there is also some sadness there, which women love.'

They discussed the man at some length until a woman at a neighbouring table reached over and said, 'I was at that meeting too and I can tell you he has my vote. And I have never voted anything but Republican!'

Suddenly it came to Ross that he saw something of Jack Freemantle's political strategy. If he could build a respectable cross-party coalition in Idaho, even if he did not win the Idaho Governorship, he would make a very attractive candidate for a senate seat in neighbouring Washington, and then anything was possible. A decent showing in Idaho for a Democrat after sixty years in the wilderness and the presidency would also be something the Democrat bosses would have to consider. And a Democrat who won in Idaho… the party would come knocking on his door if he wanted a shot at the White House. The man was nobody's fool.

Just then the CB radio that had been rumbling in the background took on an urgency and the café fell silent. There was some police emergency and it was coming their way. The words 'hostage, hostage' caught everyone's attention.

Ross and Sandy were sitting at a table right by the front window looking out at a tranquil scene of an apartment block across the street, trees and gardens, and an older man cutting the lawns in front of the café.

Barely five minutes passed and then a SWAT team arrived, a highly trained police unit offering a 24/7 response to barricaded persons, active shooting scenes, and high-risk search warrants. Ross made to get up and Sandy put her hand on his arm.

'Ross, we have our own fish to fry.'

He shook his head.

'Just come away from the window.'

They moved to a table further back and sat down again, watching keenly as the heavily armed team deployed round the apartment building. The CB radio kept a running commentary. It seemed a woman and her lover were in one of the apartments and a jealous former husband had taken them hostage and was threatening them both with a gun.

Ross noted with wry amusement that the old man cutting the lawn just kept going, his rhythm little troubled by what was taking place not fifty feet from him across the street, the lines of his cut as straight as they had been ten minutes previously.

A shot rang out, a man jumped to the ground from a first-floor balcony and was apprehended by the police. And just like that it was over. The hostage-taking ex-husband had taken a bullet and was on the way to the hospital, the woman was shaken up but OK, and her lover had a sprained ankle in his jump from the balcony. Everyone in the café went back to eating and drinking, barely commenting on what had just taken place. The lawn cutting outside continued, the lines arrow straight.

Ross asked for his tab, paid up, and he and Sandy strolled out to the Jeep.

'Well! That was something,' she said. 'Did you notice the guy cutting the lawn just kept on going?' Ross chuckled. 'Probably a vet, or deaf and blind. This place can be a bit different at times.'

As they drove north to the ranch he noted the sky had darkened considerably and a wind was buffeting the Jeep. He turned on the radio and soon heard a weather forecast. 'High winds, dust storms and possible rain on the way for the Panhandle. Winds up to 60 mph with the threat of falling trees. Be careful folks!'

Ross put his foot down and felt a surge of affection for the old Jeep as the great engine pushed them back into their seats. It was just an hour's drive to Sandpoint and he would make time while he could before the rain hit. He was worried about the horses. But soon enough, visibility was down to a hundred yards at best in the dust cloud, and he and the rest of the traffic on the I-95 slowed, pushed around by the wind.

And then it started to rain. It looked like blood on the windscreen as the dust from ploughing to the south around Boise was lifted into the sky, carried north on the violent airstream and then carried down by the driving rain. It was like a scene from the Apocalypse. Ross would have pulled over but concern for the horses kept him going, although his speed was down to 30mph. They crawled into Sandpoint and he dropped Sandy at her home and then took off into the hills to the ranch.

By the time he got there, the worst of the storm had passed over and he found the horses grazing peacefully enough in their pasture, although both were soaking wet. He left them to it and went in to get a coffee.

The first thing he did the next morning was to call an old friend, a fellow former SEAL, now selling real estate in Chicago in the black middle-class suburbs of Roseland, Auburn Gresham, and South Shore on the South Side. Wesley Williams had been the go-to IT and comms legend in the unit and still did some consulting on that front, although his property operation in Chicago gave him a very good living.

Ross came straight to the point after the usual joshing stopped. 'Wes, I need some of your IT athletics.' He did not explain the why and what of it; there was no need. 'I'm checking this guy out who is running for Governor of Idaho as a Democrat.'

There was loud and sustained laughter down the line. 'You kidding? Brave guy! I meant to ask how are you enjoying life in that redneck paradise? I hear its whiter up there than a china plate. Is that so?'

Ross told him. 'A mixed-race couple – black guy, white girl – were shot in Spokane a few months back, so we are now down to zero black dudes here now. Pure white is how they like it up here. I'd invite you to come visit, but I don't know you'd enjoy it here; the barbecue doesn't touch Chicago.'

Wes said he would see what he could find on Freemantle and the next day called back. 'Clean, clean, clean. Not a damn thing. Well, some minor traffic violations going back years. But he is either damn near pure or he has someone better than me cleaning up his backtrail. Very difficult to do these days.'

'OK, Wes, that is helpful, or actually it's not. I was hoping to find some dirt. Can I ask one more favour? Could you check out how long he has been interested in the whole environmental issue, and how well briefed he is, who he is in touch with and just how serious he is about the whole environmental deal?'

Wes was his usual prompt self and within another day Ross had his answer. 'This guy could pass as an Environmental Professor with a handful of PhDs. He is one well briefed motherfucker. He's been at it for ten years at least and he knows all the big hitters here in the US and abroad. He's built a very impressive coalition of academic and activist support.'

'When you say activist, how activist is that?' Ross asked.

'I don't think any of his contacts are doing shit like Greenpeace, ramming fishing and whaling vessels, but among them there are some pretty committed folks, it looks like.'

'Wes, you still drink bourbon, that cracker juice?'

'I do, my man, I do!'

'OK, there is a case on its way to you. You are a bloody genius. Don't ever get fat and lazy mind. I might need you again, and you'd better be able to run!'

They laughed at the reference to running and scenes from another time, another place, another continent, flashed before them. Different as they were in terms of race and class and culture, their brotherhood was not in doubt.

Ross put the phone down and swore. 'Damn! This isn't going to be easy.'

CHAPTER 12

Ross could only wonder at the strange role of coincidence in his life, something he had mulled over many a time when in a philosophical frame of mind. There were things that he had experienced that left him wondering about this phenomenon. That strange feeling crept over him as he checked his online banking details. A not insignificant amount had been deposited in his account just two hours previously – the exact amount he had requested for research expenses. The depositor was listed as a horse outfitting operation in Montana. He checked it out with a phone call. A very friendly guy on the phone thanked him for the horse he had sent, adding that it was working out great. The Agency had not lost its touch, he had to admit.

He called Wes and asked him to provide two or three of the activist organisations that Freemantle had been in touch with over the past few years. The names when they arrived made him smile – Greenpeace headed the list, then there was a woman named Hester Townsend who had been one of the organising committee of the Greenham Common protest in the UK, which had quietly circled the NATO-US Airforce base that carried nuclear weapons on its patrol planes, and forced them after two decades of noisy protest to leave. And finally, an intriguing name, the Sons of Aryan, based just south of Sandpoint. Not much was known about them, other than they were led by a blowhard conspiracy theorist whose ideas were decidedly racist.

He sat down at his computer and started to dig. Greenpeace he knew by reputation, actions and results. They had made a significant impact on whaling, he knew. But some of their victories came as news to him.

In 1971, a small group of activists set sail to Amchitka Island off Alaska in an old fishing boat called *The Greenpeace*. Their mission: to stop a US nuclear weapons test. Although the voyage was racked with personal conflict, and failed to stop the test itself, it sparked a storm of publicity that ultimately turned the tide. Five months after the group's mission, the US stopped the entire Amchitka nuclear test programme. The island was later declared a bird sanctuary.

In the 1970s and 1980s, Greenpeace campaigned for a ban on nuclear testing. In 1974, Canadian activist David McTaggart took the French government to court. He won: that same year, France announced that they would end their atmospheric nuclear testing program. The Nuclear Test Ban Treaty was eventually agreed in 1996, forbidding all nuclear weapon test explosions or other nuclear explosions.

Through the 1960s and 1970s, the Scottish government permitted mass killing of seals around the Orkneys and Western Isles because they 'interfered' with commercial fishing. But in 1978, Greenpeace intervened. The Greenpeace ship *Rainbow Warrior* trailed the seal hunters' vessel for two weeks, preventing the start of the cull and sparking a public outcry against the killing. Eventually, the planned cull was massively reduced, and then shooting seals was completely banned in Scotland.

Ross felt that it would be perfectly legitimate for Freemantle to be in touch with Greenpeace, which these days wore a cloak of respectability thanks to their impressive track record, which proved that they were on the right side of history. It made him wonder why he was on the side he found himself on.

Hester Townsend, on the other hand, sounded almost too good to be true. She was a key player in the Greenham Common protest, a group of some 70,000 women who over a

20-year period got rid of a nuclear armed air force base in Berkshire, England. In 1981 she had helped to set up a group of women, angered by the decision to site cruise missiles – guided nuclear missiles – in the UK, and organised a protest march from Cardiff, Wales to RAF Greenham Common Air Base near Newbury in Berkshire. Here they set up what became known as the Greenham Common Women's Peace Camp just outside the fence surrounding the airbase. Their long running and gritty protest, which was essentially nonviolent, with the odd fence-cutting attack, lasted an unbelievable 19 years. In the end, their persistence paid off and they could legitimately claim victory. In 1992, at the 'end' of the Cold War, RAF Greenham Common closed and, in 1997, the land was returned to the public as parkland.

Ross was impressed at the doggedness evident in this long-running intervention to halt the presence of a nuclear facility. He had to admit that there could be no better group than this and Greenpeace for Freemantle to be speaking to. He wondered how the Greenham Common women had been able to maintain the necessary enthusiasm and dedication over the 19 years needed to outlast successive UK governments and the military.

The Sons of Aryan were possibly another matter. Ross booked himself a trip to England to meet with Hester Townsend and then to Amsterdam in the Netherlands, where Greenpeace was headquartered. Sandy kindly agreed to babysit the ranch and the horses while he was away. His approach to both Greenpeace and to Hester was straightforward. He asked for an opportunity to pick their brains on how to campaign against the nuclear sites in the Pacific Northwest and he received a gracious response from Greenpeace and a rather more eccentric one from Hester, who also recommended Greenpeace as an essential stop on his research tour.

She wrote, 'Young man, I admire your concern and your activism, but I am an old woman now, fast approaching 90. I am not sure if my advice would be worth tuppence, but you are more than welcome to pop in.' She provided her address and some directions.

His flight was uneventful, but it gave him the time while crossing the Atlantic to run his motives through the wringer once more. He could not help but compare this mission with others that required him to cross the ocean. But this time he would not be putting his life on the line. That said, if he was successful and managed to uncover anything compromising about Freemantle, his life henceforth would be free of any and all commercial pressures. He daydreamed of the places he would enjoy taking Sandy to, places he had discovered over years of rest and recuperation in Asia, Thailand, Bali, the Philippines, Indonesia, Malaysia and Vietnam, places of fabled pleasure that held only good memories, but also a remembered sense of loneliness that would not be the case with Sandy.

He hired a compact car at Heathrow Airport outside London and drove down to Dorset. The final few miles of the three-hour trip took him down extremely narrow lanes bordered by hedgerows some 20 feet tall, bedecked with cow parsley, wild roses and honeysuckle, whose scent filled the car. Passing only the occasional pulling-over spot, he felt like a fieldmouse moving through its territory on grass runs hidden from the sky. Now and then he was forced to back up when some red-faced farmer in a Land Rover came hurtling round a corner and showed no sign of retreating. Ross gritted his teeth and reminded himself that here he was a guest.

When he reached Hester's home, he could not help himself from taking some quick shots on his phone to share with Sandy. It was England at its chocolate-box best – stone walls covered in ivy, half-hidden under a thatched roof which looked like an oversized hat. On the roof ridge perched an owl made of wood.

Hester was a tall, imposing woman whose seeming severity was belied by a very sweet smile. She offered him Lapsang tea and crumpets with raspberry jam in the rose garden. In a field behind the cottage two horses grazed contentedly in lush pasture grass.

'My granddaughter's hunters,' Hester offered, when

she noted his appraising eye on the grey and the chestnut, large upstanding animals who looked as if they could keep up a good gallop in the hunting field. 'They are a mix of Thoroughbred racehorses crossed with Irish Draughts, to give them some bone. They will go all day with Chloe, who rides at something ridiculous like eight stone. Horse mad girl.'

Ross asked if she rode. 'Not for some years now, but I used to ride a lot, although I never really took to hunting,' she said.

They made some small talk about the area and then got down to business. He said, as he had in his emails, that he was concerned about the nuclear sites. He asked how she had managed to maintain the nearly 20-year commitment at Greenham Common and how she and her group had managed to deal with the police presence and the political and media pressures.

'Well, I suppose it was the first time those opposing us had ever run into a wall of bloody-minded women. We sort of wrong-footed them all the time, and it helped that some of the British media rather admired what we were doing.'

She was a fascinating woman, still intellectually sharp, and she answered all his questions with a great forthrightness that spoke of unshakable integrity. Ross thought she must have made a forceful and impressive addition to the leadership group at Greenham back in the day. As the talk wound down, he asked her for her impression of Jack Freemantle, who was leading the fight in the Pacific Northwest against the nuclear sites.

Hester was unequivocal in her support of the man and his aims. 'I found him very straightforward and committed. If you are asking me if he is using this issue for political purposes, I would say yes and no. I don't doubt his interest and his passion to stop the madness but he is a very smart cookie so the political value of his actions would be plain to him too. And I don't hold that against him. I'm only sorry you don't have more politicians with that kind of commitment to this issue in America.'

As he was taking his leave, his understanding of Hester

Townsend's savviness jumped ten notches. 'Commander McCallister,' she said, smiling, 'It's not every day that a military man switches sides. Are you sure you are here to find out how to stop the nuclear waste protest or how to stop Jack Freemantle?'

Caught on the hop, Ross moved into his most charming self. 'That's a very fair question, but if I was here trying to learn something to incriminate the anti-nuclear fight, it would be rather foolhardy to break cover by coming to you, wouldn't it?' His answer seemed to satisfy her. As he drove back into the maze of protective lanes, he smiled at the thought of someone so sharp at 90. 'Respect, ma'am, respect,' he muttered.

In Amsterdam, the message from Greenpeace was the same. The meeting on a very spartan ship with the Head of Communications, Kees Meertens, was brief but enlightening. They very much approved of Freemantle and thought of him as a friend, but one who would not wish to compromise himself and his followers by any action that could be interpreted as illegal.

Kees laughed when Ross put a blunt question to him. 'If you mean would he ever countenance any physical attack on the sites, then no. He is coming at it from a very political and media-nuanced position. He hopes to persuade people of his position, not risk hurting anyone by direct physical action. The Greenham Women, one of whom you've just met, put much more on the line. How do you say in America? They had more skin in the game.'

It had been a pleasant break from his ranch routine, but was ultimately a failure and a waste of time. He wondered for the thousandth time why his handlers were so keen to be shot of the lawyer when patently he represented no threat whatsoever, other than his potential to persuade enough people to enable him to bring about political change that would allow for the closing of the facilities. There simply was no dirt on the man.

Then on his return to Idaho, seemingly out of the blue,

he received an invitation from Freemantle to join him for dinner at Cedars, the floating restaurant on Lake Coeur D'Alene.

He did not ask what the reason for the invitation was – he had a feeling he knew – but he accepted anyway. The restaurant had been an unassuming, down-home kind of place in the Nineties, but it was now home to fine dining, and the water no longer lapped around patrons' feet.

Freemantle was already at the table when Ross arrived and they ordered swiftly, both choosing seafood. As soon as their meal was served, Ross found himself being cross-questioned about his trip to Europe. Freemantle clearly smelled a rat. Ross remained calm, enjoying his meal. He had expected something of the kind.

'Jack, you will understand that I felt it necessary to check you out with others who have taken on the authorities over nuclear sites. If Sandy and I are going to commit to this fight, I don't want to be part of your election campaign, if that is all this is.'

Freemantle relaxed somewhat. 'Good. I understand. That is perfectly legitimate. But it seems a great deal of effort by a private citizen to fly to Europe just to check me out?' There was a moment of slightly strained silence, and he continued, 'You won't be surprised that I have also been doing some digging, and I understand that you have had a very distinguished service record, followed by work for agencies of which I have some knowledge.'

As they sparred, both men gave little away of their real feelings. It appeared that sweet old Hester Townsend had not entirely bought into the tale Ross had spun her and had made a phone call to Freemantle to ask who Ross was.

Ross said, 'Well, you will understand, given my background, that I don't want any part of any activity that is going to impact my freedom to live my life as I wish, nor embarrass anyone I have ever worked for. I decided to proceed with caution and am pleased to say both Greenpeace and Hester speak highly of you. Both assured me that you are not about to lead us into any compromising action at the nuclear sites. And to answer your question about the reason for the trip, it was mainly to connect with travel organisations in London. They are keen to know what we can offer their clients in tailor-made safaris into the mountains. Our marketing is beginning to attract European clients.'

There was a tangible sense of tensions lifting as they ordered coffee. Ross decided to seemingly throw caution to the wind. 'But what about the Sons of Aryan? What would I find if I visited their compound?' he asked.

Freemantle was discomfited but looked him directly in the eye. 'You will find that I visited them following an invitation to discuss my stance opposing the government's approach to the nuclear threat to our communities in Idaho. We ended by agreeing to disagree; they wanted actions that I would not be comfortable with.'

Ross nodded. 'That doesn't surprise me.'

The conversation then moved on to how Freemantle's political campaign was going and whether the nuclear waste issue was helping him or not. Latest polls showed that he was in fact making gains even among Republicans unhappy about the possible threat to their children and grandchildren. The evening ended well, with both men feeling that the air had been cleared, and with a greater sense of understanding and mutual respect between them.

As they left the restaurant, they paused to look out over the lake. Freemantle turned to Ross and said, 'You must know that if you come out publicly backing me, your endorsement would carry very significant weight, given your background and service record. I would like you to think of a role in my campaign to stop the government's half-hearted clean-up plans.'

Ross was silent; he had not foreseen this.

'No need to say anything,' Freemantle said, 'just think on it and let me know.'

As he drove the hour and a half home to the ranch, Ross admitted to himself that he had reached a 'shit or get off the pot' moment. Jack was a shrewd operator. If he accepted his offer to get involved, it would be a case of having a possible enemy inside the Freemantle tent rather than outside 'pissing in'. And if he proved to Jack that he truly was a friend, then he had his name as political capital.

He could not see how this game was going to end, but from his wrestling days he knew that to win you had to get down and dirty with your opponent to test his mettle and find his weaknesses. He was in two minds still about where his loyalty ultimately lay, but he would try to get a discreet throat-hold on Jack.

CHAPTER 13

In the days that followed, Ross worked hard on his property. He put up solar panels and battery banks, drilled for water and struck lucky, putting in a well and starting a rudimentary garden. The horses were on holiday and getting fat.

The late summer and early fall meant he had time on his hands for once, and he took hold of his chainsaw and axe to fill up his woodpile for the coming winter. In these parts, winter was a serious business and you needed to be ready for it. Both the cabin and his Jeep needed to be winterised, but those could wait. He found the woodcutting deeply satisfying, both the work and the sense that he was stocking up a store of warmth and fuel for cooking. As he wielded the axe, his mind turned to scenes of Christmas, which this year promised to be a good one as he had Sandy to share it with. He thought too of the animals preparing for winter, the squirrels and bears in particular, laying in stores of fat and in the case of the squirrels, hiding a cache of nuts to see them through the hard time. He felt a close affinity to both species as he chopped. His friend, the robin, was in close attendance, as ever.

He acknowledged that something profound had happened to him to bring about such change within. It was, he thought, having a home of his own at last, set in a beloved landscape, and having someone to share it with, someone he thought of as exceptional in so many ways.

This Country I Call My Own

Sandy, it turned out, was something of a cooking maestro, her French heritage showing up clearly in her choice of dishes she chose to prepare, traditional Breton mainly. Smoothies also entered his life, both vegetable and fruit. Mexican and Thai cooking styles were part of her repertoire too. He found himself putting on weight for the first time in his life. She ate a great deal of cheese and fruit but ran it off with little trouble. And she had green fingers too, as the thriving plants in the small polytunnel showed with their exuberant growth. He enjoyed watching her garden or cook and in the mornings her eyes watched him back over the white and blue rim of her French-style coffee bowl.

Ross had reached a point in his life where he saw himself as part of nature, not superior to it in any way. When he moved through a landscape now, he moved through a universe of living things, all of which had some form of consciousness he could not explain. At first, on his return to the US from the various theatres of war, he had sensed this change in himself and thought it was the effect of war-weariness, of the PTSD weirdness. But now he knew better. He had devoured all the scientific papers he could lay his hands on which addressed this subject.

He came to understand that everything living, and some of it as inanimate as rocks, had an energy of its own. And all of it was now at risk because of the poison that man had buried in the very soil, the wellspring of life on earth. Increasingly, Ross felt himself at odds with the task that he had accepted from the Agency. His head had said yes to the task, but his heart was in revolt. If his position had not been clear before, it was increasingly so now. Despite all the money on God's earth, he could not see himself living at peace with himself if he acted on the brief required of him.

He knew he had to contact the Agency to report on any developments and he wavered about what to tell them. The fact that he had already spent some of their money on the research trip to Europe made him hesitate to say he had changed his mind. He reasoned that if he told them the truth about how squeaky-clean Freemantle was, it would buy him time, time he would be given if he added that he had so won the man's trust he had been asked to join his team. This, he knew, would be seen as a major win, having one of their own in the enemy camp, though Ross could no longer think of Freemantle as the enemy. The quality of the man and his reputation with some impressive people had wrought a sea-change in Ross's attitude.

He made the call and it went as expected. 'Great work. Just keep us posted the moment you have anything substantive we can use.' He undertook to do just that and made a second call to Freemantle to say he was considering his offer and would like to know more of what would be expected of him. His presence on the ranch meant that his availability would be limited to a very part-time role, he explained.

But as is the way of life, any decision on this front was suddenly put on hold when, to his surprise, Ross found himself involved in planning a wedding on the ranch. His wedding to Sandy.

Sandy explained that her father was not well and had at best a year to live. He had successfully fought off leukaemia for years but now his readings were close to a terminal point and despite blood transfusions, he would not live long. At the age of 30, Sandy very much wanted her father and mother to see her married and settled.

Ross asked her what she had in mind. 'Do you want us to fly to Quebec and get married there?'

Sandy shook her head. 'No, I want to get married here on the ranch, so that my father, mother and brother can understand my life and you, and see that I have a home and a place here in this community. It's important to me to do that for them.'

They spoke about the arrangements needed to hold a wedding in such a relatively remote spot that was still very rough around the edges. Sandy just smiled and said, 'If you let me organise it, all you will need to do is buy the wine and turn up on the day.'

It sounded like a sweet deal to Ross and he gladly

agreed. What happened next rather took him by surprise. Sandy said she would need a month to set it all up and described what she had in mind. He held both his hands up and said, 'I'm in your hands.'

It was a joyous thing, the thought of marriage to Sandy, but it was also painfully obvious that for the wedding itself he had little to offer, not even a best man, no family and no friends to speak of. He was very much a lone wolf. Sandy made flight and hotel plans for her parents and brother and got the ladies from the Hoot Owl Café in Sandpoint to agree to help with the catering. And then she received a surprise that moved her greatly. Her class of seniors, the 17- and 18-year-olds from the 12th grade, thirty in all, volunteered to assist, as did Sky Jensen, a favourite and highly creative former pupil who had graduated two years previously. And they were as good as their offer.

The family of one of the boys ran an events company and a huge marquee was brought out to the ranch to cover the round corral. Wooden pallets were placed across it and a plywood floor nailed in place with a red carpet covering it all. Chairs and tables were set up on either side of an aisle, and a raised dais for the officiating priest created at the far end. It all seemed to happen as if by magic.

A bank of portable toilets was trucked in and a massive rotating spit roast was set up next to the woodpile. Before Ross could blink, the ranch was a wedding venue.

He drove into town with two of the boys, who kept calling him 'Sir', to fetch cases of beer, cases of red and white wine, a case of champagne and soft drinks too.

As the ranch was transformed, it struck Ross that he was not just marrying Sandy, he was being wed to a community, and the thought brought him a strange, bittersweet pleasure.

Sandy arranged a photographer and, crucially, a priest, a Catholic priest who did not object to marrying one of his flock to an Episcopalian. All he asked Ross was, 'You do love the girl, I presume?' Ross grinned and admitted that he did indeed love the girl.

Two days before the wedding, Sandy's family flew into Spokane, and Ross and Sandy drove to collect them. As she had said, her father François was frail, but her mother Marcelle had all of Sandy's fire and energy and she hugged him. Her brother Jacques was almost as tall as Ross and said he was honoured to be his best man. The warmth of all three was tangible and Ross felt much relieved, as he had worried about how Sandy's family would take to him. They in turn were impressed by his French, rusty though he felt it to be.

Sandy spent a day showing them the sights in and around Sandpoint and the ranch and took them to her school for a meal in the cafeteria. That evening they all returned to Sandpoint for dinner and then she dropped them at their motel. François seemed to be holding up to all the excitement.

He found a moment to take Ross aside and taking his hand, said, 'This is for me one of the happiest days of my life. I can see how happy you make Sandrine. She is a wonderful girl with much courage, much determination and big dreams to change the world. Too much for most men, I think. She has done well to find you and you are blessed to find her. Promise me that you will always take care of her as I know she will take care of you.'

Ross gave his promise with a great sense of emotion, knowing full well that in all likelihood he would not be seeing Sandy's father again.

The day of the wedding dawned bright with a promise of warmth and clear skies. Sandy was driven to the ranch by one of her friends and teaching colleagues, Marty Gibson, with two of her former pupils, Sky and Storm, who acted as bridesmaids. Her father was just able to walk her down the aisle to give her away and then join his wife at the front of the congregation. Altogether, they were some 70 strong and not a single one of them from Ross's side. Many of Sandy's fellow teachers were there as well as her friends from college and her pupils, who had done such sterling work on the marquee.

The ceremony in the flower-bedecked tent was

charming and Ross could not take his eyes off Sandy, who was more beautiful than he had ever seen her in a gown of cream lace that her mother had selected for her in Quebec. He wore his best navy suit and his ribbons and medals on his chest, something Sandy had asked him to do.

'You may not have a living family at this wedding, so I want everyone to see what we and this country owes you, so that they will understand that we are now your family.'

Hearing this, Ross had to hold hard onto himself. He was silent, for he could not express to her how much her words meant to him. But she saw the effect of her words and she hugged him. In that moment, both of his own parents and his brother stood with him, as real and tangible as when they were alive. For Ross, that was the moment that he felt himself wedded to Sandy for life.

The rest of the wedding day was a blur. He recalled being joshed by the ladies from the Hoot Owl Café who told him not to be a stranger and if Sandy did not work out, he would be welcome to choose one of them as a replacement. He thanked them for the offer and for what they had produced in the way of outstanding food and flowers and for looking out for Sandy when she did shifts at the café.

Jacques, although shy, made a more than acceptable best man's speech, teasing him a little for capturing his sister's heart when so many had failed, and thanking him for making her so happy.

In his own speech, Ross made a point of speaking some words of thanks in French to Sandy's family and he thanked Sandy for making a lonely bachelor a husband as well as a citizen of Sandpoint, which was very well received. And he thanked Sandy's students for all that they had done to make the day memorable.

'Finally, I want to thank the ladies from the Hoot Owl Café, who sent Sandy to wait at my table on that fateful day. I'd just popped in for a coffee and a doughnut and look what I found.' He turned to his wife, glowing with joy by his side, the circlet of white daisies shining in her dark hair, and the dress selected for her by her mother, of a beauty that only

Paris or Quebec could produce. 'I found this beautiful woman who not only served me a doughnut, but she also filled up the hole in my soul.' There was not a dry eye in the marquee after that.

Ross spent the rest of the afternoon walking the marquee to thank everyone for coming and at around 4pm, he and Sandy finally had some of the delicious beef barbecue and some red wine. A four-piece school band struck up at around 7pm and there was dancing both in the tent and outside, watched by Rincon and Buddy, who looked somewhat spooked by the goings on.

By midnight, the last guest had left. Sandy and Ross sat by the outside fire-pit and toasted themselves with the last of the champagne, which Ross had stashed in the Airstream. It was a beautiful night, and they sat up late recalling the highlights of the day. Ross then picked Sandy up and said, 'Mrs McCallister, I think it's long past time we went to bed!'

In the morning, he made the call he had been putting off for some weeks. He called the Agency and briefed them on the research Wes had done for him. He reminded them that on his trip to Europe, Freemantle had come up smelling of roses. 'The guy is squeaky clean.'

There was a silence on the line and then the answer he had been dreading. 'Keep digging.'

CHAPTER 14

In the days immediately following the wedding, Ross found himself living in a new reality, one in which he was suddenly very much a member of the Sandpoint community. It was a novel and unsettling experience for one who had lived so much of his life on the edge, or in the shadows. On trips into town to get fuel, hardware and food, he found himself greeted with cheerful waves, nods and even handshakes from well-wishers.

'Thank you, thank you,' became his go-to phrase. But he was totally unprepared for his welcome at the Hoot Owl Café when he popped in for a coffee and a doughnut late one afternoon. As if on cue, the ladies who ran the place broke out into the chorus of *Simply the Best* by Tina Turner. They sang with huge grins, 'Better than all the rest. Better than anyone!'

Ross felt himself blush deeply for the first time in years, managing a half-hearted wave and what his army buddies would have described as 'a shit-eating grin'.

After leaving the café, he popped into a bar for a beer on the way home as a means of calming down. His welcome in the low-lit pub was more muted, but he was made to feel very welcome. It may have been the beers forced on him or the weirdness of the situation that made him take a wrong turning when he left the bar in the dark, but he suddenly found himself in a new tract of housing in Sandpoint and as he did U-turn after U-turn to get out of the maze of new builds he suddenly drove into a scene that might have been painted by the Flemish artist Pieter Breughel the Elder. What he saw made him pull up momentarily in astonishment.

It looked like a scene of the 'Hunters in Snow' crossed with 'The Wedding Party' dinner in the village pub. The whole street was lit up by arc-lights and dead elk lay across the bonnets of hunting vehicles. The neighbours were all out in the road, barbecuing, drinking, dancing and butchering the deer. He had stumbled into that local Panhandle fall fixture, the return of the deer hunters.

As he slowed down and then pulled up, his vehicle was recognised and mobbed and he was half dragged out by many hands, some of whom he recognised from the wedding. A beer was put into his hand and a roll bulging with barbecued elk liver thrust into his other hand. That weird grin was back on his face. He stayed longer than he had intended, and it was midnight before he reached the ranch.

As he explained to Sandy why he was so late back, starting with the Hoot Owl Café singing and then the bar and then ending with the street party, Sandy started to laugh quietly at first and then with tears streaming down her cheeks. Ruefully he joined in. It had been a most discomfiting and discombobulating few hours for Ross. The next morning, when he went to unload the Jeep, he found among the purchases he'd made the previous day a burlap sack containing a huge joint of elk meat.

For someone who felt he had never belonged, never truly had a home, had lived out of tents and sleeping bags, broken-down bombed houses or caves, in hotels or guest houses in more countries than he could remember, this reaching out by a community to embrace him, to welcome him, was something that took some getting used to and he felt the need to examine it to process the whole thing. He knew it was all down to Sandy's good standing in the community. She was a much-loved and respected part of this place, and he was now the beneficiary of that. It felt good, but at the same time very unsettling. Just at the point in his life that he had decided to withdraw as much as possible from the community of people, he was suddenly engulfed by it.

But the local community had much to recommend it, he thought, recalling his wrong turning the night before and what he had driven into. The elk hunters would have full freezers to see them through the winter and Ross wondered how many communities still lived like this in the lower 48 states, living only in part from supermarkets, yes, but also from salmon and trout taken from lake and stream with moose and elk to further bulk up their pantries and freezers to slim down their food costs. He respected anyone capable of such self-sufficiency; it was after all something he aspired to himself.

This was a community of people who had denied themselves the lure of California, Oregon and Washington's Pacific coast, a people who had hunkered down here in the eastern lee of the Rockies, settling for less in some ways, for a less trammelled or glamorous life, a life of relative hardship thanks to the short growing season and the winter snowdrifts. A place still remote in some ways.

He had to admit that there was a dimly seen pioneer quality to these people who had rejected both the ease and the frantic rush of cities. This were a community not overly set on wealth creation or fame, but who sought a good life based on older values. They were not a replacement for the Native Americans whose way of life had maintained the wealth of wildlife and who had lived in harmony with the land, but there was in the settlers, too, a nod in that direction. He knew many were as concerned about rampant capitalism as he was and also feared the damage that climate change might bring. These were people who Ross felt he could fight for.

Ross and Sandy had agreed not to have a honeymoon away but instead to use the fall weather to ride into the mountains to camp for a week. Ross borrowed a mule to haul their camping gear and food supplies and a light tent. The horses were grass-fat so they took things slowly, making just 20 miles on the first day before making camp by a stream.

The trees were well on the turn and the landscape glowed gold and red and green as if to celebrate with them.

As Sandy busied herself getting dinner ready, Ross flicked a fly in the river and soon had two fat rainbow trout to smoke above the fire. The days and the nights that followed rolled into each other in a similar pattern, and the newlyweds were profoundly happy in each other's company. A morning or afternoon would go by with barely a word spoken, just a smile and a hand pointing something out. This silence between them was something they both valued and acknowledged that it added to their appreciation of the landscapes they traversed. In ways they barely understood, they felt the land enter them and they became increasingly at ease with it.

The mule, typically, was a bit mulish at times, but they soon realised that if he had a mind of his own he was often right in the choices he made. Thanks to him they avoided a number of snares that otherwise would have created problems, once quicksand and once a cougar sunning itself on a rock above the trail they had wanted to take. They renamed the mule Solomon for his wisdom, Solly for short and he too became a team member. On their return to the ranch, tired and sore but joyful, they made an offer for Solly which was accepted, and Rincon and Buddy had a new partner.

One morning, as Ross was mucking out stables, he received a call from Freemantle. 'Is that offer of a ride still on the cards?' he asked. Ross assured him that it was and a three days later they rode out together.

They were about half an hour into the ride when Freemantle asked Ross what his position was on joining his fight against the nuclear waste storage sites. Ross had been expecting the question and he said, 'I'm sorry it has taken a while, but if I can help you can count on me.' He explained that he had just got married and that he'd had a hugely warm reception from the townsfolk in Sandpoint and from surrounding ranch neighbours. 'Sandy has taught a lot of their kids.'

'Congratulations Ross, I heard that you guys had got

hitched. You are a lucky man. Sandy is a fine young woman; I hear such good things about her.'

Ross thanked him and pulling Rincon up, he looked at Freemantle and asked, 'How exactly can I help you?'

Freemantle said, 'If you can face it, I'd like you to join me on speaking platforms now and then and to lend your name in support of the cause. I think that as a decorated veteran and a commander at that, it would help us greatly to get traction.'

So here it was, finally, the fork in the road, the time to choose, to make what Ross knew would be a fateful decision. Ross said he would do what it took, knowing as he did that it would raise eyebrows at the Agency, who would wonder what the hell he was up to. He knew full well he was also opening himself to a lifetime of toil, as he would be kissing goodbye to the Agency money and any future chance of having friends at court as it were, unless Freemantle made it to the Governor's mansion, and that was a very long shot indeed. Such an outcome was unlikely in such a staunchly Republican-voting state.

Ross asked Freemantle if he wanted to ride high or low. And how much time he had.

'Let's go as high as the day allows. You are joining me on the high road Ross, so let's go high!'

They did not speak much after that as they were on and off the horses, constantly climbing for height and helping the horses by taking the weight off their backs on the switchback trail. The scenery was spectacular with majestic trees, huge skies that changed as the cloudscapes moved, and the brooding mountain peaks that they worked their way towards.

After a few more hours of riding, Ross felt Rincon begin to lose his edge, and he knew that Buddy, being older, must be feeling it too. He looked above him and saw a spot that would make a good place to rest up before heading back as promised. The trail had narrowed down to a rocky ledge but still wide enough to allow for reasonable access.

They were just turning to pass up a switchback when

Ross heard Freemantle yell and saw him and Buddy slip off the crumbling trail and cartwheel down the mountain side with a small avalanche of rubble following them down. Ross was off Rincon in a flash and rappelling down on the rope fixed to his saddle, but when he reached Freemantle, he was beneath the horse.

Ross checked Buddy and saw with horror that his front legs were broken. There was nothing for it but to shoot the horse, putting him beyond pain, and then struggle to push him off Freemantle. Thanks to the steepness of the slope, the old horse slipped down the mountainside into a brushy ravine and suddenly there was a ringing silence. Freemantle's legs and pelvis looked crushed and he was slipping in and out of consciousness.

Ross looked up and saw that Rincon, good horse that he was, was keeping the rope holding him taut. He feared to move Freemantle, who was now totally unconscious. Ross reached for his phone and called Sandy for help. By the time the medevac chopper arrived, Freemantle was deep in a coma. The medics looked Ross over but he said he was fine, so Ross went to calm Rincon and held him while the helicopter took off for the flight into Spokane.

Sandy called to see if the helicopter had arrived and he assured her that they had Freemantle and were on their way with him to hospital. She asked if he was injured, and he said a few scrapes from getting down to help Freemantle and sadly had had to shoot Buddy and then edge him off the injured man.

'Oh my God Ross!' she gasped. 'Poor Buddy!'

It was a long ride home. As he rode, his mind, so used to situations like these, went into automatic crisis control. There were no witnesses as to what had happened, other than the medevac helicopter crew, who had only seen the aftermath of the accident.

Freemantle had been stopped, that was for sure, but not in a way that Ross had wished or intended or, to be fair, that the Agency had asked for. Would the Agency believe that, or would they think he had gone rogue? If Freemantle lived, would he remember what had happened? When Ross reached home, he assured Sandy he was OK and put Rincon into the paddock with the mule. The loss of Buddy bit deep.

The moment he got inside, he called the Sheriff's office and briefed them on the accident. They said they had already heard from the medevac team and the hospital. Freemantle was still in a coma, but stable. They asked him to come in to give a full statement on what had happened. He said he was on his way. He then called the Agency. Not surprisingly, they were already briefed. He explained in minute detail exactly what had happened.

'Ross, when you brief the sheriff's office, tell them exactly what you have just told us but none of the context. Freemantle was a friend who shared your concern about the nuclear waste sites, that's it! You guys were out on a Sunday ride, end of story. Accidents happen in the mountains. And Ross, don't beat yourself up, this is not the end of the world. Mission accomplished.'

Ross put the phone down and looked at his hands. The old tremor was back.

CHAPTER 15

'Mission accomplished!' The words rang in his ears and would not stop. He slept badly and his night horrors returned with a vengeance. Ross knew the figures: experts estimated that 54 per cent of suicides among people living with PTSD were directly related to the condition. He knew he was treading a fine line. As a senior officer, he'd ridden shotgun on this issue with men in units under his command and he recognised all the symptoms in himself. The world started to close in on him.

The day after the accident, local sheriff Jake Williams and his deputy Mike Silver, two FBI men and a tracker arrived at the ranch in two all-terrain vehicles. Ross shook hands all round and felt the eyes of the two FBI personnel hard on him. He looked back coolly, as usual, wondering how they would handle themselves when things got rough. He wondered too how much they knew about him, how much his army unit would have given them and more crucially, his Agency. They asked a few brief questions about how he came to know Freemantle and he told them as much as he could. That he was concerned about the local environment and had attended a lecture by Freemantle in Coeur D'Alene, been impressed and the beginnings of a friendship had started. They knew of his trip to Europe and who he had spoken to there.

'Seems like a long way to go to check out

environmental activism,' the more senior of the two said.

'Well, it wasn't just to see them, my main reason for going was to check out interest from UK tourist organisations who want to arrange trail riding here. But I also wanted to have the views of Greenpeace and Mrs Townsend on Freemantle who told me he had had contact with them. This nuclear waste stuff is going to get more heated before it is resolved, and I chose to live here to have a quieter life.'

They left it at that and said they wanted to see the site of the accident. There was just a trace of an emphasis on the word 'accident' that Ross noted, as he was meant to. Ross and Sandy joined Jake and Mike and the tracker – known locally as Wild Willy for his dreadlocks – in their vehicle and directed them for the hour it took to reach a point just below the final bluff where he and Freemantle had ended their ride so disastrously.

They left the two vehicles and climbed the ever-narrowing horse trail up to its steepest point, with Willy in the lead. At the point of the landslip he motioned them to stay back, and he clambered up and around the rockfall, clutching onto brush. Once back on the track, he looked closely at the stony ground of the path.

'The back horse, he stepped back quick!' he said indicating the marks on the ground. He then pulled himself up the rock incline to a point above the trail which commanded a view of the whole approach.

He let out a yell and called, 'Bear sleep here or wait for deer coming up the track!' They then all struggled up to join him and he showed them the flattened grass and tufts of bear fur where an enormous animal had rested and waited in hiding. Willy said that it was impossible to tell if the bear had been there during the incident or whether Buddy had scented the bear's hide-out; maybe a shift in the breeze had given him the scent missed by Rincon seconds earlier. He'd involuntarily stepped back, his back left leg going over the edge which crumbled and he then lost his balance and fell. It was all there to see for those who could read the signs.

Further up the trail, you could also see the marks made

by Rincon to brace the lariat rope holding Ross as he tried to pull Freemantle clear. They then made their way to the place that Buddy's fall had been broken, trapping Freemantle below him. The signs here were clear too, the thrashing of the horse's rear feet as he tried to gain purchase to pull himself back up the slope which must have impacted the rider beneath him and the blood trail from the bullet that ended his life. Then Willy moved further down in a controlled slide with Ross and Mike following. There they found Buddy's remains in thick brush, badly mauled by predators and birds of prey. Lying in the bushes was Buddy's skull with the single round hole where Ross had ended the old horse's life. Ross cut the saddle free from the horse's carcass and dragged it back up the mountainside.

The five men and Sandy stood looking down the mountainside. The sheriff said, 'Hell of a fall. The horse stood no chance. It's just as you said, Ross, and now we have the signs to corroborate it, and even the reason poor Buddy took that step back. Any horse scenting bear would have done that. Looks like an ambush spot the critter used before.'

Sandy took Ross's hand in hers and they made their way back down to the vehicles. Ross felt an enormous sense of relief that the evidence so exactly matched what he had told the sheriff. The FBI men had little to add, just checking the time it had taken to reach Sandy on the phone and get the chopper to the site.

Despite being free of any suspicion of evil intent, Ross increasingly found himself creeping out of the bedroom quietly in the dawn light to avoid waking Sandy. Watching the sunrise brought him a little peace that calmed his night horrors. He had once been told by a very tough sergeant after a particularly brutal encounter in Afghanistan, 'Son, just remember this, tomorrow the sun will rise as usual.' It was, on the surface, the most anodyne of comments, meant to reassure, and indeed it had done just that. It had stopped the horror and despair he'd felt, and a burden had been lifted off him. It was true; whatever terrors the day brought, life would go on, the sun would rise once more.

This Country I Call My Own

As he sat sipping coffee outside the cabin he had built with his own hands, the old magic worked once more. There was a peace to be had in just being, letting go, drinking the coffee, feeling its warmth enter his body and the caffeine taking hold as the sun warmed his face and hands. His thoughts turned to the beautiful woman who had just joined her life to his and who was warming his bed even now. He threw the coffee dregs out into the yard and slipped quietly back into bed, watching Sandy sleep.

And it was in that time of watching her sleep that things within him were resolved. It was not a conscious thing, he felt no decision had been made by him, but the choice facing him, to unravel or to hold fast and survive had been made for him. Like tempered steel, his mind and body had been stressed once more, and once more had come back into true equilibrium. Despite the PTSD and the hand tremors, he was after all a veteran and if that counted for anything, it counted in these moments when you are being threatened with disintegration and you said, 'No! Hold fast.'

From the earliest days of his military studies, he knew that the great French general Napoleon Bonaparte and many others since acknowledged this strength in their veterans, those battle-hardened by violence. 'The first quality of a soldier is courage, the second is perseverance!' And he had witnessed it himself at first hand. The veterans were the shock troops needed to lead an attack or to offer cover for a retreating army. These were not boys who could be overwhelmed with the horror of battle, these were men who had integrated the horror so that they could deal with it. Ross felt himself coming together, a sense of girding up his loins, as the old saying had it. He felt more whole than he had for some time. This too would pass, this latest horror, this time too would be history, and he would go on going on, both for himself and for this woman who now added such a powerful reason to live his life to the fullest. The words of the poem *Invictus,* dimly remembered, whispered in his head:

Julian Roup

Out of the night that covers me
Black as the pit from pole to pole,
I thank whatever gods may be
For my unconquerable soul.

In the fell clutch of circumstance,
I have not winced nor cried aloud.
Under the bludgeonings of chance
My head is bloody, but unbowed.

Beyond this place of wrath and tears
Looms but the Horror of the shade,
And yet the menace of the years
Finds, and shall find, me unafraid.

It matters not how strait the gate,
How charged with punishments the scroll,
I am the master of my fate
I am the captain of my soul.

Ross determined that he would live to fight another day and take pleasure in the fight or go down fighting. There was a hard glint in his eyes once more. Someone, he forgot who, had said to him, 'You can't fill another's cup if your cup is half empty.' He was determined to keep Sandy's cup topped up.

Later that afternoon, he received a coded message from his offshore bank that the exact amount of money promised him for the 'last job' had arrived in his very discreet and private bank account. Ross thought about what this meant for a long, long moment. The chess pieces in his head played their old game, this way or that way, fall back or attack. The one thing it signified was that the Agency believed he had acted in good faith and manufactured the 'accident'. They knew his horse skills and his track record for jobs even more demanding of finesse. In the end, he pigeonholed the information under 'Hold for now, do nothing'.

Ross took Sandy with him the next evening to visit

This Country I Call My Own

Freemantle at Providence Sacred Heart Medical Center in Spokane. They barely spoke on the drive down from the ranch, enjoying the sunset. Freemantle was still in a coma, but his pelvis was pinned and his legs too. He would live, but how much of the old Jack would wake, if ever he did, nobody could say. There was some concussion, too, hardly surprising, said the young woman doctor who showed them to his room. She said Freemantle would need at least six months of further surgery and a year to recover. His run for the governorship was indefinitely put on hold.

Lying in his hospital bed, he looked pale and much smaller than they remembered him, like a boy. Evidence of support and high regard were all about him in the flowers and the cards that decorated the room. The nurse who stayed with them once the doctor left said that Mrs Freemantle came each day to read to her husband, but that as yet there had been no flicker of recognition or return of consciousness. She said that once his surgery had settled down and he remained stable, he would be moved to Seattle to be closer to his wife, children and friends. The drive home seemed much longer, as the Jeep carried them into the dark of the night.

CHAPTER 16

There was an urgent need to replace Buddy as winter was coming and there would soon be fewer horses available for sale. Ross made a note of each horse auction in the region and also scoured the sale adverts in the local news and horse press, and he turned up a few likely sounding animals. It was always a complete lottery when buying a horse, smoke and mirrors was the order of the day and outright lying the norm. Very few people selling a horse would share with you its mental or physical issues or any quirks it had – windsucking, bucking, rearing, a vicious nature – the list was endless. It truly was a case of buyer beware.

Ross traipsed around the auctions, but found nothing suitable. The razzamatazz of some of the auctions was enough to turn a horseman's stomach; the music, lights, flags, bunting and the endless hucksterism of the auctioneer's patter set his teeth on edge. How any horse behaved itself in that bedlam said much for their long-suffering nature. And how anyone felt able to buy amid this chaos amazed him. But sell horses they did. He learned to give them a wide berth or sometimes go but wearing earplugs. It was horse buying hell.

What he had going for him was years of experience with horses and his brief stint as an amateur rodeo rider. He was not without his own resources when it came to buying horseflesh. He missed Buddy every day and knew it would be a long old haul to get the new horse up to anything like Buddy's accommodating behaviour unless he struck lucky or a miracle was on offer, but there are few of these in the horse world.

He drove miles each day, eliminating options. Eventually he found an unusual-coloured blue roan, an Appaloosa-Quarter horse cross that looked useful, solid enough to be able to carry a big man and temperamentally quite chilled. He rode it in the corral and though it seemed fairly green, that was only to be expected from a five-year-old that had done little since being backed. The girl selling the horse was off to college shortly and seemed sad to be losing her horse. He asked if he could give the horse a run on the ranch and she saddled another horse to accompany him and show him the way. The horse felt fresh which he took as a good sign that it had not been drugged. There was no indication of it being cold-backed and it stood still while he mounted and then moved off smartly at his urging. After half an hour of playing around on the tracks, Ross asked the horse for a canter and it was then that it showed some spirit with a neatly executed buck before hitting its stride, but there was no grabbing at the bit or any attempt to bolt with him. He looked at the girl and she said innocently that she had never seen Blue buck before. Ross took that at face value.

But he felt that the horse, with regular work, would settle down to being a useful citizen and one he would trust Sandy on. What he particularly liked was that he would not be spending the best part of the winter backing the horse, who was well-backed already. He bartered with its owner, who showed a streak of toughness that she had not showed initially, but in the end, he picked the horse up for $12,000, subject to a full veterinary inspection.

He did not want to get the horse back home only to find that it was blind in one eye, had a heart defect, back problems or any one of the myriad leg ailments that befall horses. He made a few calls and found a vet he had heard of who could do the job the next day and asked him to run a blood test to look for drug use or anything else that signalled danger. As he drove away, he crossed his fingers. He felt he had found something useful. If the horse passed the veterinary inspection, he would keep the name but change it slightly to True Blue.

The next day he took Sandy with him to the vetting and her excitement was palpable. She loved the horse's colour, the almost-black head matching its mane and tail, contrasting nicely with the blue speckled body. Blue certainly looked the part of a working ranch horse. After a very thorough work out, the vet signalled an all-clear, other than an old injury which had left a small scar but no lasting internal damage; the X-rays endorsed that view. 'Nice horse!' he commented.

Ross had brought the trailer, hoping for this result, and so after loading Blue without any problems, they were on their way. The horse soon settled and they travelled the two hours home without incident. He had not seen Sandy this excited for some time. She wanted to know when she might ride him and he said, 'Let's give him a week to settle down and get to know the place, meet Rincon and Solly, and then he is yours to play with. You can lead him round the place every day if you like, that would be a good start.'

He made another suggestion that met with Sandy's approval. 'Why don't we get your pupils out for a weekend camp to thank them for all the work they put in for the wedding?'

Sandy leaned over and hugged him. 'That's such a lovely idea. I was wondering what I could get them by way of thanks.'

In early October the students arrived at the ranch, and each of the boys and girls in his or her own way offered him condolences for the riding accident and the loss of Buddy. But he also sensed something new from them. They seemed a little confused about who he was now that they knew more about him as a result of the newspaper coverage the accident had generated. They had seen him as a rancher, a horse packing guy, but now they knew something more of his service history, too. Sitting by the fire on Saturday night after supper, singing to a couple of guitars, there was some story telling about the old days in the area and then one of the students asked him to tell them some of his army experiences. He gave them a very brief insight and played down any heroics. It seemed to leave them wanting more.

'So what are your plans, your dreams? What do you

guys want to do with your lives,?' Ross asked as a means of directing the conversation away from his previous life. A number of the youngsters said they wanted to travel, some said backpacking in Europe, and a couple wanted to try the nomad life for a year before college, in campers like many of those they followed on YouTube, van builders turned vloggers.

The kids explained the concept of 'Patreon', the online mechanism for generating cash for a project or a cause in return for regular videos posted on YouTube.

Ross asked, 'You mean people pay to watch these campers travelling?'

They assured him that some did very well out of it. The videos covered their everyday life, cooking, building, travelling, meeting new people, falling in love. With this in mind, he watched a number of these vlogs and was suitably impressed by the ability with carpentry, plumbing, electrics and building that many showed as much as by the looks and charm of some of the characters, both male and female. What astonished him was that people, 'Patreons', paid towards the making of these videos in such numbers that it allowed the vanners to live this nomadic travelling lifestyle.

Once he'd logged on to this material a few times, the YouTube and Google algorithms continued to feed him more of the same and he discovered a world he knew nothing of, people being paid to sail around the world, horse trainers who retained followers numbering in the tens of thousands and people living off-grid in the wilds, creating food gardens, hunting and fishing and finding an enthusiastic audience for this slow, bucolic lifestyle. It was a sort of living through others that stressed city dwellers seemed to crave, as well as influencing other young and not-so-young people to take up this life, living and recording their lives and travels to earn an income to continue living the dream.

It started Ross thinking how with Sandy's help he might monetise their life on the ranch to provide another income stream, but he dismissed the idea out of hand. It would be a massive loss of privacy that ran counter to everything he craved. But it gave him a wild idea.

He wondered how a 'virtual' online protest, Greenham Common style, would work? If people from across the US and the world posted videos opposing the nuclear waste sites might these help to fund the protest at the same time as building a constituency of support? He decided to kick the idea around with Sandy. As usual, she cut straight to the chase.

'Ross, it's an excellent idea, but really? You'd finally be showing the Agency where your heart truly lies. Flagging up the fact that you had no hand in Jack's accident.' She was dead right and he put the idea on hold for now, or at least until he'd thought about it some more.

The three students who had naturally taken the lead in organising the wedding work party and who directed the weekend tent camp at the ranch spent a fair amount of time with him, the two boys, Max and Kent and the slightly older girl, the lovely blue-eyed blonde, appropriately named Sky Jensen, who seemed to have an existing joshing friendship. In his mind he thought of them as a collective and named them 'Max Kentsky' to help him remember their separate names.

In a quiet moment after lunch on Sunday, Sky surprised him by asking if there might be any work on the ranch with the horses. 'I love it out here. I've dreamed of working with horses and if you would teach me, I could drive out and help you with them.' Ross looked at this lovely girl asking for help and guidance and something made him hesitate.

'Sky, let me have a think about it and a chat to Sandy. What would your folks say? Would they support the idea?'

Sky laughed and said, 'My folks would be delighted. They would be so pleased that I've finally found something that really interests me. Once I've learned how it is to work with horses, I might then do a college course of some kind that gives me academic back-up to the practical stuff.'

Ross promised her he would speak to Sandy and later that evening, with just themselves left on the ranch after the kids had gone, he did. 'I'm not sure how you'd feel about me working with a 20-year-old girl?' and he looked at her quizzically.

To his surprise Sandy laughed out loud. 'Ross, you big fool, Sky is gay. She would not be any trouble in that way.'

Ross shook his head; he had not seen that coming.

'In my classes there have been straight, gay, bi and trans kids. You are a bit out of touch! And I know that since graduating, Sky has had at least two relationships with women older than her.'

And then, in mid-November, the first snow flew and the land was suddenly white and still, and a great peace descended on the ranch and the whole of the Panhandle. It gave Ross the time to think, time he needed badly. He had decided to keep the Agency money. He had promised Sandy an easier life and he felt strongly that whatever the Agency thought they had paid him for, he had inadvertently achieved their goal. He also felt that by his military and security service he had earned it ten times over, both by putting his life on the line repeatedly, and then the years with the Agency, working on the many discreet security actions in the Middle East and elsewhere. He felt they owed him; he'd earned it. And although he'd never had any intention of 'stopping' Freemantle in the way the accident had, the effect was the same – he had been stopped. And that was because of his involvement with him.

Ross did not tell Sandy that he'd been paid for the Freemantle job. It was something he knew would not play well with her. This would remain one more of the many secrets he carried with him, the reason he slept badly and his hands shook.

CHAPTER 17

Ross sat drinking coffee and sunning himself on the couch by the window, looking out at the view but not really seeing it. Sandy came over and kissed him on the top of his head. He reached back and pulled her onto his lap and the butterscotch leather couch took some more damage.

Later that day he watched as Sky and Sandy worked the horses. Sky was a natural; she had taken to horses as though she had been doing it all her life. She was gentle but firm with them, not taking any nonsense or allowing them to push her around, establishing herself as a leader. Soon they followed her if she entered their paddock and would snuffle her hair. She was not afraid of hard work and she learned quickly. Ross had only to show her the way he liked things done and it was set in stone.

Sandy had started giving her riding lessons on Solomon the mule, who proved a most accommodating teacher. It was as if he knew she was a beginner and he carried her gently, stopping when he felt her lose her balance in the saddle. It did not take long till the two women were riding the ranch fences together and then making small excursions out onto the forest trails.

Sky, always a bit of a wild child, once focused, suddenly found her groove and the pendulum swung in the opposite direction – one of utter dedication. Discovering a love of horses and two people whose lifestyle bewitched her, encompassing all the things she held dear, a life in nature off-grid, with a slightly unusual approach to things. Slight and petite, she nevertheless had a will of iron which meshed well with the robust antics of a horse herd. She had an almost savage hunger for life that made her seem older than her years. She was a natural leader, keeping Max and Kent devotedly in tow, and also getting along with the girls in her friendship group.

Blue settled down soon enough, other than some typical youthful high jinks in the paddock. He took his work with Sandy and Ross seriously and was much less green than when he arrived. He could now pick up on the aids almost as though he wished to please his rider.

Getting back from a trip to town, Ross pulled the Jeep over to watch a new development, Sandy riding Rincon and Sky on Blue. They made a picture that caught in his throat. He felt blessed.

Sky's parents came out for a Sunday lunch and were delighted with their daughter's progress. 'We don't know where this love of horses comes from, nobody in our family has ever shown the slightest interest in horses,' Mrs Jensen told Ross and Sandy. He could tell that they were proud of her and asked his advice on how she might use her newfound skills to find a career working with and caring for horses.

Sky got a bit flustered. 'Mom I've hardly started to learn the ropes, I'm in no hurry to move on elsewhere.'

Her mother reassured her. 'Honey, of course. It's just interesting to hear what Ross thinks about this life and how to give yourself the best chance.'

Ross explained that there were all sorts of paths Sky could take, from a veterinary career to running a horse yard, dressage, jumping or cross-country eventing, or even, in time, running her own horse packing outfit. 'She's a natural. She'll find her way. The horses and the mule love her and the barn is immaculate thanks to her. The place looks much more professional already. She is a great asset.'

He noticed Sky blushing at the praise. Her parents

agreed that if Ross and Sandy really did not mind, Sky was welcome to take up their offer of spending weekends at the ranch, using the Airstream as her accommodation.

Now Ross took Blue in hand himself for some more advanced training, getting him used to opening and closing gates without barging or hanging back, learning to stay in one spot when the reins hung to the ground, and he introduced him to some night work.

Once in a while, the sheriff's office or the mountain rescue teams would ask for local support, so it was useful to have a good night horse. In the barn, Ross kept a 'rescue rig', which had everything he would need if called out in a hurry, dry clothes, rope, a tarp, a torch, fire starters, dry hard tack and jerky in sealed plastic containers. It was rare that he needed it, but it was always there, refreshed from time to time. He wished to be seen as a good neighbour and someone who could be relied on for help in an emergency.

Saddling Blue up one evening at sunset after a day of mixed sunshine and showers, he headed out to test the young horse in the dark. The first pinewood forest they entered was lit up by the low sun and every tree trunk glowed red, reminding Ross of the brass sandboxes in European cathedrals, filled with a mini forest of flaming devotional candles, each one illuminating its neighbours. He had lit a few of those in his time for friends both living and dead. He pulled Blue to a halt and sat still, just listening to the slight wind moving the tops of the trees, birds settling down for the night and now and then the scraping scuttle of squirrels. Blue's ears and eyes kept tabs on it all as well.

Emerging from the wood, Ross looked up to see the last of the sunlight gild the mountain tops. Blue felt relaxed and so he pushed on. The grass they were wading through was still wet from the last shower of the afternoon, but above them the sky was clear. At the edge of the next stand of trees, he picked up on an unexpected sound. It was raining in the wood. Nonplussed, he sat for some moments, scanning the clear sky, thinking how could this be? How was it possible that he and Blue were dry under a clear sunset sky, when a few feet away it was raining in the wood? As he looked closer up into the trees, the answer revealed itself. A breeze was stirring the trees just enough to help them shake the water from the last shower off their leaves and that was the soft rain pattering sound he heard and what made it seem like rain falling amid the trees. It was a weeping wood. The thought struck deep, overlapping instantly as it did with thoughts of the tears he'd shed for lost comrades. He held the horse still for some minutes.

For the thousandth time, Ross noted the beauty and the magic of this place. He felt the usual sense of being alert for anything that would spook the horse with dusk falling fast now. But he had no sense of being alone. He knew he was observed by countless eyes invisible to him and he accepted that the trees too were aware of him and the horse. As he moved through them, touching trunks or moving a branch away that was impeding his and Blue's progress, he knew that the trees were telegraphing this news to each other using the fine threads of fungi underground to spread the message. He had read with astonishment the latest scientific papers on this 'consciousness' that trees had developed to warn other trees of fire, the impact of deer, or insects, or the axes of men. It made him feel a part of the energy of a 'thinking universe'. And thoughts of the nuclear poison below ground, not very far away, came to him too.

Gently pushing Blue on into darkness, Ross skirted the stands of trees to make it easier for the horse, not wanting him to trip on windfalls. He could not feel any tension in Blue and he spoke to him quietly, telling him how well he was doing and patting him with his free hand.

He noticed a mist rising in the river valley to his left and soon horse and rider were engulfed in darkness made thicker by the fog formed out of cold air meeting the last of the day's warmth. After an hour of this sightless movement, he turned the horse for home just as the moon rose to provide some dim light.

It was then that Blue stopped suddenly and planted, refusing to go on. Ross looked sharply all around him. He could not see anything that would have spooked the horse, but he trusted Blue's instinct and did not try to force him on, he just spoke to him quietly, and then to his amazement, he noticed what the horse had seen, and what was making him tense up so that his neck thickened and he felt ready to flee.

Ross shortened the reins and watched as a milk-white stag emerged from the mist. It looked like something out of a children's fairy story. It spotted the horse and rider and it raised its head and antlers, standing stock still; it was a moment of pure magic. For what seemed like minutes, the world stopped as man and horse gazed at this apparition and then suddenly it whirled away back into the mist. Blue, spooked by the unusual sight and by the wild movement, also tried to whirl away, but Ross kept him where he was until he relaxed and they moved on. Half an hour later he was rubbing Blue down in the corral, knowing that he had all the makings of a fine night horse with excellent night vision. 'You've got the right name, my friend. True Blue you are.'

And so the winter passed, with Sky spending weekends in the Airstream, helping out with the stock as well when needed. She was good company and both Ross and Sandy liked having her there. It made their winter routine of mucking out stables, chopping wood, cooking and snow ploughing the drive a lot less lonely, having her company in and around the place. And there was less need for him take on the exercising of the horses, with Sandy and Sky more than happy to oblige. The relationship of the two women was no longer one of teacher and former pupil, rather it was becoming one of friendship and a joint pleasure in ganging up to tease Ross. They also discussed him at length. One day as they exercised the horses, Sky asked Sandy. 'So how did you know he was the one? How do you ever really know?'

'Well, to begin with, I wasn't looking for a relationship. There was a lot of baggage in my wake and I was happy on my own, fulfilled by the teaching. And then at the café all the full-time waitresses said there is this guy we want you to meet, he comes in very seldom, but he is special, and I could tell this guy had really impressed them, so my heels were already dug in. I was more than ready to dislike him. And then one day he walked in and the first thing I noticed was that the café went a little quiet as he walked to a table. He is a tall man, but he moves quietly, like a big cat. I found it hard to look at him, I didn't want to. But then they persuaded me to serve him, and I went over and he just had this presence, it was like a force field.'

Sky nodded. She knew exactly what Sandy meant.

'And you've heard his voice, so you know. When he asked for a coffee and a doughnut, it was like the words just rumbled right through me. And those eyes, those beautiful, terrible, sad eyes, eyes that have seen so much pain and suffering. So when he was paying at the end of his visit and he asked if I would like to come riding, it's hard to explain what happened to me, but it felt like my heart stopped. And the day that we went riding, it was like a sort of magic happened.

'He is not a fancy talker, he is not a charmer, he is certainly no great conversationalist, but he is so very much himself he doesn't have to say much. It's how easy he is in his own skin, that complete and utter confidence in himself. I just felt protected by his force, his power, and in the easy silences between us I felt as though he was talking to me. I felt more noticed by him than by anyone I've ever met. So yes, it was easy. I just knew in my soul he was the one.

'So imagine how it was when weeks went by and I heard nothing, he did not phone or write or email or text. Nothing. And I began to think I had imagined the whole thing. Just made it up in my mind. That the connection I felt between us was all in my own mind. It was really horrible. Eventually, when I could not reach him, I began to worry that something bad had happened to him and I drove to the ranch to check on him.

'I knocked and knocked but got no reply and then finally the door opened and there he stood with a gun in his hand looking like a ghost. And that was the moment that my heart just gave up any kind of resistance, I felt my heart open and that was that. If ever I have a child, I think that is what I will feel again, such a wish, a wanting, a need, almost a madness to protect him. So no, it was easy, I knew in my heart, in my soul, in my bones that he was the one. I felt then that I would do anything for him. Anything.'

Sky dropped Blue's reins and took Sandy's hands in hers and said, 'You are lucky. He is lucky. I don't think many people get to feel what you have just described.'

Chapter 18

Just as spring arrived, Freemantle woke from his coma. It seemed that his body had lain dormant with the winter dark, and that with the coming of the light, something stirred within him. Ross heard it from the papers first and then he had a call from Freemantle's wife Michelle, who said that Jack was still weak but clear-headed and very much wanted to see him. She sounded happy but there was a note of concern when she said she understood he'd had to deal with some official pressure from the authorities after the accident. 'Ross, I do hope that is all sorted now?'

He assured her that it was and added that if it suited her, he would come immediately. He would welcome the chance to speak to Jack. Michelle agreed and insisted that he stay with them.

Ross was in the Jeep within the hour heading for Spokane Airport, where he took a half-empty flight to Seattle. Michelle had sent an Uber to collect him, and he was soon walking into their imposing home that overlooked the sea.

She opened the door herself. 'Welcome, Ross!' Her greeting was warm and bore no trace of anger or bitterness toward him. Ross was relieved, as he had not been sure how she felt about his involvement in her husband's accident.

She led him to an upstairs library where Freemantle was propped up in a club chair, looking much better than when Ross had last seen him in the Spokane hospital. 'Ross!

Good of you to come!' The men shook hands and once Michelle served coffee, they spoke about Freemantle's remarkable recovery and about that fateful day.

It was quickly apparent to Ross that Jack Freemantle had retained all of his intellectual capacity as well as his memory. He said he clearly recalled Buddy startling badly and stepping back on the trail and then falling.

Ross took him over the tracker's discovery of the bear hideout. 'It could just as easily have been Rincon and me who went over the edge. He is the more highly strung of the two horses.'

Freemantle said, 'I'm so sorry you lost Buddy. I know how fond you were of him. A better rider might have held him on the trail.'

Ross replied, 'Nobody can stop a bear-spooked horse. And you had nowhere to turn. I'm just so sorry for taking you up to that high point. I had no idea it was a bear's lookout. I've never seen a bear there before.'

Later, Ross joined Jack and Michelle for an excellent dinner. After coffee served with a glass of cognac, he and Freemantle continued their discussion. Without any preamble, Jack asked Ross how he felt about picking up the reins of the nuclear waste protest.

'I'm out of any kind of campaigning for the governorship for at least a year. But there are other projects I do want to pick up on, things close to my heart, like the nuclear waste fight.' He was honest about it, admitting that it would keep him in the public eye so that when he was ready to take on Idaho's Republicans, he would not have been forgotten. 'But I can't ride point on this. Would you consider getting involved, properly involved? Do you have the time to commit to something like this? Your background commands respect, you would get many platforms open to you, and that would be an immense asset to the campaign.'

Ross surprised him by explaining what he had been thinking about over the winter as a way forward on the protests. 'It really started with my talk to Hester Townsend in England. She is an extraordinary woman, as you know. She achieved a major victory by keeping that fight alive with others for almost twenty years.' He explained the whole YouTube Patreon concept and how it might be used to create a 'virtual community' of supporters who might also contribute financially. Freemantle saw the virtues of the plan immediately.

'Would you be prepared to make that happen? I would be very happy to speak on this issue as often as needed, my health permitting, but it's really the voices of the local people in the affected communities that will make or break this idea.'

Ross explained that he would ask for Sandy and Sky's support and he briefly outlined who Sky Jensen was. Freemantle was enthusiastic.

'She sounds ideal!' And then he added quietly, after a slightly awkward pause, 'Ross, I have something I have to get off my chest, will you hear me out?'

Ross nodded. 'Sure Jack.'

'I know that whatever brought you into my world, you came into it in an ambivalent state about the nuclear waste issue, to say the least. I am not without my own resources as regards information and background checks; as a lawyer and a would-be politician, I have to be able to make informed judgement calls. I don't want or need to know what made you cross my path, but it seemed increasingly clear to me that after you got to know me and more about the nuclear waste issue, you were genuine in your wish to help us, or at the very least did not wish to obstruct us. So you can imagine how many times I have re-run the accident in my mind.'

He held up his hand to stop Ross responding. 'Let me finish. What I want to know is that if you get involved with us you are ready, willing and able to withstand the pushback and outright attacks that will be coming your way, and secondly that any present or former affiliations you have are not going to embarrass us or the cause you have joined us to fight for?'

There it was. There was a long silence as Ross thought this through. He had suspected that this conversation would need to be had. And he knew his involvement would bring down the wrath of the Agency on his head and the loss of the money, but for his own peace of mind and a final proof that he had nothing to do with Jack's accident, he had come to the tough decision to act as he knew his father would have expected him to act and his own sense of honour demanded.

'I am ready for the solids to hit the fan, but what I can't promise is that my "previous affiliations" will not try to embarrass me and so you. If you take me on to lead this thing, I suspect there will be consequences. One of them will be flushing out who we are fighting here. That is the best that I can offer. It's for you to decide whether my involvement might be an embarrassment. But I do hope you understand that my getting involved now is the clearest indication I can make about whose side I am on. When I moved to the Panhandle, it was because I had fallen in love with the area but had only the vaguest idea of the environmental damage the region has suffered, and certainly little idea of what the mining interests planned to do, searching for rare metals for the electric car business.'

Freemantle reached out his hand. 'I can live with that if you can.' They shook hands and Ross went up to bed. He called Sandy and told her something of what had been discussed and promised to fill her in the next day. He had a great deal to think about and he did not sleep well.

The next day he flew home and collected the Jeep from Spokane Airport. Why had he not mentioned the Agency payment to 'stop Freemantle'? He did not have a simple answer to that. In part, he had hoped to keep the money that he felt he was owed. But if he was now joining Freemantle, surely the money would have to be returned? This was the inevitable first consequence of his decision.

When he reached the ranch, he found Sandy knitting something pink with balls of wool in a basket by her feet. 'Bit soon to be knitting booties don't you think? Or is there something you want to tell me?' Ross said.

Sandy grinned and said, 'Actually, Texas, it's a night jacket I'm knitting for you! I believe older people feel the cold terribly in bed.'

'You're knitting me a pink bed jacket?' And both of them started to giggle and then laugh. Sandy enjoyed teasing him. It was one of the things he loved about her. Very few people had ever thought to tease him.

He brought her up to speed on what he and Freemantle had discussed and she put her finger on his one concern. 'Ross, you came here to get away from the world to some extent and you now find yourself with a wife and a dependent girl. And now you want to get involved in the community in a big way with what is going to be a very messy if not brutal fight. The people opposing us are not going to play nice.'

He sat and listened. She certainly understood him and what his proposal meant for him and indeed for her. He sat thinking for a while when she had finished. He looked up at her and could see she was concerned, that was clear.

'You are right,' he said. 'It has been a complete U-turn on just about everything I thought I wanted and needed ever since walking into the Hoot Owl Café that day for a coffee. I wanted to be gone, just gone. But you've created a community for us here, one I am increasingly proud to be a part of. And meeting Hester Townsend just impressed me so much with what a dedicated, principled person can achieve if they stick to their guns.'

He was quiet for a moment again. And then he said, 'If we ever had children, I would like them to know that I stood up to be counted for something important, something that mattered to me, but something that was not just about me, it was something that affected the whole community and the whole region.'

Sandy was deeply moved. What he'd said filled her with pride and love for this man who was still fighting to rid himself of the horrors of his previous existence. She came and sat by him, put her head on his shoulder and took his hand. 'You're a good man, Ross McCallister!' And they sat like that for a long time. As they sat, Ross wondered what one of his favourite writers, Ernest Hemingway, would have made of this situation. Hemingway had lived at Ketchum near Boise, a good 490 miles to the south, and had taken his own life there. One of his books, *A Farewell to Arms*, taught that life was short and one should take a great love seriously and be prepared to abandon war for it. He had always admired Hemingway's writing. The man understood the craziness of war. But he had been unable to make a peaceful farewell to arms; it had taken his own weapon to do that, violently.

To Ross, coming to the Panhandle had been his own attempt at a farewell to arms, a wish to be gone from all that the bearing of arms entailed. But he had to admit that this ambition was not going so well, though much of his life was. He asked himself for the hundredth time why he was getting involved in this protest business? Why was he endangering everything he and Sandy had achieved? Why would he risk this great love he had been sent? He thought of his words to Sandy about children being proud of him one day and could find no fault in what he had said.

It came to him that maybe Shakespeare's explanation for why men act as they do – 'character is action' – was part of the answer. A man's character would inform his actions. He'd seen this played out countless times. Maybe he was just not cut out for a quiet life? Maybe he wanted some action, some danger, and also to count for something on his own terms, not as a cipher for the Government, the army, the Agency, but for himself. His loyalty had never been questioned by those he found himself fighting alongside or working with. And now he felt a growing sense of loyalty to this community and he wished to make something of his being a free agent, more than filling a bank account with ever greater sums of money. He wanted to leave a legacy that was not just 'Ex-SEAL'.

He decided that it was time to make a start on the online nuclear waste protest. He and Sandy talked it through and Sky showed them how the whole Patreon deal worked. She videoed them working around the ranch and riding the horses. Sandy persuaded him to speak about his horse packing and hunting operation in the region and to explain why he was opposed to the nuclear waste sites. She wrote a speech for him that worked well and he then put it into his own words.

Looking square into the camera, he said, 'I moved to the Idaho Panhandle because I fell in love with the area, which to me felt like the last frontier in the lower 48 states. Its physical ruggedness, which is matched by that same quality in its people, drew me here. I have had two careers, one in the armed forces serving abroad and a second one serving our country with a security service, also abroad. I was burned out when I came here and this wonderful place has given me back my health, both mentally and physically.

'I've recently got married and my wife Sandy and I want to live in a country fit for our future children and for your children. So please join us in opposing this horror that is poisoning the soil and the water table and doing untold damage to the land we all love so much. This damage is entering the bones and bloodstream of our children. We have a debt to repay, the debt to our children.'

Sky edited in some of his military images, including one of him receiving his medals from the General in command of overseas operations and one of him attending a function honouring decorated military at the White House with President Clinton. At the end of the video, there was a brief statement from Freemantle, saying he had asked Ross to lead the protest while he was recovering.

But they did not issue this or any of the videos as yet; something held him back. That something was the sure and certain knowledge that once he broke cover as a supporter of Freemantle's position, demanding a proper clean-up of the nuclear waste sites, he would be a marked man with the Agency. They would want the money back, and he wasn't ready to hand that over yet.

With Jack Freemantle urging that it was time for action and after much discussion with Sandy and Sky, Ross agreed that it was time to go live, to launch the online protest, and devil take the hindmost. But even as he agreed to press the button, he had a premonition that his life would never be the same again. It was the old feeling that came upon him just before going into combat. He looked around at what he had created on this land, and it was almost as though he saw it in an old black and white photograph; he experienced a sense of vertigo as he stood there.

They issued the video on YouTube on a Monday and the response to it took them by surprise. It went viral within a day and the press then picked up on it too. Within 24 hours, Ross was being invited onto TV, radio talk shows and political programmes and was asked if he would join an Environmental NGO. And money came pouring in as YouTube featured dozens and then hundreds of videos from people who wished the nuclear waste sites gone.

The video clips opposing the nuclear waste sites took off across the Pacific Northwest at first and then across the whole of the country. People filmed their lives and then spoke in simple but moving terms about why they were opposed to these sites near them.

It soon required Freemantle to appoint an accountancy firm and open a bank account for the money being raised for the fight. The money would be used to hire interns, to fund advertising and a PR Agency to get them more press coverage, creating a multiplier effect, raising more money and bringing in more supporters. It simply snowballed.

As the success of the videos grew, Ross found himself with almost no time to take horse packing client trips out, but Sandy urged him to keep his business alive and he found that his raised profile brought many new people keen to do spring rides with someone fighting to protect the environment.

And the landscape did not disappoint. The new leaves on the trees were neon-like in their brightness and incandescent when caught in the sunlight. The quaking aspens, native to the region, were lovely, a tree poem in their beauty, trees of light with their silver-bark trunks, the leaves glowing green in spring and gold in the fall, always a counterpoint to the darkness of the brooding pines.

CHAPTER 19

When the backlash arrived, as they knew it would, they were nevertheless taken by surprise. The Agency issued a statement that said Ross McCallister, one of their former operatives, had been dismissed from his job for increasingly erratic behaviour and now seemed to have gone rogue. His actions to endanger the phased withdrawal of the nuclear waste sites and his supposed friendship with Jack Freemantle may have been subsidised by a foreign Agency or government with a suspicious payment made to an offshore bank account as a worrying indicator that something was amiss.

Ross's phone never stopped ringing and soon Sandy's as well. They switched both off for periods. Freemantle urged him to make a statement to one of the news agencies whose film would be nationally syndicated. Associated Press sent a two-man team out to film him at the ranch and Ross thought he made a reasonably good job of refuting the Agency's charge. He argued that it was inevitable that his position would come under fire, that there had been huge efforts to own and control the nuclear fuel dump issue by powerful groups within government. And now that they were spooked by the increasing clamour for a proper clean-up by thousands of people, the person leading the campaign was always going to take some flak. He added that other forces, including the mining industry and the new mines they planned to dig for rare earth minerals for electric car batteries, were also against any growing environmental awareness in the local population.

Still on film, Ross said at the end of the interview, 'I've been under attack many times in my life by people who actively wanted to kill me. I've sat in trenches under bombardment, but I did not stay there for long. I took the fight to the enemy and that is what we are going to do here. This issue is too important to tolerate being intimidated. So you be the judge of my character and whether I have gone rogue as they charge. If you feel as we do, please join us. Do not let them silence you!'

It was powerful stuff and the news channels featured it endlessly.

And then news of a $500,000 payment to Ross's private offshore account in the Bahamas broke. The journalist who revealed the news of this secret offshore bank account had her story picked up by the *Washington Post*, the *New York Times* and the *San Francisco Chronicle* as well as all the TV networks. The story went viral on Twitter. The article explained that the benefit of a Bahamas offshore banking account was the banking secrecy which held transactions safe from prying eyes. Financial privacy was undoubtedly one of the most important banking services that some dubious clients craved, especially those who registered their companies in tax havens offshore. An unknown source had provided compelling documentation that listed Commander Ross McCallister as the beneficiary of the $500,000.

Sandy asked Ross why he had not told her about the payment. It was the first time that he felt anything other than support from her. 'Why, Ross?'

'I'm sorry Sandy, I should have told you immediately. Partly I was horrified that they thought that I had earned it. I was embarrassed about it. And then I thought that, no, damn it, I earned it, although not in the way they had intended, but the end result was the same. And finally, I said nothing because I knew I could not keep it. That I could not live with it and all that it stood for. That I would have to send it back.'

She hugged him. 'In future, don't feel you have to deal with this stuff on your own. Speak to me!'

Soon she was also involved. As a naturalised former Canadian from Quebec who spoke fluent French, suspicions about her loyalty to the US was being questioned by some media outlets.

And then Rose Carter, the school head, called Sandy in for a discussion. After some awkward small talk, she said, 'I'm sure you can appreciate our position. I've had a number of parents calling me about your continuing to teach here. They don't know what to think. Some actually asked if you were part of a terrorist cell!' She asked Sandy to take some time off till the whole issue became clearer and the school governors were content that there was no reason to ban her from teaching at the school. She said, 'There is an element among the school governors, very committed Republicans, who feel this business is a put-up job by the Democrats and that you and Ross have either willingly co-operated or you've had the wool pulled over your eyes.'

She was embarrassed but firm, and Sandy knew that it was pointless to argue. As she drove away from the school, there was a part of her that was furious, but also a part that acknowledged that she had always known marriage to Ross would not be a bed of roses, he was something of a storm petrel, a bird suited to fighting life in high winds.

During this turmoil, Sky stayed put in the caravan for the holidays before college began, but not before she'd had a heated discussion with her parents about Ross and Sandy.

'They have been nothing but kind to me. I can't just walk out on them now, when they find themselves up against people who are happy to leave our soil and water contaminated. I am with them in this fight, all the way!'

Her parents were concerned, but also very proud of the principled stand she was making. They were pleased that their daughter had found direction and had the gumption to stick to something she believed in. But both of them asked her to be careful; if things turned rough, she was to come home. They knew Sky well enough to know she had a mind of her own and a will of iron, and there was a strange satisfaction amid their concern that their little girl was an adult now. They really were proud of her. She had always walked a hard road, and this promised to be as hard, but it was about something they too believed in, so she had their support.

Ross called Jack Freemantle regularly and agreed that his former Agency seemed to have helped to embarrass him by releasing information to the journalist about a payment to the private bank account.

'Ross, what was the payment for? Freemantle asked.

'To get you to stop the protests.' Ross said bluntly. He heard Freemantle's sharp intake of breath just before the lawyer put the phone down. Now began a chess game of real and false news all wrapped up together.

Ross no longer wanted the money and he tried to return it as the only way to convince Freemantle and others that his hands were clean, but his instruction to his Bahamian bank was blocked or ignored and the money was prevented from leaving his account. When he inquired what was going on, he was told by a bank official that a US government Agency had been in touch advising them to freeze the account. They said that they had little choice in the matter once the US government got involved.

After his phone was switched off, reporters started arriving unannounced at the ranch. His raised public profile now worked against him. The press wanted to hear from him, wanted to hear his response to the charges. They wanted to know if the news of the $500,000 was true and what it was payment for.

Frustrated by his silence, the media waded into Ross's personal background. Was he a simple cowboy, or was he a CIA or FBI operative, or working for one of the shadowy mercenary operations supporting US interests in the Middle East theatres of war? Clearly it was a mystery. Truth and fiction collided. A variety of media and lobby group agencies for the nuclear industry and the mining industry went to work overtime. There were helicopters overhead at the ranch and TV crews living at the gate to his property.

Ross found his thoughts turning to one of his heroes, Marcus Aurelius, the Roman emperor who had lived almost 2,000 years previously, a man who believed in the philosophy of the Stoics. His best-known quotes ran through Ross's head as they always did when he found himself up against the odds and as ever, they helped to strengthen his resolve.

They had become something of a mantra to him and as he worked the horses and managed his chores, he would repeat them to himself softly. He knew Marcus Aurelius had had to cope with immense pressures as the head of the greatest empire the world had seen till then. So these thoughts were borne out of lived experience in the political cauldron of the time and for very high stakes.

There were some quotes that lived in his heart.

If you are distressed by anything external, the pain is not due to the thing itself, but to your estimate of it; and this you have the power to revoke at any moment..
Waste no more time arguing about what a good man should be. Be one.
Accept the things to which fate binds you, and love the people with whom fate brings you together, but do so with all your heart.

These words from a long dead man carried great weight with Ross; he had always found that they helped him immensely. And there was one more thought that life had taught him: 'Choose to be happy.' This was something that had come to him in a previous crisis, and he found that if he repeated it to himself in extremis, the thought became the deed as it lifted his mood significantly to a point where he moved from despair to happiness. He could not fathom its power, but he knew its effect. In these days he often repeated the phrase to himself as well as the words of the Roman Emperor.

But despite his reliance on philosophy, the sense of being prey, hunted like an animal, pervaded his mind. A primordial mindset that he knew of old from his days as a SEAL helped to keep him afloat. Survival was everything. But there came a day a fortnight after the story aired that Ross felt he needed a break, to escape to get away. In short, to be gone.

With Sandy's blessing, Ross took off one evening to escape the press, into the mountains with Rincon and Solomon. Sandy and Sky helped him saddle up. Both hugged him and told him to mind himself. As he rode into the hills and then the mountains, he was overcome by a sense of disgust with himself. How had he come to this point?

How was it that he had turned his back on the brutal need that had driven him to be alone, to simply disappear from society, from all humankind, or at the very least to limit his interaction with people to the few he needed, a checkout clerk, a mailman? How had he come to spout such bullshit about himself? 'Proud to be part of this community.' 'If we ever have children I would like them to know that I stood up to be counted for something important, something that mattered to me, but something that was not just about me, something that affected the whole community and the whole region.'

What utter bullshit! What drivel. He had no right to think of children, what sort of father would he be? As for being proud of this community… he did not give a good goddamn for this society of rednecks, loggers and miners, dreamers, of California Trust Funders, all struggling to find a way of living in this deeply polluted, raped and despoiled landscape. Yes, it was beautiful, but what a corrupted Eden, and about to be clear-mined for a new technology that in its way was as polluting as the internal combustion engine. This was just the place to dump nuclear waste! Where better?

It all hinged on Sandy, Sandy, Sandy. He had fallen in love with an extraordinary woman, and he'd played house, pretending for her sake to be normal. And what was he thinking when he agreed to get involved in this ridiculous protest movement? His days of belonging to some mad scheme to control or change the world was truly over. He wanted to ride into the mountains and dig himself a hole or find a cave and be bloody done with it all. He stopped the horse, pulled a bottle of whisky from a saddle bag and drank deep. The burning in his throat matched that in his heart.

But something within him argued against these negative thoughts. What of the words of Marcus Aurelius: *'Waste no more time arguing about what a good man should be. Be one.'*

He thought of the women in the Hoot Owl Café, of Sandy's students who had come through for them at the wedding, of the ranchers who lent him horses when he needed them, even the sheriff who had not given him a hard time for tying up those two idiots in the woods. He thought of those people who had come up to him in the streets of Sandpoint to wish him well and he recalled the videos pouring in from like-minded people opposed to the rape of their state. It was all down to Sandy, who had provided this entrée into her adopted community. And Sky who stood by them. He could not let them down… *'Love the people with whom fate brings you together, but do so with all your heart.'*

It was with a lighter heart, helped by the whisky and Marcus Aurelius, that he rode on his way, climbing steadily towards the heights, taking deep pleasure in Rincon's surefooted and willing pace. The horse felt happy to be back on the trail and Solly was enjoying life too under his light pack.

The spring was well established but the nights were cold, and Ross found the going harder than he had expected. His age was definitely beginning to impact on his performance outdoors. He'd been four days in the mountains and he was tired of the cat and mouse game, tired of the cold, tired of living from hand to mouth, fed up with dodging news helicopters and trackers hired by the media. He managed mostly to stay out of sight in old cabins he knew of, or his own former camp sites chosen for their tree cover camouflage. He seldom lit a fire, surviving off what he had brought with him or could forage and what his various emergency stashes in the mountains provided.

With his senses on full alert, he came across more indications of a previous presence in the mountains and the hidden valleys. There was nothing physical on the ground to prove this, but the mix of river, meadow, wood and shelter told him that these places could well have been the home of

Julian Roup

any one of the Nimi'ipuu (Nez Perce), Kalispel, Kootenai and Schitsu'umsh (Coeur d' Alene) tribes not so long ago. It gave him comfort. His old skill of sensing human presence, actual or hidden, told him he was right. He made a mental note to ask Wild Willy, next time he ran into him, if his hunches were correct, although he knew what the response would be: 'Maybe, could be.' Willy was not one to offer much on this subject. These half-felt presences also saddened him, telling him so clearly that if a whole people, with a distinct culture, evolved to survive in this place, could disappear from their home of centuries, his own time here would barely leave a mark.

When he'd been gone a week, he gambled on risking a trip to the ranch to check on Sandy and Sky and to get more supplies. He judged that few of those hunting him would think to find him there, it was just too simple and obvious. And a week is a long time in the media news cycle, most of the journalists and TV crews would have been recalled by now to work on fresher stories. Thank God for stories! The world was full of stories, a never-ending Niagara of catastrophe.

Choosing a few pitch-dark moonless nights with pouring rain and howling winds, he made the trek to the ranch in two night marches. He arrived just after midnight. The cabin was dark but there was a dim light coming from the Airstream. He could not see any sign of the press circus that had been camped by his gates. He stabled the horse and mule and then, moving silently, made his way over to check the Airstream's windows, but all the blinds were drawn. He knocked softly but the noise of the wind carried the sound away, so he reached for the door handle which to his surprise, was unlocked. Moving with utmost caution, he stepped inside to a sight that stopped him dead. Sandy and Sky lay cuddled together in bed, fast asleep. He felt deeply moved, looking at these two women whom he loved and respected.

His guess was that Sandy had not wanted to be alone in the cabin. Lowering himself onto the bed he sat watching them breathing peacefully, and it was then that he noticed that both women were naked. He was shocked and got up to leave but his movement woke both of them. They screamed. Once they recognised him, a deep tense silence filled the caravan, which was being buffeted by wind. Sandy and Sky stepped out of bed, and each took one of his arms. Seeing clearly that he was exhausted, they undressed him and put him to bed.

Sky said she would keep watch, pulled on her waterproofs and left the caravan. Ross slept with Sandy holding him. When he woke, it was just before dawn and he found Sandy gone and Sky alongside him. She was awake and watching him. 'Please don't be angry Ross. Sandy has been worried sick about you. She came to the caravan and we comforted each other. It's no big deal.' And she smiled hesitantly at him.

Shortly after that surreal conversation, Sandy returned and climbed into bed. What followed, Ross would recall in the years ahead as an experience akin to the one time he had taken LSD. He felt deep pleasure while having an out of body experience as the two women made love to him. It was all profoundly dream-like, but there was ecstasy and joy and love and a great and profound sense of letting go. And so much beauty, so much. He was borne up by an otherworldly feeling, awash in physical and mental pleasure, the bewitching beauty of the women all encompassing. He felt gifted with something infinitely precious.

Finally, all three of them slept. When they woke, it seemed that the night had been the most natural thing in the world, and of course in a way it had been. They made breakfast and ate contentedly. Ross checked his weapons and let himself out of the caravan for a quick tour of the property. All was still, there was no media presence, the rain and wind had stopped and the two horses and the mule were peacefully munching their hay nets.

Ross felt strangely grounded and revitalised by the experience of the night. There was something about the love of these two women that had the capacity to move sex from beyond pleasure to something more elemental. The experience moved him profoundly. He felt a new energy that was both physical and spiritual. It was hard to explain. This was both love and witchcraft that was as old as time. He was borne up, his spirit was refreshed and he was filled with a sense of deep happiness and oddly, a sense of power.

He found Sandy and she saw by his face that the conversation she had been avoiding and expecting was here.

'Ross, don't say a thing till you've heard me out. Please?' He nodded and she continued, 'One, no, I am not gay or bisexual. Two, this has never happened before with Sky or any other woman. Three, Sky did not hit on me, if anything I made the first move, and she tried to stop me.'

Ross was silent, waiting as promised for her to finish.

'I can't say it won't happen again with me and Sky. It has kind of opened my eyes to something about myself, and our threesome even more so. But it is you whom I truly love and wish to be with forever.'

Ross simply hugged her and kissed her head. 'I can live with that. She is a wonderful girl. But we have to be very careful not to hurt her.'

'Of course. I'm so glad that she's no longer my pupil, that would have been impossible.' She took his hands and looked into his eyes. 'It was special and joyous and very beautiful, don't you think?' And she grinned.

He smiled back. 'It was all those things.'

They left it at that, confident that their relationship was not threatened by this new development and happy with each other.

When Ross and Sky were mucking out the horses later, he told her he was just a bit confused, as he had believed her to be gay.

Smiling impishly, she said, 'I like it all I suppose. I'm bisexual. I like women and some men and I certainly like you!'

He was pleased and flattered and told her the feelings were mutual. It also gave him pleasure and a sense of increased security to know that Sandy was not alone on the ranch when he was away and had this tigress alongside her. For there was something immensely strong about Sky.

And for her part, it was his lightly worn glamour, albeit a damaged glamour, and his profound masculinity that drew her to him. There was about him the hard-earned sense of aloneness carried by some military men, by fire fighters, sea captains and bullfighters, men on whom performance under pressure, a kind of dance with death, had left this distinguishing mark. They were men apart, not entirely of this world anymore. If you watched them closely, you could see that they had seen things you would not wish to see. And they lived in two realms, this one and something other, something unknowable. And this was what passed as glamour. They were men who did not do much laughing. Ross asked, 'Did they give you a hard time at school for it? Your preferences?'

'They didn't much. Not the cool kids. They think it's fine. They don't really understand though. It's complicated.' She smiled and shrugged. She unbuckled the dungarees she habitually wore, clothing that disguised her very beautiful body, and dropped the garment to the floor. 'I'm not sure if you saw this last night in the darkness?'

As she stood, virtually naked now in the soft light of the barn, Ross could make out some tattooed words just below her navel. 'You can take my body but never my soul.' And she turned slowly, careful not to trip with the dungarees around her ankles, he saw the same words just above her buttocks. She pulled the garment back up and fastened both buckles.

'I had that done after a party where I was raped. And I started to learn about karate!'

Ross was silent awhile and then stepping close, held her gently for a long moment. He could feel the sobs against his chest. 'I am so sorry, Sky. So sorry. But you are happy now to be you?' Ross asked. It seemed to him a hard thing to live with.

'I am happy now,' she said. 'Not so much in my early teens. It was confusing. And confusing for my folks. But they are OK with it now.' She pulled Solomon's ears gently. The mule was loving it and lowered his head. 'My mom would like me to have a family someday. Kids you know.'

Ross nodded, wondering at life's complexities. Nothing was really simple. Nothing. The sense of self-disgust he had felt as he rode away from the ranch was still there, but now it battled with Sandy and Sky and a profound wish not to disappoint or lose either of them. He would have to find a way to be a good man.

Chapter 20

There was nothing from Jack Freemantle but a raging silence. He was not answering his phone. When Ross finally reached him all he got was, 'You son of a bitch! Don't you ever call me again.' Ross tried to explain, to ask Jack if he might visit him to explain, but the line went dead.

'So be it!' Ross said to himself. He thought, 'That is one less huge complication in my life laid to rest. I am no Hester Townsend and sure as hell I'm not Greenpeace either!'

The national media circus might have left his gate, but speculation about the Freemantle accident was all over the local press as it was in every local bar. Horse trainers and horse breeders were asked for their opinion on how the 'accident' might have been staged.

Jeb Jones, a respected local horse whisperer, who had a reputation as the man to go to if you had a horse too mad, bad, or broken to ride, was constantly asked for his opinion. 'You'd have to know about this bear lookout spot, you'd have to make some good noise to make sure the bear had vacated the area. Bells and human voices would do it. And for the horses you'd need mint or a strong-smelling vegetable oil, garlic and linseed or molasses, soaked cotton wool pushed up the nostrils of the lead horse which would stop him getting the bear scent. That would do it. And then you would need a little bit of luck with the wind blowing towards you.'

'But what about losing a horse he was fond of?' the interviewer asked.

'Well, I suppose the horse was getting on at 15, coming to the end of its active working life. Its financial value would have been minimal. And there was a good chance it could have survived the fall.'

The debate on the supposed mechanics of the staged 'accident' raged on and on.

It was soon evident that the local survivalists, the militias and all those opposed to Big Government as well as the conspiracy theorists, saw Ross as a government agent and though they hated Freemantle's liberal politics and all he stood for, they did not trust Ross either.

The liberals and Democrats who supported Freemantle mistrusted Ross too. And for once both sides of the media, Democrat and Republican, ran features on him that made him out to be both a dangerous man to cross, a highly decorated soldier, expert in all the arts of war and also something of a political manipulator, a Svengali of sorts.

Wes called him and asked, 'Ross, what is going on? Sounds like you landed yourself in some crazy shit with the Freemantle guy. You need any help from me?'

Ross was touched and thanked Wes for the call and the kindness. 'Hopefully it will all settle down in time. These things do blow over.'

And then his two former ranch attackers resurfaced with their story twisted to make out they were innocent hunters who Ross wanted to scare off his land because of the shit he was up to. It made for some ugly listening. It seemed that every man's hand was against him. All were on the point of hunting him down now and he had reason to be gone, truly gone from this place he'd begun to think of as a haven. But they mistook him if they thought he was going to run. He was not going to run. Ross dug in for the fight he knew was surely coming.

He stocked up on essentials that would allow them to stay on the ranch for months if need be. Sandy and Sky did most of the food shopping, but he went in to stock up on ammunition for the guns and a few other things he felt might come in handy, like flares and night-vision goggles. But his welcome felt to be wearing thin in Sandpoint.

The owner of the gun shop in Sandpoint from whom Ross had bought ammunition since arriving in the area, asked, 'You aiming to start a war up in the mountains, Commander?'

'Not if they just leave me be, Paul, not if they leave me be. But if they start anything, I aim to be the one to finish it.' News of his gearing up for war would be all over Sandpoint by dark, Ross knew, and that in itself might buy him some time.

The expected moves against him began with a direct attempt on his life. Someone had tampered with the Jeep's brakes, either while he was in town or during the night at the ranch. By pure luck he had picked up that something was amiss while driving into town. He'd had to pump the brakes to get any response. When he got out to inspect his brake cables, there was clear evidence of damage done with a tool of some kind.

And then it seemed something had been placed in their well water, making them all sick. These seemed like local actions. If the Agency had a contract out on him, it would have been over by now. He knew the Agency were in a bind. If he went public, he would destroy the last of his credibility, but he would also inflict some very serious damage on the Agency. It was a Mexican stand-off. Any action the Agency took would have to be discreet and not public in any way. But he knew they would be monitoring the situation on the ground and making use of local people who might be useful.

Ross knew that fingering the Agency would only make him look disloyal and greedy for taking 'blood money'. Good fighter that he was, he went into armed retreat mode, opting to live to fight another day and to choose the battle ground he was going to fight on.

Late one evening, as he was leading Solomon, hauling logs to the barn to be cut up for fuel, he was thrown to the ground when the mule took a shot intended for his owner and shied violently. Luckily neither he nor Solomon were badly hurt. Ross grabbed his rifle from the house and covered the ground to where he reckoned the shot had come from in good time. He quickly found tracks but no shell casing. He sent some shots in the direction he judged his assailant had run and then returned to the ranch to treat the mule. Solomon's neck had a bullet graze which bled profusely but was soon staunched and patched up. To Sol's credit he took it all calmly and stoically after his initial shy.

Ross's instinct was to pack for the mountains, to fight where he would keep the danger away from the ranch. He asked Sandy if she would take Sky home to her parents and then fly up to stay with her own parents in Quebec until this business settled down. Both women were adamant that they were not going anywhere.

Thinking about a withdrawal to the mountains, Ross hesitated. Once he was off his own ranch he would be without the considerable protection the law provided to an owner defending his land and family from attack. Out there in the mountains on his own, he would simply be an animal to hunt down, rather than a ranch owner fighting to protect his home.

The Ruby Ridge shootout some 30 years before was much on Ross's mind. Randall Weaver, his family and a friend, Kevin Harris, lived in an isolated cabin in the Idaho Panhandle and were thought to be dangerous survivalists, choosing to live apart from other communities and supposedly planning an armed insurrection.

Weaver failed to appear in court to answer charges in connection with the sale of two sawn-off shotguns, and a large contingent of US marshals was sent to arrest him. In an initial encounter, with each side claiming to have fired in self-defence, Weaver's 14-year-old son was shot in the back and killed, as was a deputy marshal, William Deegan. The next day, an FBI sharpshooter, aiming at Kevin Harris, accidentally shot and killed Weaver's wife as she stood behind a door holding her 10-month-old child. The siege lasted another ten days, and both Weaver and Harris were tried for murder but were acquitted by an Idaho jury.

The Idaho jury that acquitted Randall Weaver and Kevin Harris obviously believed that the men had acted reasonably and in defence of home and family when they resisted government agents. The defence did not even rebut the prosecution at trial, yet the jurors must have believed that the government provoked the incident.

Strangely, no legal charges against Ross had been served, not by Freemantle, nor the Agency, nor indeed the local sheriff's office which knew better than to interfere in what looked like something well above their pay grade. Nor were there charges from Republican or mining interests, as they were only too pleased that Freemantle and McCallister seemed to have taken each other off the playing board. And the IRS were strangely silent too, as was the FBI. It felt like the calm before a storm. All parties were waiting to see how things played out on the ground where Ross was preparing to make his stand.

The new mining interests certainly wanted him stopped. They feared that once the nuclear waste mess was cleared, people would not want anything to do with new mining plans that damaged the environment. They would want the new rare earth miners stopped too, and that would be an end to this new billion-dollar mining enterprise in Idaho.

Ross knew that there were some 500 abandoned mines in the Panhandle. Half of those had now been closed off but still offered places to hide up or to take the fight underground if he so wished. He had heard that at least forty people had died in the past three years in abandoned mines across the United States. The last reported death in the Panhandle region was in June 1995, when Steve Novak, the son of former Spokane City Manager Terry Novak, was overcome by carbon monoxide and died while exploring an abandoned mine near Lake Pend Oreille.

Ross figured that with night goggles, some oxygen cannisters and some hastily acquired knowledge of the mine workings, it would be possible to give any attackers a run for their money. Thinking through his options on how best to use the natural terrain, Ross also considered the lakes and the boats on them. Many of the sailboats and fishing boats carried scuba gear, and some were fitted with AIS systems that provided early warning at night or in fog of approaching vessels.

He was touched to get a message of support from Sandy's brother Jacques. 'Ross don't let them sons of bitches drive you off your land!' And he added, 'But if you and Sandy find yourselves in a tight spot, just let me know. My friend, the pilot of the firefighting helicopter I jump from, says he is at your disposal, or a seaplane if you prefer.'

'Thanks Jacques, that is an offer I will bear in mind. But believe me, they are going to need an army to move me off my land,' Ross replied, warmed by the interaction with his brother-in-law.

Ross used the lull before the coming storm to build furiously with the help of Sandy and Sky. He used his digger to excavate an underground bunker with hidden firing positions, lined it with logs and then concreted it in. They filled the bunker with stocks of water, food and ammunition. Anyone attacking the ranch would need a bomb to take them out of the bunker.

But Ross had no intention of dying like a rat in a ditch and with this in mind, he began mining the approaches to the cabin with ordnance that would cause some damage to anyone standing on them and also give away their position. He mapped the placements and showed the women the areas to avoid. He also created water-filled ditches that would slow down an advance on the cabin and he placed a number of shooting hides high in the stands of trees that commanded views across the ranch.

Now and then, as he worked his way around the ranch's perimeter fence, Ross came across the odd bundle wrapped in waterproof tarpaulin. Inspecting each one with care in case it was some kind of booby trap, he realised he was not without support from the local community. He found a number to be food parcels and as the days passed and they kept coming, he began to understand that this was the work of Max and Kent and friends of theirs. Sky admitted that she had put out a call for help and it was coming thick and fast. Soon the parcels and packages included ammunition too.

Recalling all his security background training, Ross installed and fine-tuned a camera scanning network that he could monitor from the bunker or the cabin.

His instinct told him that his weak point was the women. If they were taken hostage, his hands would be tied. He made a call to Sky's parents and told them he would be teaching Sandy to shoot and he'd be happy to do the same for Sky with their permission. They thanked him and willingly gave the plan their blessing.

'Ross, you're giving Sky skills that will stand her in good stead in this neck of the woods,' they said. Ross wondered if they had any idea of what was going down.

He decided to refresh his memory on gun law and read, 'The Office of the Attorney General for the State of Idaho advises that you may carry a weapon on your person without a concealed weapons license if you are at least 18 years old, a citizen of the United States or a current member of the United States Armed Forces, and you are not disqualified under Idaho law from obtaining a concealed weapons license. Idaho law imposes additional requirements for persons under the age of 18. A concealed weapons licence is not required for U.S. citizens and active military members. Idaho permits the open carrying of handguns on the person with no permit or licence. Idaho also allows for the carrying of long guns in public.'

Before purchasing two handguns for Sandy and Sky, Ross informed the sheriff's office that with Sky's parents' permission he was about to train both women in handgun use. The sheriff said he had no issue with this and thanked Ross for the courtesy of letting him know.

Ross selected two Springfield Armory Hellcat RDP 9mm pistols with a 15-bullet capacity which put them in the Glock category. He knew that the Springfield Hellcat was chosen by many women as their preferred choice of handgun. It came with a red dot sight which improved its hit rate considerably. And it was perfect, given its lightness, to carry as a concealed weapon.

Both women found the Hellcats easy to load and fire and with the red dot capacity they soon attained a respectable hit rate. They practised diligently and the horses got used to the crack of gunfire remarkably quickly, so that they did not even look up from grazing.

Ross figured that the ranch was safer during periods of moonlight that would highlight attackers and so he was at his most vigilant during the periods when there was no moon, or the weather made monitoring the area tricky.

When his opponents finally made their move, Ross felt he was more than ready for them. The attack came, as expected, on a night of wind and rain. Both women were terrified, listening to the rifle cracks and bullets thudding into the cabin's log walls. Ross handed them each a shotgun loaded with birdshot good for 50 yards and told them to wait until he started to fire back and then for them to withdraw quickly to the bunker.

'Aren't you coming with us?' Sandy asked. But with guns in their hands the two women were not short of fighting spirit.

'No, I am going to go and play with the boys,' he said, smiling, and took up his chosen spot and began to target the gun flashes. It was soon evident that his return fire was taking its toll. The women ran for the dugout as instructed and barred the door that would need explosives to open.

As requested, they called the Sheriff's office and reported the attack. 'Ross reckons there are a dozen good old boys with pickup trucks according to our security cameras.'

'We're on our way Sandy!' the deputy sheriff said.

Judging by the nature of the attack, Ross figured that there were at least a dozen men who had plucked up the courage to come after him. Wearing his old dark combat gear and carrying a selection of weapons, Ross quietly exited the cabin on his belly and slithered into the woods, intent on taking the fight to them.

He put as much ground as he could between himself and the cabin and then called Sandy to shoot the flares as requested. The whole area was lit up as the flares took off and gently parachuted back to earth. They provided the view he needed, the silhouette of at least six men, dressed in bulky rain gear stood out clearly and Ross made for them, being careful to stay low and move fast. As he closed in on them, helped by the noise of the wind, he withdrew a deadly three-foot-long fighting knife from its scabbard, a weapon he knew well. When he was within striking distance, he rose and slashed the leg tendons of two men whose screams brought others in to help. These Ross shot in the legs and then moved swiftly away.

He heard Sandy and Sky open up with their shotguns and it was clear they had hit one or more of the attackers. And then Ross saw one of the women, it was Sky, running at the retreating men, firing rapidly and screaming, 'Run, you fuckers, run!' She shot coolly, reloading as she raced towards them. To give her cover, Ross shot as well and the men scattered, doubling their mad dash to escape.

'He's got men in the woods behind us,' he heard one man shout and then there was the sound of rapid withdrawal. A broad, wolfish grin crossed Ross's mouth as he watched Sky, remembering his own enraptured early brushes with going berserk in the fury of battle. He knew that this experience would be deeply cathartic for Sky and he was well pleased. But like him, she would need to learn to rein it in.

After lying prone for half an hour, Ross heard the sound of distant engines and he knew the fight was over. He quartered the property, searching for wounded men but found none. His attackers had carried their injured off with them.

He went to check on Sandy and Sky and found Sandy with a bleeding cheek, where a bullet had chipped a piece off the bunker's wood lining and cut her face, but it was more of a graze than anything and they soon had her cleaned up. Sky still had the high colour of excitement in her face and was evidently buzzing from the adrenaline of the encounter.

'Thank you,' he said to both of them. 'You gave them hell!'

As there was only one road in and one out, the sheriff's team soon stopped the fleeing posse and took some into custody, some into hospital. The Sheriff called Ross to see how they had fared and he reported all well but for the wound to Sandy's face. As he spoke, Ross could hear how this news hardened the sheriff's tone. 'Two of the idiots were the mechanics who paid you a previous visit.'

'I'm not surprised, Sheriff. Those boys were itching for payback.'

'Well one of them, the big guy, is going to be walking with a limp from here on in.'

The Sheriff was more than content with his night's haul once he knew who the perpetrators were, a bunch of hotheads who had been riding for a fall for some time. Ross had done him a favour, sorting them out. And a new word entered the local lexicon: the two machete-slashed men would always walk with a slight limp after they had been 'Rossed'.

The incident only added to the local reputation Ross had, as a man not to be messed with. And strangely, as is the way of these things, his notoriety as an 'outlaw' brought in new business of all kinds, younger women, tough old hombres, urban cowboys from California who had heard of his reputation, and inevitably some characters with dubious anti-government beliefs. Sandy and Sky soon sorted the wheat from the chaff and life for Ross settled down to a steady amount of work once more. To his surprise, his neighbours were still prepared to lend him horses when needed.

Despite the sheriff's urging, Ross refused to press charges and so the matter ended there. But within days, the story emerged that Ross had a small army camped on his land, men who attacked hunters without provocation. The sheriff's office let it be known that on the night of the attack Ross, Sandy and Sky were on their own and had fought the attackers off themselves. Their evident success in defending themselves put future attacks on hold.

The Sheriff also reported that Sandy had taken a flesh wound to her face from one of the attackers' bullets. The effect of this news was almost immediate. Sandy received a call from the school head to say that the school board was content to have her back whenever she felt recovered.

As Ross worked with the horses, he figured that things could be worse. He suspected that the storm was not over yet, but he had some local support now and the love of two incredible women. His reputation, while not being one he would have chosen for himself, was not hurting him any, and in some strange way, fighting for his life and his ranch, knowing his attackers would have killed them all and burned the place to the ground, gave him a sense of deep satisfaction. There was a sense of roots being sent deep into the Idaho soil.

Chapter 21

The summer, when it came, was a scorcher, hotter than anyone could remember, and it lasted for months. Now and then, clouds gathered but then dissipated. It was hellish.

Sky made Ross and Sandy an offer they could not resist. She said she would take care of the place with Kent and Max to give them a break if they wanted a mini-holiday in the mountains. As work had slowed down considerably because of the heat and talk on the news of forest fires across the Pacific Northwest, in Montana and Washington particularly, they accepted her offer gratefully.

News of the forest fires had the effect of damping down the media's interest in Ross, providing them with a breather from further unsought attention. They provisioned for a week and took fishing gear with them to try for trout in some of the spots Ross had long been wanting to test with a fly.

'Ride safe, avoid bears and have fun!' Sky wished them as they rode out on Rincon and Blue, leading Solomon loaded with their camp gear.

'Sky, you are a life saver! And thanks for the help, Max, Kent, we appreciate it.' Sandy called back to the small group standing in front of the cabin, her former pupils who were now each in their own way so much more now.

Soon the ranch disappeared behind the first hill they crossed and then the forests claimed them. It felt like a dive on a hot day into a cool deep lake of refreshing water and the luxurious smell of the pines spoke of escape, of freedom, of peace. They smiled at each other and urged the horses on, horses that needed little urging. They too had a sense of holiday, picking up on the energy of their riders.

Ross and Sandy had picked out two favourite spots to camp rather than move on each day as the process of packing up and unpacking took hours of hard work out of each precious day. The first camp was in a lowland meadow with spectacular views to the peaks, good grazing for the animals and a pristine river well stocked with trout. They put the tent up near a stand of golden aspens.

That evening, as they feasted on fresh-caught trout smoked slowly on the fire with potatoes baked in the coals, a fresh salad salsa and sipped beer cooled in the river, Ross admitted that it was as close to heaven as he hoped to get.

'I've stayed in some pretty fancy places in my time, five-star international hotels and private homes by the sea, but I would not swap this for any of them. This is beyond five stars in my book.'

Looking at him quizzically, Sandy teased, 'How did a poor grunt soldier like you get to enjoy the life of luxury you are describing?' she asked.

'Drugs,' he said. 'I had a nice side hustle in opium poppies out of Afghanistan to Amsterdam.

She poked him hard in the ribs and said, 'You are such a bullshitter Ross McCallister! Drugs! You big fat liar.' Soon they were laughing and it was as if all the pain and anxiety of the past months fell away.

They made love under the stars and slept like exhausted children. It was a time frozen by ecstasy for Ross, and there would come a time when he would take it out like an icon, a beautiful paperweight or a rare butterfly caught in amber, and admire it afresh from every angle.

By the time they packed the tent in its second setting high in the mountains, their love was more entrenched than ever and they rejoiced in being together. The only slight concern they felt was for the smell of smoke in the air.

Ross and Sandy returned to the ranch under an ashen sky. The Panhandle was utterly quiet, no birdsong, just silence. In the week they had been gone their world had changed once more. Fire tore across the forests, leaping mountains.

The land and its people were shocked, in mourning and hurt. All interest in Ross and his doings seemed cauterised by the all-engulfing catastrophe, millions of acres of forest gone and the animals with them. People walked in a daze, traumatised by events. It was as if Ross and his little local difficulty was turned to ash by the flames, and memories were wiped, if not clean then almost. The news was all-enveloping and everyone knew someone either hurt, or killed, or who had lost their home, or was fighting the fire. It was war.

The scale of the fire was awe-inspiring and terrifying. Nobody was sure of its true scale. Some ventured a guess that it was approaching the great fire of 1910. For two terrifying days and nights – August 20 and 21, 1910 – fire had raged across three million acres of virgin timberland in northern Idaho and western Montana. Many thought the world would end, and for 86 fire victims, it did. This latest fire, more than a century on, had all the markings of another catastrophe of enormous proportions.

Animals that would normally be mortal enemies, cougars and white-tailed deer, elk and bears, moose and wolves, rabbits, squirrels and coyotes, fled before the fire, running alongside each other at times. Ross looked at this extraordinary sight captured on TV and wondered how it might apply to humans. His view was that some would use the catastrophe as an opportunity to feed better than normal, and no doubt this too happened on occasion among animal predators. He noticed the birds of prey circling in the smoke and diving for rabbits, snakes and squirrels.

The air quality was appalling in a state already beset by bad air. Idaho air quality was always getting worse; the state was among the top 25 most polluted areas in the country, an American Lung Association's 'State of the Air' report had found. Much of the drop in air quality was caused by wildfires, which were increasing as a result of climate change. No Idaho county in the report received higher than a 'D' grade for particle pollution. People in Idaho were already breathing unhealthy air.

Ross was all too aware that both ozone and particle pollution were dangerous to public health and could increase the risk of premature death and other serious health effects such as lung cancer, asthma attacks, cardiovascular damage, and developmental and reproductive harm. Particle pollution was made up of soot or tiny particles that came from coal-fired power plants, diesel emissions, wildfires and wood-burning devices. These particles were so small that they could lodge deep in the lungs and trigger asthma attacks, heart attacks and strokes, and worse.

And to this witches' brew the great fire now added a multiplier effect. Hospitals were besieged by hundreds of people having breathing difficulties and those dying as a result of lethal asthma attacks brought on by the fire.

Ross and Sandy, like their neighbours, kept a close and constant eye on the reach of the fire as it got ever closer to them. It was at this point that Sandy suggested that they offer a helping hand to any of their neighbours wiped out by the fire.

'What do you have in mind?' Ross asked her.

'Well, we have the space to put up a bunch of tents, we can borrow them from the Forestry people or anyone who has a spare bell or wall tent, and bring in some mobile toilets like we did for the wedding.'

'Let's do it!' said Ross. 'I should have thought of this myself.'

Within days they had twenty families camped on their land, some of them traumatised by the loss of their homes.

Once again, Sandy called in favours from the school, the fire brigade, the mayor's office and a team formed around her and Sky to feed the families and help them keep track of what was going on, to help them financially, medically or with counselling.

Julian Roup

News came in hour by hour of apocalyptic events, entire fire crews trapped and wiped out, water planes crashing, people burned alive in their cars while trying to escape. The spread of the fire by the second week of September was approaching a million acres destroyed.

Sandy, Sky, Ross and the two lads, Max and Kent, sat glued to the TV. Speculation ran rife, global warming, lightning, homesteaders' stray cigarettes, loggers, were all potential sources of the large number of small fires that sprang up across the region. It did not take much; a stray piece of broken glass acting as a magnifying glass was enough to ignite the bone-dry forests.

The people camping on the ranch were panicky, having been burned out once before. Ross worked to reassure them that they were safe for now and that he was keeping a close watch on the situation. If things got dire, they would evacuate to a campsite set aside for just such an eventuality on the shore of Lake Pend Oreille. Some, hearing this, packed and left immediately, wishing to put distance between their families and the flames.

Then hurricane-force gusts roared in from Washington to Idaho, turning the flames into one massive inferno. Trees by the millions became exploding candles, the US Forest Service reported. Millions more trees, sucked from the ground, roots and all, became flying blowtorches. It was an unpredictable blaze that jumped between ridges without warning and threatened multi-million-dollar houses in an area where Bruce Willis, Tom Hanks and Arnold Schwarzenegger owned homes. Private insurance companies sent crews to help protect these structures, and Sun Valley Resort used water cannons – usually reserved for making snow in winter – to keep trees and grass moist.

At one point the fire was less than five miles away from the ranch and moving in their direction. And then, as suddenly as it began, the fires died out, as longed-for rainstorms arrived and doused the remaining flames. People found it almost impossible to go back to work, such was the level of trauma across the region.

This Country I Call My Own

Slowly the remaining families camping on the ranch packed up, bidding Sandy and Ross and their team of helpers an emotional goodbye. A number of them said that if ever they needed help, they now had family in Idaho. Ross could see that they meant it. The impact of the experience was to make him feel even more invested in the Panhandle. He would not let it go.

The ranch felt abandoned after they left, eerily quiet. So Ross and Sandy saddled the horses and took off across the five miles of green land to the edge of the fire devastated country. It was like riding through an apocalypse. The horses were spooked by the smells and the sights of dead animals and the remains of huge, charred tree trunks lying like pick-up-sticks. They did not push the animals into the blackness but skirted it for a few miles before turning back to the ranch in the still falling rain.

The land and its people were in a state of shock.

And it was during this stasis, a year after trying to return the $500,000, Ross's bank alerted him that they were now finally free and able to act on his instructions. Did he wish the $500,000 returned? Almost without thinking he sent a message. 'Activate immediately.' Ross felt as though an enormous sword under which he had been living was now removed. The sense of freedom was palpable. He could see how strange that was and also wonder at the lesson this taught. Less is indeed sometimes more, he thought.

The anti-nuclear waste YouTube protests had fizzled down to a few last supporters after the first drama of Ross's divided loyalty became news. But then, almost miraculously, the protest once more gathered momentum under the guidance of an historian and human rights academic from Gonzaga University in Spokane, who also happened to be an ordained Catholic priest, the man who had married them, Father Joseph Berrigan, a Jesuit who had taught history at Gonzaga and held services that Sandy attended on Sundays.

One day, a fortnight after the fire ended, Ross and Sandy were in Auntie's, the Spokane bookstore, when they bumped into the priest. They spoke for a while, and he invited them to join him for tea at his apartment on the University campus and offered to show them one of the chapels. Sandy was keen to go, so Ross agreed, and they followed the priest as he drove back home.

After tea in his small flat he showed them around the little chapel as promised. St. Michael's Chapel, next to Duff's at Kennedy Hall, could accommodate about 80 people. It was the very opposite of the great European cathedrals that Ross was used to.

Sandy took herself off for a little contemplation and prayer and Ross found himself increasingly drawn to this simple yet complex man. There was something almost otherworldly about him. He was not much older than Ross but on his lined, ascetic face there was a lifetime of pain and suffering deeply etched. When Ross shook his hand, he felt something akin to an electric shock. They spoke for some time in the chapel which was part of the university campus where he taught human rights law.

'Gonzaga is a Jesuit school,' he told Ross. 'The Society of Jesus – more commonly known as the Jesuits – is a Catholic order of priests and brothers founded by St. Ignatius Loyola, a Spanish soldier-turned-mystic who worked to "find God in all things". Here we try to teach our students to have the courage to advocate for others. I suppose you could say it's the mantra of Gonzaga Law School.'

He said that the Gonzaga Law Department and its work on human rights included sending interns to work at an NGO in Switzerland. 'It's the Geneva International Centre for Justice, which has links to the Human Rights Council hosted by the United Nations.'

Father Berrigan explained something of his life. 'I was drawn to the priesthood as I had an uncle, a famous, or some would say notorious priest, who fought his whole life for human rights. I hero-worshipped him. He is one of the few men who I try to live up to.'

Ross asked, 'Is that why you became involved in running the anti-nuclear waste protest vlogs on YouTube?'

'I think it a very worthwhile cause,' the priest said. 'I

would say you were divinely guided when you came up with the idea in the first place.'

As they spoke, Ross found himself telling the priest something of his own life. And then Father Berrigan asked him if he wished to make a confession. Ross was taken aback by the offer but also deeply moved.

'Father, I am not a Catholic.'

The priest said, 'Ross, that will not bother God if it does not bother you.' And he smiled for the first time.

Ross to his surprise said yes and in a small confessional booth he told the priest the story of how he had come to get involved in the nuclear protest, warts and all, and something of his military background. They spoke for close to an hour until Ross recalled that Sandy would be wondering what had become of him and he made his apologies. The priest blessed him.

'Do I deserve that blessing, Father?' Ross asked.

'I believe you do. Our father moves in mysterious ways. And you married a good woman, Ross. That speaks volumes. Bless you both.'

Ross was astonished by the events of the day. He found it hard to believe that he had agreed to make confession to a man he barely knew. But he felt the better for it in some inexplicable way. It was different to unloading on a therapist. And yet, despite all this, his mind forced him to wonder at the ego and indeed the arrogance and the lack of any humility that allowed one man to say to another that he freed him of his sin in the name of an unseen god. It was all too utterly bizarre and ridiculous, and yet and yet, this was a deeply intuitive, intelligent empathic human being. Why would he choose this path, if he did not himself believe in the forgiveness he was peddling? It was aggravating and confusing and just a little embarrassing.

And yet, despite himself, he felt he trod more lightly on the earth following this encounter. Ross came away with some of the weight of his past off his shoulders, despite his cynicism, and he felt that someone truly special had entered his life. It was another of Sandy's gifts to him.

Chapter 22

The PTSD was back again following the attack on the ranch, worse than it had been for some time. Ross's hands shook and he seemed incapable of getting out of bed on some days. But the nights were the worst. He took to sleeping in the Airstream to spare Sandy and Sky his nightmares and screaming.

But for all that, life was settling back into something like a routine, thanks to the two women who took immense trouble to care for him, creating a daily plan that was almost boring in its regularity and predictability.

And then a letter for Ross arrived from England. The letter was from Hester Townsend, asking how the nuclear clean-up fight was going and telling him she did not believe the slurs against his name, that she judged him a good man, and asked if he had given up the fight.

> 'Dear Commander McCallister,' she wrote, 'I am wondering how your fight is going? There does not seem to be much news about any progress. I did not take you for a quitter. And I'm seldom wrong about people. Let me know how you are getting on. Sometimes a "pitch invasion" is helpful. It seems to dislocate one's opponents' minds and to cheer up one's own supporters no end.
> Kind regards,
> Hester.'

A pitch invasion? Ross went back to the history of Hester's Greenham Common fight and sure enough there it was – on a number of occasions the protesters had cut through the encircling fences and had almost reached the facility itself, before being violently thrown back by those guarding the airfield and its nuclear-armed aircraft.

Some 20 years before the campaign against Greenham Common airfield, the British press had carried a worrying wakeup call:

> A B-47 based at the U.S. airbase at Greenham Common, England, reportedly loaded with a nuclear weapon, caught fire and completely burned. In 1960, signs of high-level radioactive contamination were detected around the base by a group of scientists working at the Atomic Weapons Research Establishment (AWRE). The U.S. government has never confirmed whether the accident involved a nuclear warhead.

The letter from Hester seemed to trip a switch in Ross's mind and within days he had returned to the fray. He called Father Berrigan and asked for a meeting which the priest arranged for the next day at a coffee shop near Auntie's Bookstore in Spokane. He showed the priest Hester's letter and told him of the all-woman fight she had been involved in at Greenham Common, with its eventual success. And how the 'pitch invasions', storming through the fences, had made such an impact.

Ross said, 'The Greenham women created a 14-mile human chain in 1983 and took down the perimeter fence, which they described as their Berlin Wall. About four of the nine miles of perimeter fence were cut down. It created a hell of a fuss with lots of media attention.'

The priest was quiet, considering Ross's words. 'Was anyone hurt?' he asked.

'No one was hurt. They blockaded the base; they got 30,000 women there and they created a permanent peace village. And they would make that weird ululating sound that women in Africa and the Arab world do so well. This mass ululation would freak the soldiers out.'

'Maybe a "Perimeter Peace Picnic" might be an idea?' the priest said.

'Father, I think that is an excellent idea. If you agree, I'll use the event as a diversionary opportunity to make a peaceful protest of my own with your permission.' He explained what he had in mind. The priest gave him his blessing.

The next day, Ross saw the call from Father Berrigan broadcast in his gentle tones on his YouTube vlog, inviting people to attend a 'Perimeter Peace Picnic' at the nuclear dump site in a week's time.

The response was instant and overwhelming. Thousands signed up to attend.

On the day of the protest, there were at least 5,000 people camped by the fence and there was a hugely enlarged military and police presence in attendance too. The media were out in force as well and Father Berrigan's address to the crowd went down well.

'We need to shake them to wake them' he said of the politicians who were dragging their feet over the clean-up. And then he invited the crowd to shake the fences. They went to work with a will.

As the guards rushed to the most threatened parts of the fence, Ross ran, using his bolt cutters to break through the fence and then dashed for the next one, cutting his way through that as well before he was spotted. Just as the guards were about to tackle him and take him into custody he hurled two orange smoke flares at the building within and then he was overwhelmed.

Within an hour, Ross and Father Berrigan found themselves in a holding cell. The men smiled at each other.

The priest said, 'Ross, I think your Hester Townsend would be pleased with us.'

They were booked by the Sheriff and then to their

surprise, bailed almost immediately by a lawyer appointed by Jack Freemantle.

The 'pitch invasion' at the nuclear facility got huge media attention and seemed to have touched a nerve in government circles. And Ross was once more on the Agency's radar. And, as likely, in the sights of the multi-billion-dollar mining interests as well. It was a toss-up which one felt him the bigger threat. For the Agency, the loss would be reputational, for the mining interest, billions of dollars. It was a toss-up which one would come after him, or which would come first.

CHAPTER 23

Within days, Ross sensed that he was under observation and was being tracked. Deciding this time to distance himself from the ranch, he packed up his survival gear, loaded it onto the electric motorbike he had bought for just such a time, a Zero SR/S dirt bike scrambler, and took off for the high country. The bike had a 200-mile range which gave him at least a few days' off-road driving before needing to recharge it. Both Sandy and Sky offered to come with him, but he said they would hold him back from the job that needed doing and he only had the one bike.

Ross enjoyed the freedom the scrambler provided. It needed no feeding and did not live in fear of bears and wolves; it allowed him to come upon wildlife unexpectedly because of its utter silence. But he found that he did have to haul it over fallen trees and tree branches in places, unlike a horse, which would simply have jumped over the obstacle. But the gift it gave of moving silently, undetected through the woods, was intoxicating in its own unique way and he saw far more deer and bear than he would have on a horse. It would never give him what a horse did, but it certainly had its uses in his present situation.

That evening he sat up late into the night watching for anyone moving in his area, a remote and tricky place to reach. He was not sure if he had imagined it, but he had once or twice thought he'd heard the faint and distant sound of a motorbike and then once, looking up, he'd noted an eagle dive suddenly in an almost uncoordinated way, as they do when threatened by a drone, something he'd seen time and again in Afghanistan. His gut instinct told him he was being observed.

And then his patience and vigilance paid off. Just before dawn, his night-vision goggles revealed a single figure on his back trail. Observing him closely for a while, Ross realised that this was a professional deep-country tracker and possibly his killer. The deadly game was joined once more. But this time he knew the stakes were very high. He was dealing with a professional.

Ross then played a dangerous game of hide and seek in the mountains with his intended killer but each time he stopped he saw his opponent getting ever closer. He went very high to one of his food and oxygen caches and this gave him a breather as he knew he was now in better shape than the man on his trail who would have no such resources at his disposal. And chances were that he was well above his opponent by a few thousand feet.

This thought had barely come to him when he felt an enormous impact strike his shoulder and he threw himself into a rolling dive down the slope and into some brush cover. The bastard had climbed above him.

He inspected his wound, plugged it with a medical pad and taped it in place, all the while keeping a wary eye out for the shooter. After a few minutes, he scrambled down to where he had cached the electric motor bike. The shooter knew his bullet had struck him and he would know that he would be woozy with blood loss and shock. Once clear of the area, he decided to try an old Indian trick. So, instead of a horse, he left his bike lying on a gravel road alongside a dummy he pulled together, that looked credibly like a man fallen off the bike, using some logs for legs and arms and his coat and helmet to do the rest.

And then he waited and watched, his telescopic rifle sight scanning both approaches along the road and both sides of the fringing woods. It was less than an hour when he spotted movement that then stilled. The attacker was just 300 yards off, moving fast but remarkably silently through the trees. He stopped a hundred yards from the bike and the 'body' and raised his gun.

Ross fired first and his stalker dropped, with all the signs of a killing shot. Cautiously Ross approached, keeping inside the woods. For good measure he put another shot into the fallen figure. The man was dead. He pulled him deeper into the wood, cleared his bike off the road and threw the wooden arms and legs off the road too. His helmet and coat he placed on the bike.

Listening for some minutes, he could hear no sound of approaching vehicles and so moved back to the body. Using an entrenching tool, he dug a grave some four feet deep. He checked every item of the man's clothing and his weapon, not surprisingly a rifle that he recognised as being Czech made. He placed the weapon to one side and buried the man. The shot in his heart would have killed him instantly and the second in his head sealed the deal.

Having looked closely at him and his clothes and gun, he knew that the man would be untraceable. From the looks of him, probably a mountain Chechen from the high Caucuses, brought in on a contract. Ross smiled a bitter, knowing smile. A Chechen, no doubt battle hardened in the wars against Russia, extremely capable and at home in mountain heights, and a Muslim to boot, made the man the perfect choice, with no possible links to any US organisation and with a clear motive – Ross had been killing Muslims across the Middle East for a very long time. His killing Ross would look like retribution by some terrorist group.

No one would come looking for his would-be killer. The Agency, or whoever had hired him, might just be spooked enough to call it a day. But Ross knew he would now always live looking over his shoulder. It was a fate he would have to accept; it was a way of life he had lived for years.

He was now woozy from shock and blood loss. Digging a grave had almost done him in. Using the last of the bike's charge, he headed for Hayden Lake near Coeur D'Alene to hide out in a house he knew Sky's parents used only in summer. The only stop he made was to throw the man's rifle into a small lake on the way.

When he arrived at Hayden Lake he stood among some trees and watched the house for any sign of movement and when he was satisfied that it was unoccupied, he moved through the trees to the house, which commanded a good southerly view across the lake and part of the Hayden Lake Country Club golf course. Watching the golfers, he found it hard to believe that normal life continued all around him.

It took him the best part of two hours to clean out and disinfect the wound, bandage it and strap it closed. He then collapsed and slept the sleep of someone utterly exhausted. When he woke, he felt cool, with no sign of fever, so bathed and dozed some more. He ate tinned beans from the pantry and baked a pizza he found in the deep freeze. He waited for the dark and sat on the porch enjoying the sounds of small waves lapping the shore. In his teeth he held a cigar, though he did not light it. Caution and superstition were stitched deep into his DNA.

Ross felt the onset of cabin fever at the end of his second day in the summer house. This feeling was given an edge by something he'd noted as he arrived – a beautiful, deep green Indian style canoe stashed on the front porch made with Northern white cedar clothed in glass fibre. Its double-ended paddle was tucked in just behind it.

Taking a torch with him, his revolver and a hat he picked from the pegs by the front door and which he pulled down low over his face, he added a light fishing rod and reel to provide a reason for being out on the lake if he was hailed by anyone.

The canoe was lighter than he imagined. Checking for any onlookers and seeing none, he carried it down the cliff path to a floating dock, where he launched it into the dusk. A sense of boyhood glee took hold of him and, favouring his wounded shoulder, he paddled steadily to get away from the shoreline and as far into the lake as possible. There he rested and let the slight breeze move the canoe as it pleased. He swallowed some more painkillers.

A family of loons was calling and some ducks he could not make out flew in to roost for the night on a small islet – coot, mallard or teal, he imagined. A blue heron flew right over the canoe as if to give it the once over, but for the rest, it was just him alone on the lake. He now regretted his haste in leaving the cottage. If he'd thought it through, he might well have taken some lures with him and had a shot at fishing for large-mouthed bass or even a pike.

But he was content to be out on the water under a sky just beginning to show stars. He dried his hands on his shirt. The water kept dripping down the paddle as he worked it. Looking at his watch, he saw that it was almost 10pm and slowly turned the little craft around, heading back to the shore.

He wondered how he might get a message to Sandy and Sky but did not pursue that train of thought. He would speak to them once he was sure his dead stalker did not have any back-up trailing him or someone alerting the police that a murder had taken place on their patch. He would sit tight for another day or two and if he heard nothing on the news and saw nothing suspicious, he would head back to the ranch.

He brought the canoe in silently without even a splash of a paddle and clambered out at the floating dock. He left it there on the dock and checked for any hint of movement, all his senses alert as he moved up the path to the house. He knew of old that this point of the expedition was the point of maximum vulnerability. He'd given a would-be attacker an hour to hide up and prepare for his arrival. Cutting off the path, he approached the house from the rear and silently did a slow sweep right around the property. There was nobody outside or any sign of a break-in. But that did not mean there wasn't someone waiting inside the property.

Half regretting that he had taken the canoe out, he let himself into the house and checked each room. There was nobody there. Moving fast, he brought the canoe up and put it back on the porch and poured himself a stiff Scotch from the well-stocked drinks cabinet. His shoulder ached. He would not be doing any more canoeing for a while.

On the third day in the house, Ross woke to find two girls sitting on the deck. They looked much too young to be killers, but he knew he would have to get out fast. Packing his gear in the bedroom, he heard a soft tapping on the huge glass windows overlooking the lake and heard one of the girls calling softly.

'Ross, Sky sent us. We're friends. We delivered those food parcels to you guys at the ranch.'

Cautiously, Ross approached the window, watching the girls' hands splayed out on the glass as if she knew he would want to know if she was armed. The other girl sitting on the deck was turned to the window and gave him a broad smile when he appeared.

He opened the sliding glass door and beckoned them inside. Moving away from the windows to a small study he asked them to sit down.

The two girls were called Summer and Storm, friends and former classmates of Sky. They had indeed been sent by her. Sky and Sandy knew they might be under observation themselves so had sent the girls instead, quite certain of their discretion and guessing that Ross might just use the lake house as Sky had suggested it as a bolthole if ever he needed one during the winter.

The girls said they had both been to the wedding and the campout on the ranch. He recalled them now.

Summer said, 'Will you let us look at your wound?' And added, 'We've both done first aid courses.' Ross smiled for the first time in days.

'We haven't dealt with bullet wounds, though,' said Summer. But they cleaned out the mess on his shoulder, sanitized it and then wrapped it once more in clean bandages under surgical tape.

'Do you feel feverish?' Storm asked, raising a hand to his forehead. It was cool, as was her hand. There was no spread of any infection, for which he was grateful, but they handed him a small pharmacy of antibiotic drugs and creams they had brought with them.

Then they cooked a meal for him with food they had also brought along. He was still somewhat shaken by their arrival, but he sensed their concern for him and this unmanned him to a degree. He saw that they noticed his shaking hands.

Summer took out a joint and offered it to him. He grinned and thanked her. She lit it for him and placed it between his lips. He was astonished by their kindness to someone they barely knew. There was too, he felt, an almost palpable sexual tension between the three of them. And he thought, this is how cults form.

They showed him a newspaper cutting that offered a $10,000 reward for knowledge of his whereabouts and he knew it was now just a matter of greed and time, just in the way he watched it work in Iraq, Afghanistan, Syria and Libya. Some 90 per cent of people would not act on the offer of a reward, but there was always that 10 per cent who would. And who could blame them. Their need was always greater than his.

Ross knew it was inevitable that before long there would be a house-to-house search. So he kept his silent electric motorcycle with its 200-mile range charged, to get him back to high ground quickly if need be. Once more, he would be a ridge walker. Hiding in a house was proving claustrophobic for him.

The girls stayed till 10pm, cooking him another meal and leaving more food for him. He hugged them both as they left and he felt that they did not want to let go or indeed to leave.

'One day I hope to be able to thank you both and to repay the debt I owe you,' Ross said. Both girls were very subdued as they left.

Ross slipped out of the house and quietly, using forest paths, returned to the ranch. Sky and Sandy hugged him hard and all of them were a bit tearful.

'What would I do without you?' Ross said with feeling. They held him a long time.

He told them how Summer and Storm had taken care of him and Sky assured him that they were discreet and could be depended on completely. He also mentioned the reward he'd seen in the paper. They knew about it, but said the sheriff had been to visit and did not seem in any great rush to apprehend him. Everyone was hugely enjoying the fuss he and Father Berrigan had caused at the nuclear waste dump.

'At the moment, you are seen as a hero again,' Sandy assured him.

He answered the unspoken question he knew the women had. 'He's dead and buried. I got lucky. After he winged me, he was a little careless.'

They hugged him again and both women wept. And then they too went to work on his shoulder but found nothing amiss in what the girls had done.

The one thing that steadied him, as always, was working with the horses and the mule. Blue was proving to be a real find. Steady, enthusiastic, and with a kind gentle nature. He was a tremendous walker, almost a running walk, whether heading out or coming home he felt awash with joie de vivre as Sandy put it, happy to be out and going places.

Ross wondered if Blue had some Tennessee Walking Horse breeding. He spent more time with the animals than was strictly necessary until Sky complained that he was putting her out of a job.

Ross made a suggestion. 'Well, why don't you do some schooling with them? Start by watching some of the best TV videos from reputable trainers.'

Instead of turning herself into a dressage rider, Sky came up with an altogether different idea to build up their income to replace the 'lost' $500,000. Using the same technology, go-pros and other video cameras, she felt she could tap into Patreon once more, this time for themselves, given Ross's notoriety. Whatever the truth of the matter was he was the subject of huge interest.

Cheekily titled 'Gone: Off Grid', it worked as a weekly

YouTube vlog of life on the ranch, the horse packing operation, the production of home-grown food, vegetables, raising chickens, pigs and goats and offering tasty recipes. The idea was a winner when the beauty of the two women was added into the mix. Within a few weeks they had clocked up nearly 10,000 subscribers, half of them Patreons too.

Then, some months into this new regime, Sandy and Sky persuaded Ross to let them add a new venture, a 'Healing Ranch' for disturbed, troubled people or children with mental disabilities, using the horses as therapy animals. Ross hesitated over this, as it would bring all sorts of new people to the ranch and they would need more horses, smaller, quieter animals than the spirited Rincon and Blue. But in the end, Sandy convinced him that it would be seen as a positive addition to the local scene and would calm down any existing concerns people had about them. They agreed to put it on hold till the right animals were found and to maybe begin operating it in the next spring.

Nobody came for Ross, to his great surprise. The only reason for this, he thought, was the priest's involvement and the fact that the authorities did not wish to create scapegoats, which would add fuel to the anti-nuclear protest that was going better than ever thanks to the pitch invasion. It was just as Hester had predicted. The physical protest and the media coverage of it had given everyone involved a shot in the arm.

Ross saw that the Freemantle nuclear waste episode as a real fork in the road of his life, and the direction he took, the option he chose this time, was not to withdraw into himself again, putting up the barricades once more, but to engage more fully with the world. That is what he thought as his shoulder mended and he worked each day more comfortably with the horses.

Chapter 24

When Father Berrigan heard of the new enterprise – the Healing Ranch – he asked if he might visit to see how healing with horses worked. But what he really wanted was to chat to Ross on his own turf and to get a better feeling for the man.

The men went for a walk as the priest did not ride. Berrigan said to Ross, 'What is it about horses that you so love?'

Ross smiled at him. 'Father, how long do you have?' And he asked a question of his own. 'What is it about the church you so love?'

'Touché, Ross. I would say that it was a calling that would not be denied. It's my home. Why do I love it? Well, it brings me closer to God for one thing, and it enables me in a small way to help my fellow man. It fulfils me, it's my passion, in the way that making art fulfils an artist.'

'Ah, Father, I can understand that. You see horses are my passion and the landscape is my love. The one leads you into the other. It's hard, you know, when people ask, "Why do you love horses so much?" to explain it to them. It starts, if you are lucky, when you are just a kid and you get on a pony and suddenly you have speed and power and four legs and you can outrun the bullies. And the pony does whatever you ask it to do. And it looks after you and brings you home safe from the most amazing adventures. When you are on his back, you are not just a little boy, you are a prince.'

The priest asked him at what age he'd started riding and Ross told him he had been six.

'And when you are a tormented teen, the horse is always there for you, in ways that even your best friend can't be. It takes you away from your problems into another dimension. It lends you a distance and a perspective to examine your life. And it comforts you. It makes you feel good about yourself. When the time comes that you start dating, the horse is your wingman, the best in the world, because most girls respond to horses, love horses, the beauty, the romance, the independence offered, all the things the horse does for a boy is amplified if you are a girl. It allows them to go places on their own they would never dare to go on foot – into the wild for example.'

Father Berigan smiled. 'I had not thought of that. It's a powerful freedom for a woman.'

Ross nodded and continued: 'In your middle years, when you are wrestling with work and marriage and all that life throws at you, the horse is still there, still your friend, still able to bind up your wounds and make you feel good about yourself, remind you of the boy you once were. But I'm told that it's when you are old that the value of a good horse is beyond compare. You may have a bad heart, be unable to walk very well, troubled by hip and knee pain, damaged in so many ways, physically and mentally. Yet when you get on your horse's back, the years fall away, they lift from you and you are twenty again. You canter just the same as when you were a teenager. To people you pass, you are not an old man, you are a horseman. That is what people much older than me say, and at my age, I can already see that its true. And the horse does this all without speech, silently. In fact the essence of a horse would make for an amazing man, if a man could embody all that a horse is. And that, Father, is only the beginning of the story of why I love horses.'

They were silent for a while and then Ross said, 'Let me see if I can remember some words I read once that spoke to me on this subject. I forget the name of the author.' He closed his eyes and recited from memory:

> *There is a country I call my own,*
> *Some ten feet off the ground, that always feels like home.*
>
> *It is a place beyond walls, that offers endless space.*
> *There I've witnessed bronze dawns, bloody sunsets and the tapestry of trees.*
> .
> *There I move in innocence, all my actions pure.*
> *It is a gentle place, but can be tough on you*
> *With it I've crossed continents and my own inner world.*
>
> *Its language is universal, it allows me to speak to trees*
> *With it I've met both victory and defeat and the madness eased*
> *When I'm down it comforts me, when happy it celebrates too.*
>
> *It holds me aloft with the power of a great sea-wave*
> *Comes to my call and thinks of me as friend*
> *And moves with a swagger faster than I can run.*
> *It's a drug I never tire of,*
> *It's a mystery, that is hard to name –*
> *Some like to call it 'Horse'.*
> *To me it's home, this country I call my own.'*

'Ah, Ross, you too have a calling, I can see that now!' The priest put his hand on Ross's shoulder. 'You are a good man, Ross. You are.'

Ross wondered what the priest would say if he told him that the corpse of a man he had just killed lay buried, not five miles distant.

After an hour of walking, they turned down to the river and followed its course home, walking in meadow grass. As they neared the cabin, the priest stopped and said to Ross, 'Do you realise that this anti-nuclear waste protest that you, Sandy and Sky started has now reached critical mass? It's more than funding itself. Last week, we broke through the 100,000-subscriber barrier and our Patreon account now numbers almost 30,000 people. Most give small amounts each month but now and then we get a huge donation. The powers that be are trying to strong-arm YouTube to take us off air, but they say they stand for free speech and will not ban us. Word of our fight is spreading, not only across the Pacific Northwest, but across the whole country. I think we are really rattling some cages, and not only in government, but the mining interest too is worried; that is why they keep trying to take you out of play. If you want back in, to take the lead once more, I will vouch for you and stand by you. Jack Freemantle is now also of that view.'

'Father, let me think about this. As you know, I have just escaped a very troubling life, albeit that I was serving the country. And I then tried to hide myself away here in the mountains, put barriers around myself. Now, thanks to Sandy, I find myself living the most normal life I've ever lived, with the odd hiccup created from outside, and frankly I want to be a bit selfish now, to nurture what Sandy and I have here.'

'I understand, my son. And you have done more than most to bring about change for the better. You deserve some peace.'

In companionable silence, the two men walked the last yards to the cabin where Sandy and Sky were waiting by a table laden with cake and coffee.

'You two look very serious,' said Sandy. 'Have you been solving the ills of the world?'

Father Berrigan smiled. 'I suppose you could say that my child. We are certainly trying.' Over coffee and cake the subject moved to the 'Healing Ranch' project planned for the new year.

'Now that is constructive way to improve the world!' said the priest.

An hour later, Ross walked him to his car. As they were saying their farewells, Ross said, 'You know, Father, your comment about a calling and your home in the church reminded me that I too have a church, but mine is out here in nature and in fact next time you're here, I'll show you my chapel, as you've been kind enough to show me yours. I must tell you that people leave forest offerings around here to commemorate the birthdays of lost loved ones. Because the departed person loved the forest, the wife or husband or children bring gifts and cards and sometimes balloons tied to a tree. There is something deeply human in this and something religious, although I think it is a bit pagan too, maybe. It's a hangover from an earlier time. This secret, unspoken religion of the forest is part ancestor worship, part pagan veneration of a landscape, part tree worship. I understand it oh so well. The reason I call this special place in the woods my "church" is in part because the particular trees there, huge ones, really do lend a sense of religion to the place. It is always hushed and silent there. And one of the trees bears a double font made of a great cream-coloured fungi growing out of the tree's trunk, one above the other. It does not take much imagination to see it as a place of pilgrimage. And I, for one, never pass through this dell without stopping for a moment's contemplation and prayer.'

Father Berrigan asked, 'What do you pray for?'

'Father, these days my prayers are a mix of apologies and thanksgiving. I pray for forgiveness from all those many people I have killed or hurt or those I've let down, knowingly or unknowingly, out of selfishness and ignorance and sometimes fear. I have walked with fear so long it has become something of a friend. It is with me first thing in the morning and gets me out of bed and the last thing at night it tucks me in. And I say thanks for the innumerable blessings in my life. For family, both alive and dead, for old friends and surprising new friends. And for the knowledge that has kept me alive – that it's all about survival. At times, just for the next five minutes if that is all I can manage, and for longer if I can do that. It's about hanging in there.

'I also pray for kindness, that I be given the grace and patience and wisdom to be kind, as so very many people have been kind to me. And finally, I ask Mother Earth to forgive us the rape and pillage we have made of our time here. A stupidity so monstrous it mocks our arrogance. It may well mean the end of us. Amen!' He laughed. 'Forgive me Father, for I have sinned more than most, I am letting my thoughts rattle my tongue, and I am sure you have heard this a thousand times before.'

'No, no, no! Ross, you speak most eloquently about nature. And about what moves you. I am so glad you feel free to speak. And to think of the forest as a kind of church is not that unusual, I think. There are many places all over the world where people leave offerings, jewellery, crucifixes. All these objects are manmade, but they are left to link the giver with who knows what? But we do know that they feel close to that thing by being in the woods.'

Encouraged, Ross went on, 'You see, Father, when Rincon my horse and I once more enter my church, this tree-columned space, I think how few churches would welcome a horseman clip-clopping up the nave to the font. In there, you get just the faintest breath of wind high above in the branched rafters and above that only sky. The forest is mute, but it holds a horseman and his horse by a power that neither he nor I understand but which draws us back, again and again to this place, this magical place. I want to die on this land and be buried here. I never want to leave.'

As Father Berrigan drove back to Spokane, he felt refreshed and more than a little happy. A man had opened his heart to him and he saw that it was a good heart.

Chapter 25

'**G**ood heavens, Ross, what were you and Father Berrigan gabbing about? I'm beginning to get worried about you and him!' Sandy teased.

'He was asking me if I thought you'd knit him a pink bedjacket too, or one just like it in mauve!' They burst out laughing and Sky smiled. 'You guys are nuts!'

Early the next morning, Ross was up at the crack of dawn as he had clients coming, an ophthalmologist, Don Williams, and his 20-year-old son Mickey, who wanted to shoot an elk. As requested, they had provided a history of Mickey's shooting and despite his youth it was impressive, including an African safari the year before with his father in Botswana, Zimbabwe and Namibia. They provided images of gemsbok, impala, zebra and wildebeest trophies. The boy could obviously shoot. The ophthalmology business must be a good trade Ross reckoned, mentally totting up the cost of such an expedition. Ross had borrowed two horses for them as he did not want to leave the women without a horse. So Blue screamed his frustration as they rode away.

The borrowed horses, two strongly built bays from a neighbouring dude ranch, proved extremely steady. Ross planned on being gone for three days. He had done his homework as usual and had reliable information on elk numbers and grazing patterns, both from his own observation and that of a contact in the Forestry Service.

Don Williams had ridden in his youth but was rusty as well as somewhat overweight, and so Ross took things easy. Young Mickey was keen to get on and had obviously done a lot of riding. He had packed a very nice rifle, a Browning X-Bolt Mountain Pro 6.8 Western, just six pounds in weight, easy to carry on foot in mountain terrain and more than equal to the task of bringing down a high-country bull. Ross approved.

They spent the first day gaining altitude in perfect 'champagne weather' conditions as Ross termed it. They all slept well and ate with hearty appetites the steaks he had provided. Both men drank little of the beer and wine and whisky he'd packed. A good sign, Ross thought.

The next day he planned to go high enough to spot the marks where elk had pawed through the snow to get to the feed. He knew that they would often come back to such spots, especially at dawn and dusk. Judging the wind direction, he made his first cast and sure enough, they spotted a small herd on a distant hill. Mickey was all for going all out to reach them, but Ross urged caution and suggested an ambush option from a neighbouring hill overlooking the site for the evening. It would also mean that Don could be present for the kill, not having to walk for miles tracking the elk which would hold them back, as he was obviously unfit.

Despite chafing to get going, Mickey saw the sense of this and agreed. They lay up for the day resting and eating, conserving their energy and giving the horses the chance to graze. Ross made sure they all stayed below the skyline and kept checking the wind direction, which seemed fixed perfectly, blowing softly toward them. As the sun started setting, they crawled up the hill until they had a clear line of sight over the feeding spots on the hill opposite, easily within rifle range.

For Mickey, the waiting was almost more than he could stand but Ross urged him to be patient.

'I'm feeling good about this spot. Let us wait.'

As the light faded, he began to feel it was all over for the day but as so often happened, just then a bull and three does came over the hill, grazing as they went. He got Mickey well settled and Don too on the other side of his son. After about ten minutes the stag raised his head and stood silhouetted in the setting sun. He turned his head and using his antlers to scratch his rear, showing the width of his antlers and that he was trophy material. He was magnificent in his two-tone coat and noble head, his antlers a huge spread.

'Right, Mickey, take him,' Ross whispered. He watched carefully as Mickey spread his legs slightly to get more balanced, slowed his breathing and then held his breath, taking a first pressure on the trigger. The shot rang out and the bull staggered and fell.

'Nice shot Mickey!' Don said. 'Very nice!'

Ross patted the boy's shoulder. 'Well done. Let's go get him. Don, you stay here and keep an eye on the horses.' Wearing head torches and carrying skinning knives, they set off. By the time they reached the bull, there was hardly any light left.

Mickey straddled the bull, let out a rebel yell and lifted its antlers. In that moment, something turned in Ross's stomach, but he kept his thoughts to himself. Smiling with delight, Mickey asked for a photograph and Ross obliged, taking a few.

He butchered the elk, severing the head carefully, keeping the liver to one side and removing one of the hind quarters. The rest of the carcass he hauled high into a tree with rope. It was pitch dark when they got back to camp, and he grilled the liver and the steaks cut from the haunch. Father and son then made some serious inroads into the whisky. There was much laughter and storytelling.

Ross drank too, but in his case it was to wash away a bitter taste in his mouth. There was nothing at fault with the hunters, other than lack of fitness in one and a rather spoiled youth in the other, but it was enough to bother Ross and he turned in early. The next morning, he and Mickey retrieved the carcass between them, loaded Solomon with the hind quarters, head and antlers, and set out for home. They made it back to the ranch at sunset. After unsaddling the animals and setting them loose, Ross waved the hunters goodbye and walked up to the cabin.

Sandy asked how it had gone and Ross said it was the last hunt he would lead. 'I'm just done with it, with the killing. I've had a gutful, Sandy. No more trophy hunting!'

Sandy also had news for Ross. She handed him a newspaper article outlining the removal of all waste from Idaho to New Mexico – almost a year to the day of the 'pitch invasion'. 'You did it, Texas. You made the difference.' And she hugged him. Ross read:

U.S. COMPLETES NUCLEAR WASTE CLEAN-UP AT IDAHO SITE

The lengthy project to remove radioactive and hazardous waste buried for decades in unlined pits at a nuclear facility that sits above a giant aquifer in eastern Idaho is nearly finished, U.S. officials said.

The U.S. Department of Energy said last week that it removed the final amount of specifically targeted buried waste from a 97-acre (39-hectare) landfill at its site that includes the Idaho National Laboratory.

Most of the waste is being sent to the U.S. government's Waste Isolation Pilot Plant in New Mexico for permanent disposal. The Energy Department said it is 18 months ahead of schedule in its clean-up of the landfill.

Ross grinned. 'Not only me Sandy, we did it. You, Sky, Father Berrigan, Jack Freemantle, about a 100,000 people and me.' They made a copy of the press cutting and posted it to Hester Townsend. Ross added a note:

> *Dear Mrs Townsend,*
> *This is the second nuclear protest you've been involved in that has had a successful conclusion. Without your inspiration, encouragement and support I would never have got involved.*

This Country I Call My Own

Thank you so much.
Kind regards
Ross McCallister

Ross and many others rejoiced when they finally defeated the government's desire to sidestep its responsibilities for the nuclear waste piles and spent the money needed to do the best possible clean-up.

But climate warming continued to mess with the land. Summers grew ever hotter and winters more brutal, but on the upside there was increasingly less interest in mining for rare earth metals. Electric battery cars were proving to be a false dawn and environmentally damaging in their own way. Hydrogen technology began to win support from an ever-growing number of people for clean non-polluting transport.

In the wake of the nuclear clean-up win, Ross received a heartfelt letter from Jack Freemantle.

Dear Ross,
I wish to thank you for your contribution to the fight we have now finally and decisively won, in no small measure because of your efforts. As important, I write to offer you an apology for ever doubting your motives or that your heart was in the right place. If anyone should have been aware and sensitive to the power plays around this issue, it should have been me. I misread the amount of brutal pushback we got over the years from the mining lobby allied to their friends in government. If you can forgive me, I would welcome the chance to bury the hatchet with a meal in Spokane or Sandpoint, whichever works best for you and Sandy. Michelle and I would truly value that.
Kind regards,
Jack

Jack wrote back immediately, accepting the apology and the invitation to have a meal together with Jack and Michelle. And when they met for lunch, it was as if the bad blood had never occurred; both couples felt that their friendship had survived some deep and troubled waters and was the stronger for it.

Jack said he was gearing up once more to run for the Governorship. They shook on it and Ross said, 'If you can persuade the present governor to come riding with me I will see what I can do with my friendly bear!' The laughter that followed had a slightly hysterical quality.

CHAPTER 26

It was a brutal winter, even by the standards of Idaho. Some 20 feet of snow fell and icicles thick as a man's thigh hung from the roof eaves. Ross went round knocking them off and clearing the roof of snow. He worked hard to keep paths from the cabin to the barn open and worked the snow plough, bolted to the Jeep, to make a path to the county road.

Sandy and Sky worked alongside him, teasing him all the while that he was slowing down. Trees cracked open with sounds like rifle shots and they all felt some element of cabin fever. But the home fire was kept going and they ate well.

From time to time, Sky gave them space and time to themselves, borrowing the Jeep to get into town to see her folks and to visit friends. Twice she asked if she might invite Summer and Storm back to the ranch for a weekend and as the spring thaw set in Ross watched the three girls working the horses and the mule under Sandy's direction, all the animals delighted to be able to stretch their legs.

He could not explain what was changing in him, but there was an ever-growing sense of contentment. He was more at peace with himself than he could ever remember. His endless need to control things, to be in charge, to be responsible, was dissipating somewhat and he could not understand why it was happening. He guessed that it had a lot to do with the two women in his life and also his growing

Julian Roup

friendship with Father Berrigan, to whom he spoke from time to time, sharing the things that troubled him, and finding that the talking eased his mind. He no longer felt that he stood as an armed guard against the world, with a gun in each hand and knives on his hips.

He felt himself surrounded by beauty. Ross believed that when the good Lord got round to designing women and horses he must have been in the best of moods because he used everything at his disposal to create two of the most beautiful things on earth. He could so clearly remember when he first observed the combination of the two together – girls riding horses at a stable in Texas – and it was love at first sight.

The stable had been run by a Mexican American family and the combination of a day's riding in sunshine, youth, beer and that insistent commanding Spanish music, demanding a response, was intoxicating. Often at night the women and men in their Spanish costumes would dance in the firelight on a makeshift packing case dancefloor, the drama of the dance, sensual and harsh in equal measure, spoke of a deep human need as old as man's lineage. The sexually arrogant, prideful dancing, with its staccato heel drumming beat, would last for an evening but its effect stayed with him all his life. A love of Spanish guitar and of Spanish dancing was a part of his youth that kept blossoming all his life.

Years later, driving across the north Spanish plain near the city of Salamanca, the car radio offered up the Rodrigo Concerto with an electrifying effect. The vast barren plain at dusk, the music and his memories took him back to those Texas nights, the flickering firelight on the whitewashed stable walls and the heads of the horses watching girls in Spanish costume dancing, taunting, flaunting, calling out, and all that it had meant to him. It was a visceral memory that stirred in his gut even now.

Over the years, he'd had a number of girlfriends who rode. Texas offered magnificent riding country and in summer the nights were warm. He remembered one particular night, riding in moonlight with a girl who frankly rode better than him. It was unforgettable, echoed as it was by the moonlight and the bright stars.

There was something special in the relationship women had with horses. They seduced each other, he thought. He was just not sure who led the seduction, the girl or the horse. Safe to say it was a partnership that was intoxicating to observe.

A woman riding took on all the strength, mystery and grace of the horse and reflected her own mystery, strength and grace back to the animal. They were no longer two beings but one, a very powerful new thing. A man on a horse projects force. A woman on a horse was something more than that. One had only to watch the world's best dressage riders to know that what you were watching was sublime, two great artists making beauty tangible. Or simpler yet, a girl cantering a horse on a beach, manes of hair flying. What could touch that for grace?

The bond between women and their horses had to be seen to be believed. And when wilderness was added to the mix, then there was a special kind of alchemy. It was an aphrodisiac to observe a beautiful girl on a beautiful horse in magnificent wild country. Women on horseback shape-shifted into another form, allowing them access to wilderness, leaving manners and civility and civilization as far behind as a dying planet. No wonder they loved horses. And men like him loved observing them.

Ross watched as Sandy on Rincon and Sky riding Blue emerged from a stand of aspen trees, it was an image of such beauty that its power could stop you breathing.

Like so many good looking, talented, ambitious men, the number of temptations on offer to Ross had been seemingly endless, virtually each day would provide new women who would signal their interest. And, as ever, the road less travelled had held its attractions. Ross was no saint and no exception; he had walked that primrose path for decades and it had not been without pleasures and rewards. There were few women that he was attracted to that he did not learn from. He was immeasurably enriched by each encounter – new languages, new cultures, new foods, new philosophies. But he was now in a place where he felt so deeply content, so grateful and so fulfilled there was no longer any need to look beyond what he had, something he knew to be unique and precious beyond belief.

These thoughts were further embedded by his involvement with the Catholic Church and Father Berrigan. Ross spent some time studying Jesuit texts and even attending the odd service with Sandy, but rejected anything further. He just could not join another huge organisation, especially one so tarnished with scandal of every kind as the Catholic church. But his friendship with the priest added a philosophical dimension to his life that he valued greatly.

The result of his studies led Ross to construct a rudimentary yurt on a meadow commanding views down to the ranch house and barn. Now and again he would withdraw to the yurt to camp for a few days of contemplation while the life of the ranch continued to be run by the two women.

Sandy and Sky would run provisions up to him and he had his books and music. He had a very broad taste in music, from Spanish to country to jazz, blues to Motown, but his passion was opera, Puccini in particular. Approaching the camp, Sandy and Sky would hear the strains of opera wafting over the hills and echoing from the mountain sides.

Puccini – *Un bel dì vedremo* (Madam Butterfly) – one of the most devastating arias from one of Puccini's most-loved operas. Butterfly, patiently at home, sings of her hope of seeing her husband, Pinkerton, who does not deserve such love or faith. 'One fine day' he will return, she passionately sings, with one of the most extraordinary climaxes ever heard on the stage.

Sandy wondered if he did it deliberately, providing this soundtrack. She knew that he knew immediately when she was coming up the hill to the yurt, however discreetly she approached. The music had the power to hold her too, to stop her a moment in her tracks, to make her look up at the mountains, to count her blessings, and now and then to cry. But he also loved *Nessun Dorma* and *Il bobino*. Puccini's *Nessun Dorma* from the opera *Turandot*, sung by the hero Calaf who declares 'None shall sleep', an affliction that Ross knew only too well. From its hushed opening to the dramatic conclusion, Puccini took him on an incredible journey, a journey he felt that matched the path his own life had taken.

None shall sleep,
None shall sleep!
Even you, oh Princess,
In your cold room,
Watch the stars,
That tremble with love
And with hope.
But my secret is hidden within me,
My name no one shall know,
No…no…
On your mouth I will tell it,
When the light shines.
And my kiss will dissolve the silence that makes you mine!
(No one will know his name and we must, alas, die.)
Vanish o night!
Set, stars! Set, stars!
At dawn I will win!
I will win!
I will win!

Puccini's *O Mio babino caro* was another of his great loves. This aria had the power to make him weep. As soon as he heard its serene accompaniment and beautiful soaring melody, the tears would come.

Sandy was all too aware that there was a very sentimental heart under that tough hide. It was a very strange contradiction. Sky would cry when hearing this music. She could not fathom its effect, just that it shook her to her core.

'Don't cry!' Sandy would urge, giving her a hug.

After the spring thaw, the early summer turned out to be one for the record books. Warm, lazy days followed each other like languid kisses in a sweet flower meadow. One Saturday afternoon in June, Sandy and Sky invited him to join them with Summer and Storm for a picnic by the river. He strolled down, laden with wicker baskets while the women rode the horses and Solomon carried Summer and Storm. It looked like the opening shot of a movie.

While Ross spread the rugs and sorted out the food and drinks the horses and Solomon were led into the stream and washed with scoops of water. The animals loved it and thrashed the water with their legs before lying down completely to roll in the deliciously cool water.

Soon the women were as wet as the horses. They led them out of the water to graze and then stripping off their wet clothes they ran back in to swim. Ross sat bewitched by the scene, which reminded him of Paul Cezanne's 'The Bathers'.

'Come join us,' shouted Sandy. 'Don't sit there like an old man!'

Ross threw his clothes off and dived in among them. After some time they emerged, wet and gleaming as otters, and let the sun dry them as they picnicked in the nude.

Ross thought he had seen all that life could offer, but this was something completely beyond his ken. He was dazzled by the beauty and by the simple freedom these women shared. He imagined life in a hippy commune to be something like this. He was not sure how his life had reached this point

CHAPTER 27

One evening after supper, Sandy came and snuggled next to Ross on the couch.

'What's this?' he asked suspiciously. What have I done to deserve such a show of affection?' Sandy said, 'Well I think you deserve it. You are going to be a father.'

Ross looked at her to see if she was joking, but saw that she was deadly serious. He hugged her hard. 'How long have you known?'

'For a couple of weeks I've felt that something was up.' Ross was elated, nervous, excited, scared and many other emotions which he could not name, but above all he was grateful that Sandy was giving him this extraordinary gift. When they arranged for a scan, both were astonished to find that they were going to be parents of twins – a boy and a girl.

News of the pregnancy delighted Sky, who was genuinely happy for them. The relationship they had as a threesome and sometimes with one or the other was winding down, as she and Storm grew ever closer. This pleased both Sandy and Ross, who could see that a long-term relationship with Sky could only lead to heartbreak and huge complications with her parents and indeed the local community.

There came a day when Sandy was at the school teaching and Ross and Sky were alone on the ranch. She asked Ross if he had the time to join her for a ride to exercise the horses and sensing something in the way she asked, Ross agreed. After a quiet meandering ride covering some miles chatting as they rode, they made their way back onto the ranch land alongside the river and Sky said, 'Why don't we stop for a while and let them graze?' As they lay in the sweet meadow grass watching the horses, Sky put her hand on Ross's face and kissed him.

'Dear Ross, I love Storm, but I am going to miss being with you and Sandy. How can I thank you for making me so welcome in your life here on the ranch?' She pulled him down into the grass and they made love for what both knew would be the last time. As they rode home, they acknowledged that what had happened between the three of them – a love without limits, without jealousy, beyond taboos – was something they would treasure all their lives.

And so began a whole new chapter of life for Sandy and Ross. When the twins were three, he put them on a pony and led them round the paddock and by the age of four, they could ride unassisted on two gentle ponies. Father Berrigan was a delighted godfather and brought them books and read to them, as did Sandy. She and Ross taught them to love nature and shared all their knowledge with them. From an early age, it was evident that both children had a passionate connection to the land. Sandy made sure to embed that love deeply. She told them all she had discovered about her family history in Brittany and how the loss of land, the losses at sea and in war had driven the family to Canada, and how education had been their salvation.

'Land is our passion and nature fills our souls, but education is a treasure that nobody can ever take from you, and it takes up no space in your backpack, if ever you are forced to flee.'

Ross and Sandy named their son Charles River McCallister, to commemorate Ross's old SEAL compadre, Charles Stiegs Stiegler, and their daughter Clémence Willow McAlister. Clém as she was known, never Clemmy. 'I'm not clammy!' she would yell. Clémence 'Clém' McCallister was named for Sandy's late maternal French grandmother. Both kids had an artistic streak. Clém showed a gift for poetry and Charlie painted with a distinct talent, landscapes mainly and horses, but always with some element of sadness, a broken windmill, a fallen rusty barbed wire fence, a stallion with a smashed leg.

As she grew up, Clém would make time to attend poetry slams in Spokane or Bozeman. She liked people and she was the spitting image of her mother, but with a tongue on her that could skin a moose faster than a blade. Charlie was a chip off the old block but better looking, Sandy would insist, and as quiet. Getting a 'Hi' out of him was considered a major achievement.

By their teens, both twins stood tall, even without their cowboy boots, Clém at just on 6ft and Charlie at 6ft 4in. His pitch-black hair and piercing blue eyes drew looks wherever he went and Clém's swinging mahogany tresses with auburn highlights above a wide-shouldered, slim-hipped athlete's body, stopped traffic in Sandpoint. If the twins were aware of their effect on people, they hid it well. Both felt an overwhelming desire to fit in and to move beyond some of the historical family drama they were only too aware of.

But it was not easy to throw off the temperaments they had inherited. In Charlie's case, this was made manifest one day helping a friend to buy some decent cowboy boots. Charlie had made one true friend at school, David Segal, the only Jewish boy in his class. A full head shorter than Charlie, they looked an odd pairing, but David more than held his own intellectually and that seemed to cancel out the height difference. David came top in virtually all his classes without seeming to try very hard and helped Charlie with his math and science homework and prepping for exams. Charlie was no slouch, but these two subjects seemed to be a blind spot for him. Thanks to David, he managed to get pass rates and this among other things endeared him to Charlie.

The Segal family had taken a wrong turning somewhere when leaving New York for LA, David liked to joke, but in fact his father Noah Segal was a distinguished biochemist who was much sought after by the agricultural community in Idaho and he had been snapped up by the state's huge grass seed operation, one of the biggest of its kind in the world, where he ran their laboratory operation, developing new drought-resistant grass varieties.

Now and then on a Friday night Charlie would go to the Segals for the Sabbath meal and enjoy a cultural ambience so very different to that of his own family. The talk was nineteen-to-the-dozen and covered everything from US and Israeli politics to books, art, philosophy, science and music. it was hard to get a word in edgewise. Strange and exotic as it was at first to him, Charlie became a fixture, as did David at the ranch. This was a mixed blessing for David, who for years had carried a torch for Clém, but as she was almost a head taller than him, it was never going to get off the ground. It was a torment to him to be teased by her during his horse-riding lessons. But despite this he stuck it out and became a very competent rider, who more than held his own on the trail.

One day the lads stopped at the big shoe store in Sandpoint to pick out a proper pair of cowboy boots for David, who was sick of being teased about riding in his running shoes. As they walked in, they spotted a classmate, a football jock called Rob Rice, who worked there to earn some pocket money, and they headed for him to ask for help.

'Hi Charlie, what are you looking for?' he asked. And when Charlie explained that David was needing some cowboy boots, Rob laughed. 'What does a Jew need cowboy boots for? It's like putting lipstick on a pig.'

Looking back on the incident later, Charlie struggled to understand what had come over him. It was a rage so profound that he had felt an urge to kill Rob and had knocked him out cold with an explosive upper cut. All hell had then broken loose, with various people trying to restrain him, and the sheriff was called. When Charlie and David explained what had gone down, the sheriff called Ross and told him to have a word with his son.

Ross took Charlie to task, but his heart was not really

in it. He had seldom been prouder of his boy. 'Charlie, I am the last person on earth to tell you don't stand up for your friends. What you did has my wholehearted approval. But there is a but – be careful of that killing rage. I know it of old. It is a very dangerous drug. When it comes it's thrilling, because it's like a 100-foot wave of dark energy, you feel you can take on the whole world, and you simply don't care about yourself. You just want to destroy what is before you. Never give in to that rage again; it has the capacity to destroy you as well as the person you are attacking. With your size and strength, it's very easy to kill someone. And the thrill of that rage gets to be habit-forming, just like any drug. It has the power to destroy your life. When next you feel it, put the brakes on hard and act quietly and coldly. It's just as effective and you are in control, not the rage.'

The upshot of it was that David ended up with some fake snakeskin cowboy boots that he got by mail order, which gave Clém another reason to tease him, giving him the nickname 'Snaky Segal' that lasted for a year.

As the twins grew up, there were trips into the mountains the McCallisters did as a family, and these were something they all treasured. Ross would pack one of the large bell tents, big enough for six people, and they would sleep comfortably in this, each one at a different point of the compass and with feet pointing to the middle. Sandy and the twins noted that during these trips, Ross seldom suffered his periodic nightmares. Instead, he snored like a chainsaw. They discreetly packed earplugs, inserted after lights out, to ensure that they slept through this sound storm. It astonished Ross how fast they all fell asleep, barely hearing his goodnights. And they never let on.

Part of the pleasure of these trips was the $40 prize for who would catch the biggest fish of any variety, based on weight, not length. Each of the four would formally hand over $10 to Sandy at the start of the trip, which was placed into a purple velvet draw bag, and the rivalry to win the prize was fierce. The twins' rapid growth to 6ft – and beyond, in Charlie's case – made their casting a thing of beauty to observe, something that won them prizes for best and furthest cast at some of the local agricultural shows that featured a casting pond and fishing tackle suppliers.

To the frustration of Ross, Sandy and Charlie, it was Clém who seemed to win most often, even when her catch did not seem that big. There was an unspoken rule that after the weigh-in, each person was responsible for gutting and cleaning their own catch. This worked well until one day, acting on a hunch, Ross mixed up the catch deliberately, to give him the chance to gut one of Clém's fish. Removing the gills and then cutting open the gut, he found four good sized pebbles secreted in the fish's belly.

He called the family together and holding his hand open with the four pebbles said, 'Look what I found in one of Clém's fish!' Amazing! I had no idea that trout swallowed stones?'

Clém blushed scarlet, but then began to argue strenuously in her defence. She made out that Ross was trying to shame her, to win the prize himself, and that she suspected he'd placed the pebbles in the fish belly himself. 'Dad, we all know how devious you are and just how much you hate to lose at anything.'

The justice of this argument made both Sandy and Charlie look hard at Ross, who began to bluster. 'Me? I never put anything in a fish gut in my life!' But the doubt was sown and so Clém seemed to have won the argument, but thereafter the rules were changed in the fishing challenge. After the weigh-in, you had to hand in your fish to one of the others for cleaning. And of course this led in time to lead sinkers, ball bearings, earrings and on one occasion, a steel bolt being found in the fish guts. The upshot was a honing of an almost lawyer-like ability to argue the merits of the case. And a great deal of bluster and much laughter.

It became something of a family tradition to pull this stunt on unsuspecting guests, who would be desperately embarrassed when their fish were found to contain a pound or more of pebbles or lead sinkers. Some would get quite huffy or even angry, defending their honour, until the glint of laughter in the eyes of their tormenters told them something else was going on here. Teasing was a McCallister family trait that sorely tested some of the children's friendships.

This trying habit carried over into the horse riding on the ranch. Now and then – especially when a guest showed signs of thinking themselves a top rider – instead of matching them with a suitable horse, he or she would be given something immensely big, or ridiculously small, or much too sharp or almost impossible to move on. Charlie and Clém would always keep exquisitely straight faces until they could no longer and their peals of laughter would discomfit the target of the sport. It took a stout heart to befriend the McCallisters.

CHAPTER 28

The Healing Ranch programme took off slowly, with horses selected by Ross. They had to be extra careful as these horses would be interacting with people who mostly had not had much or indeed any contact with horses. It was not an easy task finding the right animals, but in time they built up a small group of horses and ponies that really liked human attention and had an innate understanding, as horses do, of what people were feeling. Sandy loved the work and took a number of courses to help her provide more effective interactions for clients and the care horses.

Equine assisted therapy as used on the ranch was a holistic, experience-based and highly specialised form of therapy that involved working with a horse, a therapist and an expert horse handler. During the sessions, clients or patients did not ride the horses, but carried out tasks such as feeding, grooming and leading them.

Sessions took place in small groups, where the aim was to help clients discover more about themselves, develop new ways of thinking and change any negative behaviours. Many of the benefits of equine therapy were thanks to the nature of horses themselves, naturally gentle and calm creatures, who were able to mirror and respond to human behaviour in subtle ways.

Many of the patients visiting the ranch struggled to articulate how they were feeling, but often found themselves able to express their emotions and feelings with their horse partners. Individuals who found it very hard to trust others or be intimate with people could often achieve a strong bond with their horse, and experience affection, acceptance and mutual respect. It was a minor miracle to observe at close hand. And equine therapy didn't just result in psychological benefits – it had distinct physical benefits too. It reduced people's blood pressure and heart rate and helped to calm physical symptoms of conditions such as anxiety and stress.

Working with horses required patience, understanding, discipline and responsibility. Horses could be stubborn one day and playful the next; this meant that clients needed to learn to be flexible, innovative and open to altering their own behaviour. By working with the horses, you could see the clients develop self-control and problem-solving skills, as well as improving their self-esteem, empathy and independence.

As the clients fed and stroked their horse partners, they found that their anxiety was reduced, learned that anxiety could be irrational, and learned that by taking things slowly and asking for support, they could achieve things that they never thought they would be able to. Some who found it impossible to share their thoughts with humans, were able to whisper to a horse about their feelings and emotions of grief and loss, and by the horse's silent acceptance they were helped.

Asked by a cynical journalist just what benefits the horses brought to clients, Sandy replied, 'Because they are herd animals, they rely on a stream of sensory data to sense safety or danger; they can also hear the human heartbeat within four feet, and research on heart-rate variability indicates that horses have a surprising ability to synchronize their own heartbeat with that of human beings. When people are introduced to the horse environment for therapy, the effect on troubled people can be astonishing to watch. You see tears, hugs, laughter, a reluctance to leave the animals in the arena. We don't truly understand what is going on, but its effects are unquestionably profound. We've had autistic children who have never spoken before, beginning to communicate. After a year with us, some of them become grooms as they love the horses so much, and some make a career out of it. In fact, I would go so far as to say that many horse riders are a self-selecting group who ride because of the unspoken therapy horses provide. I have many riding friends who say, "I ride because it's cheaper than seeing a therapist." Or they say, "Horses saved my life. I was on the point of suicide when a friend took me riding and my life was turned around." This is the sort of feedback we get every week.'

Sky's own troubled childhood, her early lack of direction, experiments with drugs and the duality of her sexual preferences, gave her something of an insight into the troubled young people who came for horse therapy healing. She was sensitive, patient and gently encouraging, and the impact this had on many of the teens was evident within a very short number of visits. She would point out things that were obvious to her, attuned as she was to the horses' responses to their human partners.

'Cindy, Wildfire is falling in love with you. Do stroke his neck.' Or 'James, can you see how Clint has started to follow you around. He wants to be your friend. Go on, give him a stroke on his face and speak to him. Tell him about yourself.'

For the worried parents, watching the change in their children often brought tears of relief and joy. Their gratitude to Sky, Storm, Sandy and the attending therapist was immense, and they would often bring gifts for the three horse handlers.

The work of the ranch changed somewhat to accommodate these new visitors. Ross added extra sleeping cabins and a dining hall, alongside paddocks in which human horse activities could take place. As ever, Sky's aptitude for turning events into strong video images proved invaluable, and the ranch increased its audience of viewers as well as visitors across the region.

The YouTube videos about the life of the ranch brought in many new people wishing to ride the big country. And the term Dude Ranch took on a whole new meaning, for many young men and women arrived looking for love. This was the result of videos made of couples who met on the ranch trail rides, who fell in love and later got married.

Ross continued looking after this trail riding operation now that there was no hunting element involved, although he still provided the opportunity to fish for those who wanted both fishing and riding.

He found the time to write a memoir of his life that he locked away in his safe. As he turned the key, the thought came to him that he was perhaps most truly the sum of his secrets. It was those things we hid from people and as often from ourselves, in a kind of willed forgetting, that most truly represented who we were as people. Our secret self was our true self. It was a dark thought.

Much as Sandy asked to read the memoir he refused. 'When I am dead, you can read it. If you read it now, you will no longer feel the same about me.' Sandy suspected that his writing of the hefty memoir could only have helped him and she was wise enough to bide her time, knowing the day would come when he would let her read it.

His paranoia still came and went, even though the PTSD seemed not as bad as it had been, or his medication mix had finally hit a sweet spot. When it was bad, now that he was a father and passionate about Charlie and Clém, he felt more vulnerable than he had ever felt before. He could never be free of the fear that the things he had done deserved punishment, whatever Father Berrigan said, and the powerful people who wished him ill had all the resources in the world at their fingertips to rain misery and hell on him and his family if they so chose. This bolstered his paranoia and stress. For he knew that hurting his wife and children would be the worst hurt they could inflict on him.

Once in a while, Sandy found him gone from the bedroom and when she went looking for him, she would find him sitting on the porch with his grandfather's shotgun across his lap, humming tunelessly to himself. But Ross was aware of how much he had to be grateful for. He spent as much time as ever with his beloved horses and also walking the woods, learning the intricacies of the seasons, observing bears whom he named and whose cubs he watched grow. He learned to know their coming by the change in the natural order, a sense of silence which affected the birds, who went quiet.

And in his reading he came across the sentence in John Irving's book, *Hotel New Hampshire*, that spoke directly to him, remembering it from his demob time with the first therapist treating his PTSD. The line 'Keep passing the open windows', referring to the suicidal desire that befell some people to jump, leaped out at him. It was a catchphrase among the Berry family, the characters whose story is told in the book. It was drawn from a tale the Berry parents told their children about a street performer called 'The King of Mice', who committed suicide by jumping from a window. 'Keep passing the open windows' was the family's way of urging each other to carry on when the going got tough. But, as ever, the horses helped Ross pass those open windows faster – their strides were indeed longer than his.

Despite the pressures of raising children, Ross still found time while riding alone to think deeply about his life and its meaning beyond the constraints and demands of the everyday. As ever, riding induced a meditative spirit in him in which he was both living intimately in the present and also with a mind cleared of all those things requiring his attention on the ranch.

He had a great concern for the way the country was going politically and the impact this had on the huge issue of the day, the survival of the planet. He was all too aware that he had played a small part in winning the fight against the nuclear waste poisoning the region, but he saw clearly how much more there was to do.

Ross figured that if humanity was not thinking about the meaning of life, the world, and its future, then mankind was truly lost. And he knew very few people who truly felt engaged enough or had the energy to think or act to change things. They plodded on with their lives like ploughmen, looking down at the furrow that the blade made in the soil, not at the bigger picture.

Speaking to Sandy about his concerns, he said, 'We are like ants crawling over the face of God, blindly unaware of the sacred nature of our journey. What we have lost in exchange for scientific knowledge and mainstream religious belief systems is incalculable. The cost to us is that we live in a two-dimensional, impoverished world, a life largely without savour or magic or wonder. Is it any surprise that our young people and our best people are always in search of fulfilment? They know instinctively that they have lost something of value, but what it is, is beyond them. Maybe the ultimate gift of this view of the world as sacred will be to help us to refocus on the profoundly important things.'

Ross said he did not wish to belittle the great gifts and blessings brought to humanity by rational scientific research or, for that matter, by the world faiths. Our lives were made immensely more comfortable by both science and religion, he believed. But progress, as it was named, had not come free, the cost had been enormous.

He knew that this appreciation of the sacred in landscape was something our ancestors took for granted, a sense of wonder, of magic, of spiritual power that was invested in us and in our physical reality. The landscape was alive for them, inhabited by explicable and inexplicable powers. The rivers sang, the trees whispered, and the very stones had stories to tell, if only one would sit in quiet contemplation and listen.

Ross's desire was not for a return to a world filled with superstition, though that was part of the lost magic; some of its loss was for the good. It was also not a plea for turning our backs on science, technology, or education. These he knew needed to be embraced, for in them lay part of our possible salvation. But they were also responsible for the culture of greed, of dominance over the natural world, of taking for granted everything given to us on this earth. Our intellect had poisoned us and our world.

His understanding of environmentalism had at its core a belief that everything was linked, and that we needed once more to worship the world, to treat it as sacred, because it was our only real heritage, our inheritance and the basis of life on earth, not only for us but for every living thing now and in the future, if there was to be a future. Around the trail campfires at night, if asked, he would speak eloquently of these things. To many, his words were electrifying.

Smiling gently, he would say, 'We need to stop long enough to understand how a belief in the sacred nature of the earth enriches everything in our lives. For if the most mundane thing, the most abject material, is filled with spirit, then we have a better understanding of ourselves as sacred animals moving through a sacred landscape. That belief makes it much more difficult to damage or destroy anything.'

It pleased him to see that his words made a powerful impact on some of his guests and he hoped that when they returned to their homes, it would not only be with sore muscles but with an expanded view on what was needed to save the earth.

When he was a boy, growing up in Texas, it was no great feat of the imagination to see the land as holy, sacred, a spiritual place, the home of those who had gone before. In his dreams he flew above it, flying as freely as a bird, experiencing that most powerful feeling of unassisted flight. No wonder then, that as he played in the woods and streams near his home, he was filled with a sense of wonder, by the presence of an unseen 'Other' that had never entirely left him. It was, he believed, the oldest known truth, that in ways we cannot comprehend, we are not alone. That we are observed, and the good and evil we do is noted. And that help is at hand if only we would ask for it.

When he was ten years old, he and some friends built imaginative city states out of what lay about them, stones, and twigs, and pieces of tile and brick. After some weeks of play, each of them had created a small world. These worlds were linked by 'ships' and 'planes' pulled on strings, vessels that traded with far-flung civilisations found behind an oak tree, or halfway up the riverbank. Ross didn't know how it was for the other boys, but the game became somehow more real and important to him than his real life. He sensed in their play something of a great truth, which he did not understand at the time. It had something of what a formal, ritualised dance in tribal society seeks to make, a sense of the great wheel of life celebrated in the shorthand of the movements of the dance, a unifying spiritual experience, linking the profane to the sacred.

He read widely, and now and again a writer alluded to 'the Other' in some way. And the experience of various tribal peoples that he read about fascinated him and led him to study anthropology. He knew from his reading about the 'spiritual presences' felt by the troops of the First World War, that they believed protected them. He also devoured books about nature and the spirits of the woods, and children's books with their magic doors into other worlds.

Among his books were some now discredited writers, Lobsang Rampa, (the pen name of Cyril Henry Hoskin), author of *The Third Eye*, Erich von Däniken, who wrote of the markings on the Andean desert in *Chariots of the Gods* and Carlos Castaneda, whose book *The Teachings of Don Juan: A Yaqui Way of Knowledge* revealed truths that emerge in drug-induced states. All of this writing seemed to touch on the issues that fascinated him, access to a world beyond our understanding.

The fact that these writers had turned out to be unreliable witnesses was of no account to him. Sometimes the way to a truth was shown by fools, the illiterate, or by the innocence of children. These writers were in their way all seeking to articulate belief systems that spoke of ways and means that were not currently available or fashionable. They tapped into the great human hunger to understand why we are here, to make sense of this world, and in this they showed something true.

Man cannot and does not entirely live by bread alone. We want more. We want to return to Eden, to innocence, to a life lived with meaning in harmony with the universe. And it was for this that Ross sought.

He read the book *The Songlines* by Bruce Chatwin, which revealed how the Australian Aborigines sang their known world into existence. Using song, they created word and melody maps of their world, which allowed them to walk securely down the song lines that offered safe passage in a harsh landscape. They combined the sacred and the profane and honoured their world with their culture. It was all of a piece. The land was their culture and their culture was the land.

Ross knew that the Romans believed that to walk was to effect a cure. There was something in the act of going on a journey, however small, that offered the opportunity to experience the world and the world it disguised. There was a gypsy in all of us. We walked as a species out of Africa and colonised the world. By walking, we took ownership of the earth. In walking lay a sort of redemption, and thus the pilgrimage was born.

His time in the Middle East had taught him that to travel was to open up the potential for being opened up. The Muslim is required to make the journey to Mecca at least once in his or her lifetime. It is a spiritual journey of enlightenment, and Ross wondered whether it was the journey or the experience in Mecca itself that offered the greatest lessons.

He was saddened by the fact that today we were tethered to our homes as never before; fear of the world kept us there, as did the warmth, security, TV and computers. For many children and adults, the landscape was *terra incognita*. For many, the world beyond their street or town was an unknown world, and this at a time of the greatest social and geographic mobility man had ever experienced. People lived within the blaring noise of our culture and its total lack of contemplation. Ross knew that his predecessors on this land, the native Indians believed silence was sacred. Out of silence and contemplation came wisdom.

Where was all this taking him? Ross did not know. Maybe nowhere. But he knew he was in search of something to help him understand his life's journey. He sensed that he had missed much, that he was impoverished with the richness of the twentieth and twenty-first centuries. He yearned to get a glimpse of God's face before he passed into the silence of death. He did not choose to be one more unthinking ant.

He listened to the call of the wild, to the song of birds, the rush of water, the wind in the trees. He would stop and look into the gloom of the woods and note the new growth, the slow silent turning of the world. He picked up stones and caressed them. For in doing these things he was honouring the world and healing himself and giving a chance for the Other to manifest itself. He knew this might take a lifetime, it might never happen, but at least he would not have travelled unaware, blind to what lay about him, to beauty.

He believed that a door had to be opened if one was to receive a visitor. All one could do was to wait and listen and be ready by the open door. Ross knew there would be new challenges to face in the days and years that lay ahead, but for now, he let slip the lines and felt the breeze take him out onto a dark sea. Who knew when or how his journey would end, but he would go with it, walking to meet it in this, his chosen landscape, his gone to place. His place of refuge. This country he called his own.

CHAPTER 29

And so, the years went by, as they do. And then at the age of 60, with the children in their teens, he had a breakdown of sorts, brought on by his PTSD and general stress. With it came an enhanced and all-encompassing paranoia about authority figures. In broad daylight, Ross attacked the mayor's office in Sandpoint, smashing in the locked security door with a length of steel pipe, cutting himself badly in the process. The sheriff was there in minutes and Ross was promptly maced and cuffed and put in a holding cell in a restraint jacket. A doctor was called and diagnosed a psychotic episode.

When Sandy and Sky showed up to take him home, he was semi-comatose with a drug the doctor had administered. When the drug had worn off, they asked him why he'd attacked the mayor's office and he said that in his confusion he'd imagined the mayor must have signed off on all the mining rights that so polluted the region. He stayed home for a few months, wandering off whenever the mood took him, sometimes half naked, into the woods. Sandy, Sky and Storm spelled each other in caring for him, as did Charlie and Clém. He was seldom left alone for any length of time. The twins had a good and detailed understanding of the effects of PTSD, having been briefed by Sandy over many years, and they had also done a great deal of reading themselves. If anything, the understanding gained made them love their father more, knowing the monster he wrestled with.

Finally, to protect him and to give them some peace, they had him placed in a clinic that specialised in the treatment of veterans. It had bars on its windows and its doors required voice entry and exit from within by warden-nurses. But they knew their stuff, and there Ross made significant progress.

Towards the end of his stay, Ross took up a position by a window which offered him a view of the mountains from dawn to dusk. He sat there day after day, just looking, and thinking about returning to the high places. His rosary was always busy in his hands as he counted off the beads and the days to his release. He walked and talked and breathed and ate, he listened to music and he smiled when Sandy and the children came to visit and the four of them held hands and walked in the lawned gardens. Although still here, part of him felt gone.

Just before being released he asked the doctor who had directed his recovery if there might be another psychotic episode. The doctor hedged his bets. 'It's hard to say for sure Ross, we are still learning about this condition. But I would say that if you stick to the prescription we give you, avoid stress, eat well and exercise, chances are you will be fine and will live a very long and useful life.'

That was enough encouragement for Ross. Sandy persuaded him to continue his treatment as an outpatient and to get some help from a therapist too. They found a woman in Spokane who had an excellent reputation and came highly recommended as someone who had significant success with PTSD cases. Once a week, religiously, Ross would attend her clinic where he met a number of other veterans whom he befriended. Those friendships also played a big part in bringing him to better mental health.

Looking back on what he termed his 'Last Hurrah', Ross came to see and understand that stress had a cumulative effect. He had arrived in the Panhandle deeply war-stressed to a profound level; the subsequent stresses of fighting for his life and for the ranch, the media camping on his property, becoming something of a national figure for a short while and then the anti-nuclear waste protest, had all served to tip him right over the edge.

'It's like ramming a car into a brick wall,' his therapist explained. 'It is only a matter of time before the car collapses. And you are not made of steel, Ross, you are flesh and bone.' Ross worried about passing on his stress to Sandy and the twins. He'd had enough therapy to know something of intergenerational stress and how it secreted itself in the DNA. Fanciful as it had seemed to him at first, he only had to notice his own hand and face gestures and expressions in his son and the tics in his voice to realise that more was passed on than one realised. It was the same with horses, why not humans too?

Ross asked his therapist to explain this issue that had troubled both him and Sandy since the birth of the twins. Her words were troubling and gave them a lot to think about. 'One of the things I would ask both of you to do is to monitor the twins' interpersonal behaviour with friends and family. Studies are showing us clearly that trauma – of the kind you carry, Ross – can be passed down to future generations. Dr Fabiana Franco says that intergenerational trauma is defined as trauma that gets passed down from those who directly experience a traumatic incident to subsequent generations. Intergenerational trauma may begin with a traumatic event affecting an individual, traumatic events affecting multiple family members, or collective trauma affecting larger community, cultural, racial, ethnic, or other groups/populations, known as historical trauma. Intergenerational trauma was first identified among the children of Holocaust survivors, but recent research has identified intergenerational trauma among other groups such as indigenous populations in North America and Australia. In 1988, one study showed that children of Holocaust survivors were overrepresented in psychiatric referrals by 300 per cent. The subjects were selected based on having at least one parent or grandparent who was a survivor. Survivors face many challenges when they are parents, including difficulty bonding to and creating healthy emotional attachments with their children. Dr Franco identified four adaptation styles amongst the families of survivors: Numb, Victim, Fighters, and Those Who Made It. Survivors who become numb seek silence by self-isolating, have a very low tolerance for stimulation of any kind, and are minimally involved in raising their children. Victims fear and distrust the outside world, try to remain inconspicuous, and are frequently depressed and quarrelsome. Fighters focus on succeeding at all costs and retaining an armour of strength, making them intolerant of weakness or self-pity. Those Who Made It are characterised by their pursuit of socio-economic success but also by the ways in which they intentionally distance themselves both from their experience of trauma and from other survivors. Children experience and understand the world primarily through direct caregivers and are, therefore, profoundly affected by their parents' behaviour. Children both mimic their parents' behaviours and learn to navigate future relationships based on how they learned to relate to their parents. Enduring coping mechanisms may be forged out of efforts to avoid and or 'fix' a parent's abusive behaviour, anger, depression, neglect, or other problematic behaviours.'

This description and the advice that came with it echoed loudly with both Ross and Sandy. They had instinctively known to look out for and guard against behaviour that would upset the twins and in this they had been remarkably successful, up to a point. They agreed to try harder.

In time, Ross seemed to have recovered fully and the old energy flowed back. The ranch became a model of its kind, operating off-grid, with its own fruit and vegetable gardens and a few head of cattle, pigs and sheep. But his pride and joy was a small horse stud operation, crossing American Quarter Horses with Irish Draughts that produced show-winning stock and Ross's reputation as someone with an eye for making clever breed decisions spread. His animals were bigger, rangier versions of the classic Quarter horses. His stock were 17 hands tall and with the kind, docile temperament of both parent breeds and with enhanced endurance and weight carrying capacity. They made ideal trail horses.

Ross loved the way his horse breeding operation joined two branches of historic Spanish breeding in the Old World with New World horses. It was a matter of historical fact that Spanish blood formed a significant part of the Irish Draught horse. This was the direct result of the wrecking of the Spanish Armada on the Irish coast in 1588. Many of the horses survived by swimming ashore and leaving their DNA in the bloodstream of the cold-blooded draught animals used on the Irish farms.

The Spanish Armada's disastrous landfall upon the coast of Ireland in September 1588 cost them a large portion of the 130-strong fleet sent by King Philip II to invade England. The Spanish fleet was blown north and west around the western Irish coast. As many as 27 ships and perhaps up to 9,000 Spanish soldiers and sailors lost their lives off the Atlantic coast of Ireland, either through drowning or being killed by English troops or Irish chieftains after they were washed ashore. But the horses that survived that treacherous swim were treasured by the horse-loving Irish who quickly saw the benefits of Spanish blood on their own stock – a much more agile and athletic animal evolved that allowed their riders to cover much greater distances.

And then there were the mustangs of the Americas that descended from the horses brought by the Spanish Conquistadores, which escaped and ran wild for centuries, providing mounts for the Native Americans whose lives were transformed by this gift. This bloodline was later bred into the American Quarter Horse. So, on the McCallister ranch in Idaho, the twin heritage of Spanish breeding was fused into a new animal that looked as beautiful as its legendary history was fascinating. Their temperament added to their reputation. But once in a while all that hot Spanish blood found a way to manifest itself afresh.

This Country I Call My Own

Clém had inherited some of her mother's French temperament and was at times as mercurial as her chestnut mare Molly, who would only suffer grooming, tacking up, or riding by her. Molly was quite capable of giving passers-by a nip or a cow kick. She was a proper madam. But with Clém she was all sweetness and light. They chose not to breed with Molly as she was just too sharp, and above all they wanted placid temperaments in their horses, most of which would end up as trail horses.

They used a chestnut Quarter Horse stallion with a flaxen mane named Lucky Dip who stood at 16 hands and six Irish Draught mares, all around 16.3 or 17 hands, four greys and two chestnuts, all bearing Irish girl's names, Meghan, Maeve, Clodagh, Siobhan, Sinéad and Niamh. The mix produced horses that were built like middle or heavyweight hunters, true Hunt Master's horses, deep chested with great heart room, handsome blood heads and quarters on which one could hold a picnic, and plenty of good flat leg bone. They could turn their hooves to most jobs around a farm, take you riding or hunting, not too precious to carry a pack, and they could jump like stags or pull a cart. They were handy, with temperaments that endeared them to their new owners. They liked people. A big 6ft 4 man did not look out of place on their backs; he looked just right.

The horses were attracting attention in the 140 fox hunting packs across the US and Canada, from New England, New York, to the Carolinas, Michigan, Maryland, Kentucky and California, where their heart and big striding boldness over fences, hedges and ditches allied to their elegant conformation and sound temperament were attributes which attracted big bucks. They were agile and athletic too and in taking care of themselves, they took care of their riders.

'Those five-legged McCallister horses', as they became known for their habit of finding an extra leg in an emergency, regularly topped prices at the auctions of hunting horses. Given the start in life they got from the twins, it was hardly surprising the stock was so sought after.

The success of the stud meant that Ross could now afford to take the horse packing business easier as Charlie and Clém got more involved with it; both of them were as enthusiastic as he was about the high country.

Sky and Storm were ranch fixtures, driving the online video operation and helping with the Healing Ranch side too.

Jack Freemantle continued to tilt at windmills of every kind, especially environmental issues which won him support from a constituency in Seattle and Washington State generally, but he made little inroads into winning the support of Idaho voters, who remain to this day wedded to the Republican Party after 60 years and counting. Every time Jack put his head above the parapet, the GOP issued a much-favoured cartoon of Jack being chased over a cliff by a fierce Idaho grizzly. The Governorship of Idaho remained beyond his grasp.

'You know Jack,' Ross would tease him, 'putting your head up only to have it smashed again and again is kind of like a definition of madness. What do you get out of it? Except sympathy from Michelle. My God, she is a long-suffering woman.'

Jack would smile. 'You are a fine one to talk. Don't think I haven't noticed that you limp a little these days, ever since that pinto stallion put you in the dust and then stomped you good. Why do you keep doing it?'

'Touché!' And they would declare a truce, with Ross offering Jack a cigar, a Cohiba Behike, of course. 'Don't smoke these on election days. Someone might shoot you,' Ross warned.

It was all going so well, maybe too well. Ross sensed this and his instinct was to double his vigilance. But when disaster struck, it came out of the blue.

CHAPTER 30

It was one of those clear, softly warm Idaho fall days when the aspens gleam gold against the blue sky, the richness of the harvest is in, and the smell of baking pies seems to scent the world with wholesome goodness.

Ross was working with the horses when he saw the sheriff's car come barrelling down his drive. This was never a good sign, but he braced himself for news of someone lost or hurt in the mountains that needed help to mount a rescue. Time seemed to slow as the sheriff walked, almost stumbling, toward him. The man held up his hands as though to show he was at a loss for what needed saying. Ross asked brusquely, 'Just tell me! What is it?'

'I'm so sorry. I have terrible news. Sandy's dead. There was an accident.' Ross felt that his heart had been cut out of him and he found himself kneeling on the ground with no memory of how he had got there. The sheriff helped him to his feet. 'A hit-and-run driver ran the lights in town and hit her,' he said. 'She died instantly.'

Telling the twins the news of their mother's death was the single most difficult thing life had ever demanded of Ross. He wept as he told them, and found that they comforted him. They were devastated and seemed unable to believe it at first, just as he struggled to accept it. Like him, they asked why? He told them that there was no answer to that question. Life and death held a randomness that at times blessed the evil and cursed the good. It was just how things were.

Ross was deeply grateful for the way the twins helped each other to cope and how Sky was there for them and for him. He flew Marcelle and Jacques down for the funeral. They hadn't seen each other since François's funeral in Quebec.

For the two days and two nights that they stayed with them, Marcelle never let go of his hand during all the daylight hours. When he asked her why she held his hand, she said, '*Mon Cherie*, these were the hands that cared for my daughter for twenty years, the hands that loved her, the hands that held hers when my grandchildren were born. Why would I not want to hold your hands? They are as close as I can get to Sandrine now.'

Ross wept great heaving sobs, and Marcelle comforted him, holding him close she whispered repeatedly, '*Courage, mon brave, courage!*', which totally unmanned him. The sounds coming out of him chilled her heart, but also told her all she needed to know about the depth of his love for her beloved daughter.

They scattered Sandy's ashes by a grove of aspen trees that grew near their swimming place in the river that she had loved so much. It was an easy walk from the ranch house and it comforted Ross to feel her close. After the funeral, Ross spoke to Jacques, who had taken the news of his sister's death very hard. He gave Ross some surprising news about his life.

'You will not know this, but I volunteered to fight your fire all those years ago. When I saw how close it was to your ranch, I felt I had to come. I said nothing because I did not want to worry you and Sandrine. Some of my friends came too, and some of them I lost.

'When I got home, I said to myself, "Jacques, you are getting too old for such heroics." So some years ago, I bought myself a small bar with my savings and some help from Maman. My friends in the fire service, the police and the military, they seem to like it. So now I am putting fire in their bellies instead of a fire putting us in its belly. I named it the Fire-Pit, but the decor is all water, rivers, lakes, the sea and some underwater scenes. Customers who walk in are a bit confused when they first arrive. But when they see the photos, they understand. You can have enough of fire.' He invited Ross to visit and said that there was a spare room for him. And at the pub, all the Scotch he could drink. 'With your Scottish heritage, you will feel at home there.'

The twins welcomed the time with their grandmother and uncle, exotic figures to them that they had not seen much of in their 18 years. She was their only surviving grandparent and had spent a few Christmases with them over the years, but their Uncle Jacques they barely knew. They knew he had been a fireman, and they knew he had not married and had no children, but he did have a partner, Cecile, whom they had not met. But that was it. They took him to see the horses and standing there with him among the smell of sweet hay and straw, he told them how their mother had learned to ride at a stable in Quebec and had collected small china figures of horses, some of which she had left with him, and that he treasured.

'Come visit me in Quebec and I will show you something of your French heritage.' They both said they would, knowing that it would never happen. But they said nothing about that. This silence and reticence ran deep with them all.

Charlie was intrigued by one of the letters of condolence with its Israeli stamps from someone called Motke Rutenberg. The writer offered his condolences and wished Ross 'long life'. When Charlie asked his father who Motke was, Ross told him something of the man's background in Mossad and added that Motke had once saved his life and that he had returned the compliment – 'but Motke's was the bigger save.'

Ross was not much help to the twins, who felt the loss of their mother was almost too much to bear. But their closeness was a great help in surviving this time and they spent a lot of time with Sky and Storm as well, working with the people who came to spend time with the therapy horses. They truly began to understand the capacity that horses have to heal. From time to time, they joined Ross on his expeditions and learned much of the country he knew that they had not as yet fully explored.

The death of his mother made Charlie an even quieter boy. But his natural reserve only added to his gravitas and he was now taller than his father. It was just as well the McCallisters were breeding big horses; he needed a tall mount. When Ross saw the young man on his favourite horse, Chancer, an imposing dapple-grey gelding, he would catch his breath.

It did not pass Ross by that more and more of the horse safari business they were getting came with specific requests for the twins to act as guides. Clém was the perfect foil for Charlie. Whip-sharp and outgoing, she charmed everyone but there were no flies on her, just the one on her name, as the family in-joke had it. That French accent on the first 'e' in her name was something that irritated her and yet she had collared it for use in the shortened version of her name.

But around the trail campfires at night, it was Clém's singing voice that held everyone's attention. Something happened when she sang and her singing voice, so like that of Karen Carpenter, shocked at first. Her rendition of Billie Holiday's *I'll Be Seeing You*, *Strange Fruit* and the old country favourite *Tennessee Whiskey* received rapturous applause. But the true magic happened when she sang the Carpenters' songs including *For All We Know* and *Rainy Days and Mondays;* these were the ones everyone wanted to hear again and again. Singing these songs at this tough time brought tears to her eyes and thickened her voice ,which only added to her allure.

Clém had attracted male attention from the age of 14 but for all his good looks, Charlie's entanglements with girls were fleeting, ephemeral things. 'He just doesn't seem to notice how girls hang on every word of his,' Clém would complain to Sky on behalf of her gender. 'He is just blind to it. His horse gets all his attention. He often does not even know the girls' names!'

The land continued to make its own impact on local

names for boys and girls. Each new generation continued to bear the geography of the place with many more named Rain, River, Aspen, Summer and Storm. It was as if the land invaded the language with this lexicon of natural phenomena in the names it lent its human inhabitants.

CHAPTER 31

Sandy's death triggered a mental tsunami in Ross. He felt that he had not been absolved of his crimes in the Middle East. He thought deeply about all that he had done there and all that had happened to him since coming to the ranch, since making his home in the Panhandle. All his old trauma and guilt was resurrected.

He searched and scoured his memory for clues, for warnings, for signs that this catastrophe would befall him, seeking for indicators which would have allowed him to forestall it, or indeed to stop this terrible retribution that he had always, at some deep subconscious level, expected.

Like so many who live on the edge of danger, or are immersed in it, Ross was subject to magical thinking, he was not immune to it. He dreamt at night about signs he had missed, things that might have warned him of this terrible price he had paid with the loss of Sandy.

And then it came, the sudden profound revelation that he had indeed been warned, but blindly had not heard the warning, had seen it but had not understood its true meaning, its significance. His deep spiritual feelings illuminated this revelation that had come too late, but which he now needed to act on.

Ross finally remembered the weeping wood and the milk-white stag in the mist, and realised that these things were signs that had been sent to him, signs whose message he had not heard nor understood. Their message that he needed to beg, to pray, for the absolution of his sins. He was astonished that he had missed these things. These signs from his own land, from the sky, the woods and the earth, from one of its noblest creatures. How could he have been so blind to its significance. He had sat beside that weeping wood with his mouth agape, and then like a fool, had thought the stag caught in the sacrificial, smoking mists had just been a rare, pretty sight.

He saw now and understood that the stag was the equivalent of the biblical ram, from the Old Testament. It represented Abraham's sacrifice of the perfect, pure ram, killed to save him from having to kill his own son Isaac, as God had demanded, to test his faith that God would return his son from death. The white stag in the mist had been the clearest message that a sacrifice was demanded.

The weeping wood, he now saw clearly, was the living embodiment of all the pain and suffering he had inflicted on countless people in his years of active military service, and it needed to be atoned for.

Ross did not question this, he believed it profoundly. He felt it was the urging of the wild consciousness of this sacred space, this high country, this place of great hills and mountains to which he prayed, to which he lifted his eyes to ask for help.

He began to fast and kept it up for days that ran into a week. He prepared dishes of bitter herbs and as he fell asleep, he dreamt that a sacrifice, a great sacrifice, would be required of him, another one. It came as no surprise to him, he had felt this calling in his soul, in his bones, since Iraq and Afghanistan. He had thought the loss of Stiegs had been his payment, but he'd been wrong.

Ross took himself off to see a clairvoyant, who confirmed his need to absolve himself of sin. Seeing his evident pain, the sense of loss that came off him, and seeing the wedding ring, she asked him how long his wife had been gone. He told her it had been six months.

'Do you have to ask her to forgive you?'

'I do,' he said, and she told him to take something truly precious to him and to bury it as a token of his failings. And to then speak his apology aloud to his wife. It confirmed all that he felt.

He also made a fresh confession to Father Berrigan, whom he asked to drive out the evil spirits within him. Father B came out to the ranch, concerned for Ross, prayed with him at his church in the wood and gave him absolution. Sky and the twins were deeply troubled by all this. They simply did not know what to think.

And then one moonlight night Ross led his beloved old horse Rincon to what would be a blood sacrifice. They stopped by Sandy's grave and he prayed for forgiveness, forgiveness for being blind to the need for a sacrifice, to find absolution before she became the sacrifice. Ross raised the gun, putting it to Rincon's head and then paused for a long moment. He wept and screamed at the sky, 'Will this be enough? Is this enough? Forgive me. Forgive me!'

And then something inexplicable stopped him from his course of action. He thought of all that he and Rincon had been through together, the logs for the cabin hauled, the miles travelled, the country seen, the mountains climbed, the loyalty given, the sweetness, the gentleness and the friendship. And he thought how Sandy had loved this horse, the one he rode on their first ride together. And he lowered the gun. He could not do it. There had to be an end to killing.

As he lowered the gun a flash of white in the near trees caught his eye and for a split second he imagined he saw a white ram. But then a figure stepped out from the trees and he realised it was Sky in her nightdress. She walked to him and took his hand.

'I knew you would never do that. Killing solves nothing, Ross.' He let the old horse go, free to graze in the night. Holding Sky's arm, he walked back to the house.

Somehow this near killing of his horse brought him to his senses and finally he felt absolved. He had some peace with himself. A sense of that peace came to him out of the woods. He walked among the trees, stroking their trunks in passing. He walked into the river for what he felt to be a baptism of absolution.

In the days, weeks and months that followed, Ross would take a horse and a tarp and disappear into the highest country he could reach on horseback. Once again, the region had a ridge walker. He haunted the forests, keeping out of the way of his own clients led by the twins, and off the trails used by other horse packing outfits. He gave the foresters, the loggers and the hunters plenty of space and he carved out a territory for himself that allowed him complete silence for weeks. He would, from time to time, return to the ranch to get a fresh horse and more supplies, and then after a day or two of catching up on the ranch operation, he would disappear again. He felt that it was best that he be gone from the ranch, that his presence there was like a lightning rod, attracting disaster.

Once in a while, if he had been gone too long, the children or Sky would hunt him down and camp with him for a few days, checking up on him. He was always glad to see them, but by now he had an aura about him of someone who was not fully present anymore.

Chapter 32

For Sky, the loss of Sandy was a tearing of her soul for so many reasons. She had loved Sandy with all the passion of first love. And she loved the twins with a bond just as strong as motherhood itself. Children were something that she had denied herself thus far. And then there were her complicated feelings for Ross that she had bottled up for two decades. She had truly loved Ross and still did. She had given him up with a heavy heart, not wishing to wound Sandy, her other love.

What sort of relationship would she and Ross have had, built on the certain destruction of Sandy whom both loved? Now, close as she and Storm were, that other half of her called out with a hunger born of twenty years of denial, of unfulfilled passion. She wanted Ross with a determination that set her on a course for fulfilment or destruction.

And as ever with Ross, when in dire straits, he turned to a woman for comfort when comfort was offered. His history of a boy who lost his mother at a very young age had set him up for this response and he did not dismiss Sky's loving advances. She said nothing, but was simply there for him. Knowing as he did that she had also loved Sandy made it somehow easier, almost fitting that as their minds and hearts recalled her, their bodies did as well.

They were discreet, but not discreet enough for a teenage girl of Clém's sensitivity and insight. Some deep female intuition had told her subconsciously for years that there was more between her parents and Sky than met the eye – she had just been the last to know. She sensed something in the relationship of her parents had once included Sky and she kept her own counsel.

But when Storm found out, she lived up to her name and barrelled off the ranch like a cyclone. She brooded in Sandpoint for some weeks and when she saw that Sky would not return to her, she left for a horse ranch in Florida to work with physically disabled people.

Before she left, she told Clém of her anger. 'Ross has returned to his old ways, his history. He has just picked up from where he and Sandy and Sky left off years ago. To me it says that Sky never really loved me, she just waited here all this time for Ross.'

It said much for Clém's maturity and her love for her father that she did not act on this information. She waited and watched, deciding for the first time in her life to keep this information from Charlie.

Thus Clém took on board her first major secret, one that would define who she was as a person and what she would become – a woman who had fully inherited her mother's compassion and love of people in all their messy complexity. Her mother's words echoed in her mind, '*Chérie*, do not judge! People are fallible, complicated, damaged. Until you can walk in their shoes, it is wise not to judge. Let God be the judge.'

And so Clém did not judge. But she felt compelled to speak to Sky about something she needed to understand as a woman. 'Sky, how can you love someone who is almost not here with us some of the time? He is like a ghost. How does that work?'

Sky smiled at her. 'Clém, when you love someone, you don't stop loving them when they die, nor when they are sick, nor when you fight, the love is like a deep underground river, never visible but always there, running powerfully underground. If you are lucky to find a true love, one that lasts, it is made up of a whole history of events and times that ebb and flow, the joys and the wounds are all part of it. And with your father, I found someone who even if he is only half present at times, is still more of a man than most men I have known. And our history together over so many years allows me to fill in the gaps when they come.'

For Clém, these words brought a sense of peace and acceptance that she could not fully understand. It spoke profoundly to her of what she aspired to be as a woman and in a way set up a signpost for what to look for in a life partner.

Gradually, things on the ranch settled down once more into a routine much like the one that had included Sandy, even though she was gone. Clém helped Charlie to get some grasp of what was going on between Ross and Sky. At first he was angry, but kept it bottled up as was his way, but when he saw how Sky stood by his father and helped to keep the show on the road, he began to see something of what his father saw in her and also that she embodied something of Sandy.

As happens when you love someone deeply, something of them becomes part of who you are. He was helped by the fact that he too loved Sky and always had, she was in effect a second mother to him, something he had barely acknowledged to himself previously.

As time worked its healing on them all, it also provided new gifts. Just when Ross felt that his life had plateaued and ahead of him lay gentle decline, life provided a new challenge and a new opportunity. He and Sky were sitting beside the high-fenced lunge ring watching the twins backing some of the four-year-old horses.

'Damn, they can ride!' Ross said aloud, speaking his thought. 'Is it bad of me to be so proud of them?

'You are right to be proud of them!' she said, and continued. 'You have been a wonderful father to them and you are going to be a wonderful father to our own child.' Ross was caught utterly by surprise. Sky took his hand as he looked at her, his mouth slightly ajar.

She put her finger to his lips. 'I know what you think, you are too old to be a father, but you are not. Life is not finished with you yet, nor am I! And remember I am lucky to be having this child, I don't have much time left to be a mother.' She watched the huge smile cross Ross's face and knew that all would be well. Sitting there watching the children they and Sandy had raised, they thought about the new life that was coming.

Ross hugged her so hard that she squealed. Charlie and Clém pulled their horses up, wondering what was going on. Ross and Sky walked to the fence and he said, 'Sky has just told me you are going to have a new brother or sister.'

Abandoning their horses, the twins vaulted the corral fence and hugged their father and Sky, yelling their delight. This astonishing news gifted a surge of energy to Ross. He and Charlie worked together to create a bedroom for the new arrival.

Ross also put into play an idea that had come to him almost as soon as Sky had broken the news to him. He purchased a parcel of land, just over 1,000 acres that adjoined the ranch. It had recently come onto the market and Ross believed that with the extra pasture it provided he could extend the number of beef cattle the ranch ran as well as provide more grazing for horses.

After Axel was born, Ross took his new favourite horse, a big, raw-boned grey gelding called The Drifter, up into the hills and from a favourite lookout point surveyed the extended ranch – the McCallister spread – and the words of his old friend Stiegs came to him. He spoke them aloud. 'Land is true wealth.' And then he added, 'But Stiegs, I must tell you that a good woman and children is even greater wealth. I am sorry you did not live long enough to know this.' And he thought of his blond-haired, blue-eyed son, just born, who Sky had named Axel.

As he sat his horse up on the mountainside, he felt as if he was standing on the back of a ship watching its wake, the wake of his life cut across the ocean of time and it was a very zigzag course. But now the boat seemed to have steadied at last, and the wake ran true, straight back to the horizon.

With the help of the twins, Ross worked to integrate the two spreads into one 1,500-acre ranch, setting up new fences and gates that allowed for a free flow of cattle and horses between the old and the new land. In honour of its new size, he and Charlie built an elegant entrance arch to the ranch with its name, The McCallister Ranch, in wrought iron.

They spent some time at auctions buying cattle to add to the herd and new young horses to add to the remuda. Life on the ranch was busier than it had ever been. But Ross still made time to get into the hills, usually as a way of settling a newly backed horse and to let it experience something of what its working life would be like.

He had been gone a few days, not long enough to worry Sky or the twins, when there came a call from one of the forestry staff to say that they had found a grey horse wandering loose with no tack or any gear. Had they lost one? When asked its colour and sex they realised immediately that it was The Drifter, the horse Ross had taken on his current trip into the mountains. The twins and Sky set off to search for him. They found him lying peacefully against a tree, his head on his chest, seemingly asleep. His camp, as ever, faced east to the rising sun. He had no pulse. All three of them were silent. It was just too enormous to take in, to believe.

Ross was indeed finally gone. He had achieved what his heart yearned for, a final solitude amid the beauty of the mountains.

The autopsy showed a massive coronary as the cause of death. In a way this helped the twins; it made sense to them that after their mother's death, their father had died of a broken heart. After the funeral at the ranch, they took his ashes to the same place by the river where they had buried Sandy's ashes and buried his alongside hers, beneath a tall aspen tree.

Holding the twin's hands, Sky said, 'Ross you are not gone, you live on in our hearts and your body is now part of the land you loved. This country you called your home. You are with Sandy, now and forever. Amen.'

They camped out there for a night, alongside the ashes

of Ross and Sandy, and the next day walked back up to the ranch house. They were silent on that walk back, their minds filled with the beauty all around them and the memories of their parents and each of them with a distinct sense that Ross and Sandy walked just behind them, watching them safely home.

Charlie answered a call some weeks later, which turned out to be from the lawyer Jack Freemantle, who had an interesting proposal. 'Charlie, would you, Sky and Clém object if I started a fund to commemorate your father to thank him for his work on cleaning up the nuclear waste in Idaho and Washington. I think it would be a great way for the thousands of people who he brought to the fight to thank him in a tangible way.

'I know he left you guys with new acres and a bigger mortgage and this would be one way to clear that. It would be a wonderful way to ensure that what he started not only continues, but helps you guys to develop his ideas further. Have a chat to Sky and Clém and let me know what you decide.'

Charlie thanked him as profusely as he was capable of and that same night over dinner shared the idea with Clém and Sky. Both were pleased and agreed immediately, delighted that Ross would be honoured and remembered in this way. Within days, Jack had a petition up calling for funds to commemorate Ross and the work he had done, and not surprisingly, there was a huge and generous response. When the final amount was calculated, it came to three times the amount of money Ross had given back to the Agency that had called for Jack to be derailed. It not only paid off the mortgage but put a sizeable sum into their investments. Some of the money was earmarked for a fund to pay for patients who needed horse therapy but could not afford to pay for it and another amount was a contribution in Ross's name to continue the fight to clean up the environmental damage to the Panhandle. It was another part of the legacy Ross left in the mountains of Idaho.

Now and again, on returning from a horse packing trip with clients, Charlie and Clém would report coming across a bear that had wandered into camp, seemingly unafraid of man and almost tame, and they guessed that it had known Ross in the high country when it was a cub. This too was part of their father's legacy.

There was never any question about Sky staying on at the ranch. She was utterly committed to being there for the twins and she continued to oversee the running of the place. Both Charlie and Clém found the time to thank her for what she did for them.

Charlie surprised her by saying, 'My father and mother both loved you and I can see why. I love you too.' She wept and hugged him. 'I love you too, Charlie McCallister. So much. Thank you for saying that. It means more than you can ever imagine.'

And Clém hugged her one day in the horse barn and said, 'Promise me you'll never leave?' Sky hugged her back and said, 'I promise, Clém. I will never leave while I have breath in my body. They will have to carry me out of here feet first. I love you guys!'

And so the bond formed with Sky took on a whole new life of its own with a second generation of McCallisters, the bond between Axel and his twin half-siblings.

Among the visitors to the ranch were an increasing number of international groups attracted by the YouTube videos, wishing to ride the mountains and forests of the Idaho Panhandle that they had watched at home. Some fell in love with the place and set up homes in the area.

The McCallister twins felt that this too was part of their parents' legacy and their heritage, creating a more international mix in the local community. And these days, among the many accents and languages heard in the Hoot Owl Café are accents and languages from Europe, Asia, Australia, and South Africa.

Father B, as the twins called him, was true to his promise to be a good godfather and made regular visits to the ranch to check up on Clém, Charlie and Axel. They found his kindness and his long friendship with their mother and father deeply helpful in mending their wounds.

Six months after Ross's death, they asked the priest if he would like to see the place where Ross's body was found, his last camp in the mountains. They were walking back from the aspen grove by the river, where he had said a prayer for Sandy and Ross.

'I would dearly love that, but how? I can't ride a horse, nor a motorbike for that matter.' The twins shared a conspiratorial wink, and both said at the same time, 'Geronimo!'

The priest, suspecting a joke, asked, 'Who is Geronimo?' and Clém explained, 'He is the kindest, gentlest mule we've ever had. He will look after you! We will give you a big sheepskin covered saddle and you will be fine. We can walk you in within a day and a half.' And so it came to pass. The next weekend, Father B was helped onto the mule, a stout grey animal with long-suffering eyes, and they set off quietly.

The twins treated him with great respect, helping him mount and dismount when nature called. Charlie knelt down on all fours so that the priest could use his back as a mounting block, with Clém holding the priest's arm.

'You know I have always wondered how my forbears, the Jesuit monks in Europe, felt when riding their mules, and now I know. It was pain!' But Geronimo took care of him, sensing his wobbliness in the saddle, and he never put a foot wrong.

That night, they camped by one of their father's old haunts and Charlie caught trout for supper. Over supper, Father B told them something of his conversations with their father. 'He had his own calling, and it was for nature. I thought at one time he might become a priest because his knowledge of philosophy and literature and music showed me what a deeply intelligent, complex and sensitive man he was, and so filled with compassion. Though not enough to forgive himself for his failings, as he saw them. I tried my best to lighten his load, but he was stubborn and insisted on carrying his own sins. Your father was a special man. A very good man.'

Before they turned in for the night, they shared a few shots of whisky. Clém asked if her godfather would like some liniment for his muscles. He thanked her and gingerly applied the salve to his calves and knees. A few minutes later, they heard him snoring gently. The twins smiled at each other. There was something in this pilgrimage that was profoundly healing for them.

That night the twins slept deeply, dreamlessly, until dawn and then, as happened with them, they both felt their father close to them.

It took them a few hours after breakfast to get to Ross's last campsite and there they had to help the priest off Geronimo and support him for the few steps it took to reach the tree for him to sit against. They sat there in quiet contemplation for some while. The priest asked Clém and Charlie if he might say a prayer for their father and he did so quietly, as though addressing a child, and then to their surprise, he sang the Latinate version of *Ave Maria* used at Catholic funeral masses. At its conclusion, both the twins wept quietly.

The priest hugged them silently and then said, 'Your father was an incredible man. I am so proud to say he was my friend. And so very glad to call you my godchildren. Your parents were so proud of you. They loved you so very much.' As he spoke these words, the twins felt a lightness of spirit enter their hearts and they returned home more whole than they had been since the death of their parents.

The trip back was slow and painful for the priest, who walked for a good part of the way. But finally, they got him back to the ranch without mishap, gave him lunch and warm hugs. All three felt uplifted by their time together. Although the priest promised himself he would not be repeating his time on Geronimo.

A few days later, Charlie found another letter postmarked

Israel, condoling with him and Clém on their father's death and once more offering that strange phrase, 'I wish you long life'. And then a sentence he had to go to an online dictionary for. 'Your father was a true mensch and a great friend of Israel.'

To Charlie, his father was something of an enigma and there would forever be parts of his father's past that would remain a closed door. He showed the letter to David Segal, who surprised him by saying, 'He is right, Charlie, that is just the right word for your father, and for you. You are both menschen.'

That night, as Charlie lay in bed listening to the owls calling and the breeze moving the aspens, he thought about what people said of his father and how deeply loved his mother had been, he thought about friendship and what his father had said about rage and anger and the need to put a brake on them. Life was going to be more difficult than he had at first imagined. But he would try his best to live up to his parents' legacy and be a good man. He had seen one up close and personal, so he had no excuses.

When clearing out their father's safe, the twins came across his memoir and both read it, fascinated and saddened in equal part. It filled in much that they had suspected but could not be sure of and some things that were entirely new to them. From these pages their father emerged as complex, troubled, but ultimately as someone who had tried his best to be a good man. They showed it to Sky, who was equally fascinated and moved.

Ross's memoir was not just his thoughts. In Africa they say that it takes a whole village to raise a child. This is as true in the case of a book; it takes a whole nation and its culture to produce a book and sometimes more than one culture. The protagonists make their own demands in the writing of a book, as do its first early readers of the half-formed text and then its first editors add their own input and all are represented in the richness of the document. In Ross's memoir this was certainly true, for he had taken great trouble to read the history of his country's conflicts in the Middle East and he had spoken to and interviewed a number of his old friends and his commanding officers. He had begged, borrowed and outright stolen material to blend into the broth that boiled down to his book. And it made a rich and compelling brew. 'It would make a helluva movie,' Sky said, holding the manuscript.

The next time Bob Redford stopped by the Hoot Owl Café, as he did from time to time when heading up to Whitefish, Montana to visit friends from the film industry, he found the manuscript placed on his table and was told there was no charge for the coffee.

Three years later, *The Ridge Walker* made a very well-received appearance at the Sundance Festival, with the twins and Sky in the audience.

Today, those who ride the Panhandle mountain ranges speak of seeing the ghost of Commander McCallister from time to time, fishing his favourite spots at dusk. He is becoming something of a legend in the mountains and there is great local pride in having this latest ridge walker as part of their rich heritage. In some strange way, Ross McCallister never entirely succeeded in disappearing. He is far from being gone. He lives on in this country he called his own.

EST. 2019

BLKDOG

www.blkdogpublishing.com

Printed in Great Britain
by Amazon